Fortunate Son

The Dublin Trilogy - Book 8

Caimh McDonnell

Caimh McDonnell

Visit my website at www.WhiteHairedirishman.com

First edition: November 2024

ISBN: 9781912897476

In loving memory of Stu Who and Janey Godley – Scotland sure knows how to build 'em right.

Author's Note

Welcome dear reader to this, the eighth book in the Dublin Trilogy.

I'm happy to report that the best thing about reaching book seven was that people finally stopped sending us emails to check if we understood the meaning of the word 'trilogy.' However, as an author I feel it is important to break new ground and seek fresh challenges, which is why this novel – in case you've forgotten, book eight in the Dublin Trilogy – mostly takes place in London. For too long the word *Dublin* has been getting away scot-free, while *trilogy* has been taking an almighty beating. I'm not sure how I'll manage it, but I intend to find some way of similarly abusing the word *the* at some point in the future. Also, before anybody asks – I am not planning to relocate the series entirely unless, of course, I do. I'll be honest, nobody is more excited to find out what is going to happen next than I am.

I should also clarify that this book takes place in January 2001, following on from The Family Jewels, which alarmingly makes it some form of historical fiction. Luckily, the amount of research required for this was limited as, by complete coincidence, I moved from Dublin to London at almost the exact same time the book takes place. You never know: Bunny may eventually become a writer living in Manchester with his long-suffering wife and never-suffering dogs. I'd like to pretend I'm not that lazy, but who am I kidding?

And don't worry if this is your first Bunny book, it can be read as a standalone. I can't remember what I've written in previous books, so you'll be fine. And I urge you to check out the link to the bonus Easter egg video you can find in the back matter – where you can see your humble author discussing what happens in the book. Please note, despite the name, this Easter egg does not contain chocolate.

Happy reading!

Caimh

Chapter One

January 2001

Bunny was sitting in silence. Or at least he was trying to.

"I thought she was a very friendly lady," said Declan Fadden Senior, the grandfather of Deccie Fadden, who was seated to the left of Bunny.

"Oh, yeah," agreed the aforementioned Deccie, who was on Bunny's right. "She seemed to really enjoy her work."

Bunny drew a deep breath before speaking. "Remember how I said I didn't want to talk about it?"

"Right," countered Declan Senior, "but you weren't talking about it. *I* was talking about it."

"Granda has you there, boss," agreed Deccie. "You never said we couldn't talk about it. Only that you didn't want to talk about it."

"I meant us. I meant that I didn't want us to talk about it."

"Okay then," said Declan. This was followed by a thoughtful pause from the older man. "Did you mean just now or ever?"

"Now." Bunny then took a second to consider his reply. "Actually, ever. Don't talk about it ever."

1

"To you or—"

"Anyone," said Bunny firmly. "Don't talk about it to anyone. Never discuss what happened today with another living soul." He turned to Deccie, the thirteen-year-old assistant manager of St Jude's Under-12s hurling team, who was quite possibly the biggest gossip on the planet. "And that goes triple for you."

Deccie had the temerity to look affronted. "I never say nothing to nobody never. I'm a sphinx."

"A what?"

"Body of a lion, head of a man, wings of an eagle. The Egyptian lad."

"Are they famous for not talking?" asked his grandad, genuinely interested.

"Oh, yeah. Well known for it. It's them that the sphincter is named after."

"What?" asked Bunny, despite himself. That was the thing with Deccie. Even when you didn't want to ask follow-up questions, somehow you still felt compelled to. "No, it isn't. Is it?"

"It is," said Deccie. "I've seen it on TV."

"What channel?" asked Declan.

"I dunno."

"What have we said about this?"

Deccie reeled off his reply as if learned by rote. "Don't believe anything you see on TV unless it's on RTÉ."

"That's right," confirmed his grandfather. "Only the national broadcaster."

"Is that not a bit prejudiced?"

"What? No," said Declan, suddenly defensive. "I'm not prejudiced. I just ... Facts are important. You need to get them from a trusted source."

"And that's not the Brits?"

"I'm not saying that," replied Declan. "It's just ... Things like the news, you want to make sure you're getting the Irish perspective."

"Right."

2

"And history," added Bunny.

"Oh, yeah," agreed Declan Senior, "definitely history."

"Well, that goes without saying," said Deccie.

"But other stuff," said Declan, "that's fine. Mostly. Take that David Attenborough. You can trust him. He seems very on the ball."

"Knows a lot about otters," confirmed Deccie.

"He does. So you can believe him. But when it comes to other facts, like news and history ..."

"Probably geography, too," added Bunny.

"Yeah," agreed Declan. "Geography is a very sticky area. The British made up a lot of it by just swanning in and naming a place, regardless of what the locals were already calling it. History may be written by the victors, but geography is written by the lads with the big maps."

"Very true," said Bunny. "They weren't even that good at the names. I mean, they called Ghana the Gold Coast. The first country in the world named for where it was and what they were nicking from it. Lazy."

"Very lazy," concurred Grandad Declan. "So don't go trusting them on geography."

"Or sport," continued Bunny. "Get all your sport from the Irish channels, too."

"Oh, RTÉ for the sport every time," said Declan, nodding in agreement.

"And besides," added Bunny, "you should only be watching the GAA." Bunny's dislike for all things soccer was well known.

"Yeah," said Declan Senior, considerably less emphatically. "And I'm not even saying don't ever watch the news on the BBC and that, but if something big happens, turn over to RTÉ to make sure they've got it right."

Deccie gave another nod. "Seems reasonable."

His grandfather paused for a second. "Also, I'm not going to ask any further questions about this, but I don't want you watching any more programmes about sphincters. God forbid your granny were to

3

walk in. In fact, don't go into the double figures on the channels. 'Tis the Wild West up there."

"A lot of it is very educational."

"That's what I'm afraid of."

"Could we ..." Bunny stopped himself at the sound of the irritation in his own voice. He took it down a couple of notches. "Could we perhaps sit in silence for a few minutes?"

"Oh, yeah," said Declan. "Absolutely. Great idea. I love a bit of silence, me."

"You do," agreed his grandson. "You're always saying that."

"Very good for the soul."

"And," said Deccie, "when we're at home, if we're quiet, we can hear the Watersons – that newlywed couple next door – moving the furniture round."

Bunny glanced at Declan Senior, and the briefest of looks between the two men confirmed what he suspected.

"Yes," said Declan quickly. "They're settling in. Lot of furniture to move about."

"There must be," said Deccie. "They're at it all hours. That poor Mr Waterson must be exhausted. She's got him on the job morning, noon and night, Granny says."

Bunny found himself watching Deccie carefully. If he was trying to wind them up, there wasn't a trace of it on his face. He would say the lad would be a hell of a poker player one day, but he'd already caught him trying to run his own card game after football practice, and they'd needed to have one of their little chats.

"Well," said Declan Senior, in an effort to move the conversation on. "It's their first home – they've a lot of furniture."

"They would do," offered Bunny, trying to help the older man out.

"She'd want to make her mind up," said Deccie, "or the poor fella is going to throw his back out. She's always saying, 'Yes, there, right there, that's the spot,' and then clearly she's changing her mind—"

"Anyway," interrupted his grandad, loudly. "Silence. Bunny was hoping for a bit of silence. So let's do that now."

"And she's yelling at him to keep going—"

"Absolute silence," said Grandad Fadden, his voice a mix of determination and desperation. "Three, two, one, go!"

Silence did indeed descend upon the group.

It lasted eleven seconds, which Bunny strongly suspected was a Fadden family record. The most surprising thing was that he was the one who felt compelled to break it.

"It's weird, isn't it?" asked Bunny.

"It is," confirmed Declan.

"It's because we're naked," said Deccie.

"For the last time," said Bunny, "we are not naked. We're wearing towels."

"Well, we're not not naked, are we?" countered Deccie. "If the three of us were walking down O'Connell Street like this, people wouldn't be pointing at us, going, 'Look at them three fully clothed eejits.'"

"We're in a sauna," said Bunny. "We are appropriately attired for three men in a sauna."

As far as relaxing days went, it had been the most stressful imaginable. The trio were spending it at the new male-only spa off Parnell Square called Kanin. They were there because Declan Senior had won a spa day for four people in a raffle. Bunny's raffle. Technically, it was the St Jude's raffle, but for the past month people all over Dublin had been referring to it as "Bunny's bloody raffle", or a less polite approximation of those words. The pitch belonging to St Jude's Hurling Club had been beset by a serious drainage problem and Bunny needed to get it fixed before a twelve-year-old got sucked into the mud, never to be seen again. Hence the raffle. Before Bunny could "persuade" people to buy tickets, he needed to "persuade" other people to donate prizes. That was the difference between a raffle and extortion, although the line was admittedly blurry. The spa day for four was one of the prizes that had been offered to him, persuasion-free, by a very nice Danish man called Elias Jensen. He and his wife, Patty, were the owners of Kanin and lived in an apartment near the St Jude's training ground.

The problem was, no man Bunny knew wanted to go on a spa day. It appeared Irish males were inherently distrustful of such places. It also appeared to be a fundamental difference between them and the Danes, which the Jensens didn't understand, even when well-meaning people had tried to explain it. Bunny had been relieved to find out that the couple had made a ton of money from Patty inventing a new kind of plastic or something, because Kanin was the single worst business venture he'd ever seen.

Not that the place wasn't very nice. On the contrary, it was done up very smartly. The kind of music people who talk about auras think is relaxing was piped into every room, and the whole place smelled like a really nice bath bomb had gone off somewhere. Still, on the night of the raffle, person after person had come up to claim their prizes, and, as Bunny had feared, the spa day voucher had sat there uncollected. The bottle of sambuca Bunny had added as a joke had gone before it, to a man he knew for a fact had been on the wagon for almost twenty years. This was not an entirely unexpected turn of events, but it didn't make it any less awkward.

Bunny wasn't proud of what he did next, but with a bit of sleight of hand he'd pulled out the number of the ticket he'd given to Declan Senior earlier that day. Which explained their presence here today. There were only three of them because the non-existent fourth person had called in sick. Not really – they hadn't been able to find one.

The pedicures and manicures had been alright, despite neither Fadden having nails in need of cutting. Bunny found out later that Deccie's grandmother had spent the weekend scrubbing and grooming the duo to within an inch of their lives so they wouldn't "show her up". Deccie even had a rash from where she'd gone at him with a scouring pad. Bunny could have happily gone without seeing that. The massages had been OK-ish, except for the fact that Declan

Senior had refused his because he'd been "a happily married man for fifty-six years". Bunny had awkwardly explained that it was just a massage, but Declan had been insistent: "Only Bridie gets to lay her hands upon my body. That's the oath I swore in front of God and the good folk gathered in St Brigid's Church on that fateful day." He had at least partaken in the cucumber-and-yogurt face-mask treatment, of which Deccie had managed to eat an embarrassing amount.

It was only out of a desperate need to be polite that Bunny had agreed to the waxing. He hadn't known he had a hairy back because, well, it was his back. What kind of a narcissist has the time to align mirrors, or whatever, to look at their own back? He'd first become wary when the nice Thai lady's face had lit up. She'd appraised him the way a seasoned mountaineer would probably appraise K2. As she'd started, he'd tried cracking a couple of jokes, although he couldn't say which of them he'd been trying to put at ease.

Bunny had lain there on his stomach, his face peeking through a hole in the table, while the Faddens had watched on, keen observers. If they'd not been there, Bunny would have yelled at the therapist to stop after she'd pulled off the first strip. But they were there, so, summoning reserves of courage he'd not known he possessed, he let her continue. He'd given the St Jude's hurling team enough tub-thumping speeches about sticking it out when things aren't going your way, that he couldn't face making himself look like a total hypocrite in front of his assistant manager. It was a hell of a time to find out that, apparently, the opinions of a thirteen-year-old and his grandad meant so much to him. The pain had been excruciating, like nothing Bunny had ever experienced before in his life, and that included getting shot. At one point, Deccie had been moved to comment, "Jesus, it's like watching someone pull up carpet with their bare hands."

Bunny wasn't entirely sure, but he thought he might have blacked out for a while. He distinctly remembered promising God he'd give up drinking if He made it stop. He hadn't. After about twice as long as your average ice age, the ordeal was finally over. He felt incredible afterwards – mainly because the pain had stopped. The smiley little Thai lady, who Bunny was now convinced was the first stone-cold psychopath he'd met in his career in law enforcement, had said something about going downstairs. Bunny, in his weakened state, had readily agreed, envisioning a cup of tea in his future, before Declan Senior had stepped in: "I think Bunny is alright for the downstairs area." He then added pointedly, "Aren't you?"

Even the therapist had looked relieved when Bunny reversed his earlier decision, which would have been a tad uncomfortable had Bunny any remaining capacity to feel pain.

Declan Senior studied Bunny's back as Deccie poured yet more water on the sauna stones. "I think the bleeding has almost stopped," he said, before averting his eyes. "Sorry, we're not talking about it. I forgot. Still, though – this'll all set you up nicely for your holiday next week."

"D'ye reckon?" said Bunny, without much enthusiasm.

"Oh, yeah. You can relax on the beach with your newly hairless back. Ye won't know yourself."

"What's this place you're going called again?" asked Deccie.

"Mauritius."

"And where is it?"

"It's ... Do you know, I'm not actually sure. I just know it's hot and it's all inclusive. So, I'm going to have a week of sitting in the sun, drinking drinks with little umbrellas in them."

Bunny had booked the holiday on a whim one particularly bleak December day while monumentally hungover. He hadn't had a holiday since he was a kid, and he couldn't really afford this one. Still, once he'd confirmed that it was too late to change his mind, he'd found himself really looking forward to it.

"If it's sunny, why would your drink need an umbrella?" asked Deccie.

"It's just a thing they do."

"You'd want to watch that," said Deccie ominously. "There was a thing on telly last week about weirdos putting things in people's drinks. On RTÉ," he added pointedly.

"I think I'll be OK," said Bunny. "I just want to be somewhere hot and relaxing."

"You already are," observed Deccie.

"No offence, lads," said Bunny, "but this isn't exactly what I had in mind."

"Why is it so hot in here?"

"You're in a sauna, Deccie."

"Yeah, but I mean, what's the point of it? Us sitting here like three big hams in a butcher's shop window, sweating our—"

"Language," interrupted Declan Senior automatically.

"—you-know-whats off."

"It's good for you."

"But how?"

Bunny glanced at Declan Senior, who seemed disinclined to take this one.

"It's the heat. It makes you sweat."

"And that's supposed to be good, is it?"

"It, ehm ..." Bunny vaguely remembered something that seemed relevant. "It opens up your pores."

"Your what?"

"Pores. They're like little holes on your skin."

Deccie raised one arm and peered at it intently. "Are you still feeling funny after the waxing, boss?"

Bunny was swiftly experiencing that familiar feeling of a conversation with Deccie Fadden running away from him. "They're little holes, and the steam, it opens them up, and it's good for you."

Deccie looked alarmed. "I'm supposed to be going swimming tomorrow. What happens if these holes are still open? I could drown!"

"No, you won't. Don't worry about it."

Bunny leaned back and closed his eyes, silently praying for this day to be over. "After this," he said, "we've just got the mud bath, and then we're done."

"Oh, I told them we weren't doing that," said Declan Senior firmly.

"Yeah," agreed his grandson, who despite his drowning concerns had resumed putting water on the rocks, "if we go home covered in muck, Granny will hit the roof."

"You don't go home covered in it," said Bunny. "They wash it off ye." He was ninety-five percent certain of this.

"So, what's the point of that, then?" asked Deccie.

"Ara, I don't know."

"Don't worry about it," said Declan Senior. "I signed us up for that whatchamacallit – ironic litigation, whatever that is."

Bunny had taken a couple of deep breaths before one of the remaining parts of his mind that hadn't fallen into a stupor kicked the rest of his brain into action. His eyes flew open and he sat bolt upright.

"You don't mean colonic irrigation, do you?"

"Maybe I do. I'm not great with accents. That might have been what that nice Mr Jensen said. Why, what's one of those?"

Bunny literally didn't know where to start. Despite sitting in a sauna, a chill passed down his spine and into areas he was of the firm opinion should remain un-irrigated. He was lost for words.

There was no way this day could get any worse.

It promptly did. Through the steam, he was aware of the sauna door flying open. A voice he recognised ripped through the air like a chainsaw. "Bernard McGarry, I need a word."

The trio froze in the kind of mortal terror that can only grip an Irishman in the very particular situation of being not not naked when a nun comes storming into the room.

Chapter Two

People who knew Sister Bernadette would often describe her as a "force of nature". They did so because it was a lot more polite than the more accurate description of "walking nightmare". She was five foot nothing and of indeterminate age. A combination of healthy living and near constant scowling means that the only way to effectively estimate the age of the average nun is to cut them open and count the rings. Not that Bernadette was anywhere close to the average nun. She was a member of the Sisters of the Saint – an order that, rumour had it, had been excommunicated and whose members took a considerably more proactive approach to solving the world's problems. The simplest explanation of the difference between the Sisters and other nuns is that Bunny wouldn't be in the least bit surprised to discover Bernadette kept an illegal firearm secreted under her wimple, and he'd pity the person who tried to find out if she did.

Her withering stare had the effect of making most people feel as if they'd inexplicably left the house without wearing trousers. The fact that, at this point in time, Bunny was already trouserless, having only had time to grab one of the Kanin's fluffy robes and a pair of complimentary flip-flops, made him feel especially vulnerable. Bernadette had left the sauna and was waiting for him in the now ironically named "relaxation room". On his way in, Bunny assured the hovering Mr Jensen that everything was OK, as if a nun storming into his place of business was something he should probably expect to happen again in the future.

As soon as Bunny opened the door, he was confronted by Bernadette sitting in an armchair, glaring up at the ceiling.

"What the hell is this noise?" the nun demanded.

Bunny consulted the screen beside the door as he closed it. "It says here that it's sounds of the rainforest."

"And that's supposed to be relaxing, is it?" she scoffed. "I guarantee you that whoever came up with such nonsense has never been to the rainforest. It is not a relaxing place. I've got a scar – somewhere I won't be showing you – from a logger's axe that can attest to that. What are you doing here?"

"What am *I* doing here?" echoed Bunny pointedly. "Shouldn't that be my line? You're in a male-only spa, Bernadette."

She rolled her eyes. "How refreshing. A space just for men. This place reeks of the patriarchy."

"Actually, I think that's lavender," he said, sitting down in the chair opposite her. "Now, what can I do for you? Come to think about it, before we get to that, how the hell did you know I was here?"

"Finding people is one of my many talents."

"And that's not an answer."

"Well spotted. I need you to find a seventeen-year-old boy called Sean Malone."

"Has he been reported to the Gardaí as missing?"

"He's in London, last we know."

"They have police over there, too."

"They do, but I'm sceptical of how motivated they'll be to find a seventeen-year-old runaway, and the clock is ticking. His mother's name is Orla and she's dying. Cancer."

"I'm very sorry to hear that," said Bunny. "I should tell you, though, I'm off on my holidays in a couple of days, so I can't go to London."

Bernadette nodded as if in acknowledgement, but she kept going regardless. "Sean hasn't had it easy. I won't go into all the details but he decided to run away to London to find his father. Daniel Martin. An incorrigible gambler and small-time conman. At least he thinks he is. The only thing he's worse at being than a husband is being a father." She leaned forward. "Sean is a good lad, but he's got problems. I'd be worried about drugs and God knows what else. Orla was hoping he'd go to London, meet Daniel, realise he's not the image of a father he's built up in his mind and then come home again."

"And now," said Bunny, "you're thinking she hasn't got the time to wait for that to happen?"

"There's that," conceded Bernadette, "but there's also the other thing. Sean's been gone for six months now, but each week, without fail, he's sent his mother a letter, telling her how he's getting on. They may be more creative writing exercises than truthful accounts, but he was still sending them. At least he was up until last week."

"He might have just missed a week."

"He never misses a week," said Bernadette firmly. "He knows his mum would worry and he would hate that."

"Does he not ring home?"

"No, because I don't think he'd be able to bear listening to her begging him to come home. He's a good lad, just ... confused. He's seventeen and full of anger, but he loves his mum."

Bunny nodded. He'd known more than enough teenagers to know that things were rarely simple. "So she's worried about him?"

"She was already worried. Now that he's stopped communicating, she's beside herself. The woman is desperate to see him one last time."

Bunny nodded. Sentences beginning with the words "I'd like to help but" kept popping into his mind, although none of them reached his lips. Instead, he went with, "Could you not go looking for him?"

"Normally I would do, but there is another situation I am

required to deal with." Bernadette sat back. "Believe me, you do not want to know the details."

Bunny didn't doubt it. The Sisters viewed laws as things that happened to other people.

"If it was Dublin," said Bunny, "then fair enough, I'd sort it out. But I don't know anyone in London. I'd be staggering around in the dark."

"If I had a better option, I wouldn't be here. I have a couple of leads for you to follow. You could be done in a day. When does your flight leave for your holiday?"

"Four days' time. Saturday."

"Perfect."

Bunny shot her a sceptical look. "If this was as straightforward as you say it is, you wouldn't need me."

The nun fell silent for a few seconds then shrugged. "There might be a complication or two. Nothing you can't handle."

"Such as?"

Bernadette began patting her pockets. "I've got the number for a contact in the Met Police – he should be able to help you track down Daniel's address. I've also got Sean's letters so you can go through them."

"The more you talk, Sister, the more convinced I am that another shoe is about to drop and it's going to smack me right on the back of the head."

From inside her habit, Bernadette produced a bundle of letters and photographs held together by a couple of elastic bands. She pulled a picture off the top of the pile and handed it to Bunny. It was of a young lad and his mother. Him hugging her, messing for the camera – the two of them beaming away, amid fits of laughter. The resemblance was there for all to see in the dark, red hair, aquiline noses, strong jaws and deep, chestnut-brown eyes.

Bunny stared at the image for a long moment. He knew full well what this was. It was easier to say no to a hypothetical situation than to a reality you could picture in your mind while walking out the door. He was damn sure Bernadette knew that, too. The woman had always played for keeps. "I believe you were about to get to the problem part?"

"Not a problem, a lead," she replied, pulling out another photograph and handing it to Bunny. "This was included with one of his letters a few weeks ago."

Bunny looked at the picture. Sean looked different in this one – more careworn, thinner, but the same beaming grin was still there. He was holding up his fist. And the hulking man beside him was holding his own fist aloft next to Sean's. "Is that—"

"Yes," said Bernadette, "I'm reliably informed it is."

"Stevie Brandon, the heavyweight boxing champion of the world," finished Bunny.

Bernadette got to her feet and handed Bunny the bundle of letters and photos. "Keep these safe. There's a mobile number on the top envelope there. That's the Met Police contact. He's a jittery sort, but he can help. Oh ..." She patted her pockets again and produced a bound-up roll of sterling notes. "I won't ask for receipts, but be sensible." She tossed him the money. "I expect an update every twenty-four hours. There's a taxi outside, double-parked, for you. You should hurry. Your flight leaves in just over an hour."

"I've not got my passport or—"

He stopped as she produced a passport from yet another pocket. "Here you go."

He took it and opened it. "This is mine!" He looked up at her in shock. "Did you break into my house?"

"You really shouldn't leave a key under a flowerpot. Have a nice flight."

Chapter Three

Eighty-seven minutes later, Bunny found himself in a window seat on the six-thirty flight to Heathrow wondering what the hell had just happened. He'd been planning on heading to O'Hagan's for a couple of pints, grabbing a curry on the way home and then watching *One Flew Over the Cuckoo's Nest* on telly. A damn fine evening all round. Now he was off to England, looking for a kid he didn't know in a city he didn't particularly like. He'd been in London before, and his overriding memory of the place was of crowds of people rushing everywhere as if something was on fire.

Bernadette's larcenous incursion into his house had extended only to grabbing his passport. While he could have done with some toiletries and other luxuries, such as a change of underwear, upon thinking about it, he'd rather do without them than have to cope with the image of Sister Bernadette going through his undies drawer. After clearing security, he'd had just enough time to grab some socks and a T-shirt from one of the godawful tourist shops, and some briefs from a men's boutique.

Bunny had never bought clothes in a boutique before, having to work up considerable energy just to drag himself into any shop in the best of circumstances. As he'd strongly expected, the difference between a boutique and a shop was about a fifty percent mark-up and a smell of sandalwood, or something like that. This place hadn't even sold boxer shorts, so instead, he'd paid the price of a decent bicycle for a pack of three briefs. When Bunny had queried the price the young fella behind the counter had attempted to explain the revolutionary engineering involved in these undies. All Bunny wanted was to keep his nether regions at an appropriate temperature and an approximate location – he wasn't trying to land his bollocks on the moon. It felt as if capitalism might have peaked back in the nineties, and now people were only improving stuff into obscurity.

Sitting in his window seat, he was feeling uncomfortable, and it wasn't because of his current or future knacker packaging. It was because of the wad of handwritten letters from Sean Malone to his mother, which was balanced on his knee. He'd only glanced at the first couple of paragraphs of the top letter and already it felt like a horrible invasion of privacy. Still, needs must. He had precious little to go on and he needed to find this young fella fast. Bernadette hadn't said exactly how long poor Orla had left, but he got the impression it was weeks rather than months. Bunny pushed his qualms aside and resolved to get on with it. Aside from that, it looked as if he had nothing better to be doing anyway, seeing as the aeroplane was still sitting at the gate. The rising murmur of tutting around him indicated that this hadn't gone unnoticed by his fellow passengers, either. On the upside, on an otherwise full flight, Bunny appeared to have lucked out as the aisle seat beside him remained free.

The letters were a difficult if not particularly long read. It was a one-way conversation, a son writing every week to reassure his mother that everything was going great. Sean mentioned a couple of times that he'd ring soon, but evidently he never did. It was obvious that he loved his mother, and was worried about her worrying about him. Who writes letters in this day and age? People who can't stomach the idea of a direct conversation.

Sean might have been trying to reassure his mother, but he was terrible at keeping his lies straight. In one letter, he'd found a lovely place to live near Tottenham Court Road, and a couple of weeks later, he was "still living in Balham". Bunny didn't know a great deal about the geography of London, but even he knew those two places were on opposite sides of the river. Sean also made reference to working on building sites and making good money, but he referred to all the English lads he was working with as being nice. Again, Bunny was no expert, but he'd wager the price of an over-engineered pack of briefs that most of the casual labourers on any site in London wouldn't be English. Building sites the world over were full of workers from other countries, willing to put in hours of hard and often dangerous work to find a foothold for themselves in their new world. Bunny double-checked the dates on the letters, clearly added by Sean's mother to keep track of things. They confirmed that he'd talked about hoping to sort himself out with a mobile phone, three weeks after claiming he'd lost the one he supposedly already had. This lad would be depressingly easy to trip up in an interview. Along with the letters, some pictures had been included. In addition to the one of Sean and Orla Bunny had seen earlier were a couple more of Sean, one where he was beaming over a birthday cake and another holding an excited looking dog. There was also an older picture, or rather half a picture, showing Sean's father, Daniel Martin, favouring the camera with the kind of smile that could get a man elected. He looked a little taller than Sean but the familial resemblance was obvious to see.

The letter which had accompanied the picture of Sean with the boxer Stevie Brandon was the only one that gave some form of concrete lead. Sean's excitement at the meeting was evident – he said not only had he met the heavyweight champion of the world but he'd also got a job helping out around the gym where the fella trained. That would be Bunny's first port of call in the morning.

He didn't know much about Stevie Brandon aside from some sketchy details. Bunny had boxed in his younger days, but he hadn't followed the sport much beyond that, bar watching the Olympics every four years. Boxing was, more often than not, Ireland's best chance at a medal, the nation having proved better at producing fighters than runners. Bunny recalled that Brandon was born in England but had some Irish roots through his father. Normally, while the Irish were touchy at the merest suggestion of anyone laying claim to one of their sporting stars, they would have an even better shot at a medal if bandwagon-jumping ever became an Olympic event. The thing that sent this particular wagon off the rails was that Brandon Senior had, by all accounts, been a nasty piece of work, his son's ability to take a punch having been trained into him at a young age, it would appear. The father then disappeared and the son ended up in care.

Bunny knew this only because one of the lads in the pub had once told him that Stevie had also killed his father and dumped him in the Thames. He had it on good authority. As always, the authority in question was someone who knew someone who definitely knew all the facts. One of the first things you learned as a police officer was the importance of being able to smell that kind of bullshit from a way off. The story was probably an urban myth, but it had done the rounds enough times for plenty of people to believe it, because they thought that hearing the same story from two different people somehow made it true. Regardless, Brandon was Bunny's best chance at finding Sean, so he and Bunny would be having a conversation as soon as possible.

This reminded Bunny – the first thing he'd do when the plane landed was get hold of one of those *A–Z* maps, as he didn't have a clue where he was going or, come to think of it, where he was going to stay. This was assuming, of course, that they'd ever make it off the runway in Dublin. As he'd been reading the letters, the tide of discontented conversation had swelled around him steadily. They'd been sitting there for nearly half an hour now.

Bunny was about to ask what was happening when a large man

19

stomped through the aircraft door and shuffled down the aisle. It didn't take the world's greatest soothsayer to see where he was heading. Suddenly, Bunny's prized position as the winner on this flight – he who had a row all to himself – was in serious jeopardy. Not only was the extra space gone but the new arrival also looked like one-and-a-half seats' worth of man about to be squeezed into one. As he made his way down the plane, his fellow passengers greeted his arrival with a wave of dirty looks and muttered grumbles. Showing a quite remarkable facility to misinterpret basic social cues, the fella nodded his head and kept saying in a strong Dublin accent, "I know, I know. Unbelievable. These people. Unbelievable. Unbelievable."

As he drew closer, Bunny realised the man wasn't actually that big. Or, at least, a lot of the bulk he was carrying wasn't actually him. He appeared to be wearing several layers of clothing. Under his very stretched jumper, Bunny could spot a hoodie sticking out, and he guessed there were a few T-shirts or shirts under there, too. He was also wearing two pairs of trousers, clutching the waistband of the outer pair to hold them up, as he wasn't able to fasten them over the pair underneath.

"Unbelievable," repeated the man as he wedged himself into the seat beside Bunny. "Absolutely unbelievable."

Bunny tried to reposition himself as he now found himself sharing his seat with what appeared to be a solid portion of this man's wardrobe.

"Unbelievable," he said yet again.

Bunny could sense the man's keenness to have a conversation, so he steadfastly focused on the view of tarmac out the window, to avoid making eye contact.

Dissatisfied, the man nudged him. "You're not going to believe this."

Bunny sighed. "That's what I keep hearing."

"They wouldn't let me bring my bag on. I bought a ticket like everybody else and they wouldn't let me bring my bag on the aeroplane."

"How big was the bag?"

"That's not the point."

"I think it is. 'Tis a rule."

The man ignored this. "I wasn't going to let them win. We have to stand up for ourselves. The little guys."

"You're not that little any more."

The man ignored this, too. Bunny got the impression that to this guy conversation was like a river, in that it flowed only one way and involved quite a lot of babbling. "You'll never guess what I did," he said eagerly.

"You took all your clothes out of your bag and you're now wearing them."

"How'd you know that?" asked the man, the disappointment evident in his voice.

"Because I'm the poor sod having to sit beside you while you take up all that room."

"I think it's a genius idea," the man said defiantly.

"I'm sure the writers of *Friends* did too, seeing as they had it first."

"It's a matter of principle."

"Is it?" said Bunny. "Where's your bag now?"

"I had to dump it at the gate."

"And how much was it worth relative to how much you were going to be charged for checking it in?"

"That's not the point, it's—"

"A matter of principle," finished Bunny. "Yeah, so you said. Fair play to you. You're the Mahatma Gandhi of air travel."

"Is he that cricketer?"

Bunny was already deeply regretting his participation in this conversation. "Yeah."

"Never liked it, meself. Terrible sport."

As it happened, Bunny agreed with him, but he'd rather eat his own shoe than make such an admission at that point.

A member of the cabin crew came up to them, looking flustered. "You need to put your seatbelt on, sir."

"I'd love to," the man said pompously, "but I'm afraid it doesn't fit around me."

"Right," said the flight attendant, and Bunny could detect the unmistakable exasperation of someone who wasn't paid enough for this level of hassle. She turned and called back up the aisle. "Siobhan, we're going to need the extender."

"Yeah," proclaimed the man loudly, like he was the town crier, "this is what you get for your dragonian rules."

"Draconian," said Bunny reflexively.

"See?" insisted the man. "He agrees with me."

Two rows ahead on the left, the head of a small bald man popped up. "Would you stop being an awkward prick. I'm going to miss my connection."

"Me?" said Not Gandhi. "None of this is my fault. I'm standing up for the little guy."

"Could you sit down for him instead?" shouted a female voice from behind them. "Some of us have places to be."

"It's a point of principle."

This prompted the angry little bald head to pop up again. "You can shove your point of principle up your fat arse!"

"Hey! Who you calling fat?"

"Yes," agreed an elderly lady across the aisle. "He's not fat."

"Thank you," said Not Gandhi.

"He's wearing all of his clothes," continued the woman, a notable edge now in her voice, "because he's a pain in the backside who can't follow basic rules."

Bunny's seatmate jabbed a finger towards the flight attendant. "None of them are allowed to talk to me like that. I demand an apology."

The flight attendant tried to smile. "Let's all just calm down."

"I will not calm down. My civil rights are being infringed upon."

At this point, much to the flight attendant's obvious relief, her older colleague turned up. "What's the problem, Eva?"

"This *gentleman*," said Eva, imbuing the word "gentleman" with the kind of barely suppressed rage that only people whose job involves having to deal with the general public at their worst can understand, "is having some words with the other passengers, Siobhan."

"Right," said Siobhan, raising her voice. "We all want this aeroplane to get off the ground as we all have schedules to keep to, so let's keep quiet and get going." She held a seatbelt out to the man. "Your extender, sir."

"No," said the man, folding his arms. "Not until I get my apology." His demand was met with a chorus of agitated tutting. "It's a matter of principle."

"Sir—" began Siobhan, but she didn't get any further as she was interrupted by the bald-headed man, who was now out of his seat, trying to clamber over the passenger sitting beside him. "That's it, I'm going to kick the living crap out of this idiot."

"Sit down," ordered Siobhan, to no effect.

Enough was enough. With difficulty, Bunny got to his feet. "Right. This bullshit ends here." He pointed at the bald man. "You. Seat. Now."

"Not until I've had a word with your buddy."

"He's not my buddy. I'm just the poor sap who got stuck in the seat beside him. Worse luck, I'm an off-duty member of An Garda Síochána, so get back into your seat before you do something daft."

"I want you to arrest him," said the man beside Bunny gleefully, "for threatening my life."

"And I want you to shut up and put your seatbelt on now."

"Can you not arrest him?" asked the older lady from across the aisle, pointing at the walking wardrobe.

"Sadly not," said Bunny, "because, despite my lobbying, being a fecking gobshite isn't currently against the law."

"I'll have your badge," cried the gobshite in question.

"We don't have badges, ye fool. Now, put your seatbelt on right now or else I really will arrest you."

"Arrest me?" squealed the man. "For what?"

Bunny paused for a second then pointed down. "Public indecency. Your trousers are open."

"What? But I've another pair of trousers beneath them."

"And I'm sure you can explain that to the judge. I don't even want to go to London but I fecking have to, and believe me, if I have to get off this aeroplane to arrest you, it's going to go badly for you."

"You all heard that," shouted the man. "He threatened me with police brutality."

"We didn't hear a thing," came a female voice behind them, followed by a murmur of assent.

"Put the belt on," ordered Bunny.

"I am not exposing myself," said the man.

"I can see his winky," shouted the older woman.

This took Bunny aback, and he looked down again. "Really?"

"So can I," said another woman, two seats further up, raising her hand.

A wave of other raised hands swiftly passed up the plane, with more and more passengers attesting to being able to see the man's genitalia.

Bunny looked at Siobhan and Eva, the two flight attendants, who shared his bemusement. "Well," he said, "this is quite the I-am-Spartacus moment, isn't it?"

Bunny took the belt from Siobhan's hand and held it out to the man who'd just metaphorically exposed himself to about eighty people. "Last chance. Put this on now and don't say another word, or else I'm dragging you off this plane."

The man's mouth flapped open and closed a couple of times before he snatched the extender out of Bunny's hand and began buckling himself in.

Bunny sat down and, while Eva helped the man get belted in, Siobhan looked down at Bunny. "Thank you," she said in a quieter voice. "Would you like a complimentary drink when we've taken off?"

"That'd be grand." His seatmate was glaring at him now and

Bunny smiled back. "And in case anyone is wondering, as soon as we fly out over Dublin Bay my jurisdiction ends, so if a door were to mysteriously open and a certain individual were to plunge to his death, that'd be a matter for the coastguard." Bunny lowered his voice and leaned into the man. "I never did like the coastguard."

Chapter Four

I n the time-honoured tradition of people everywhere who've had a thoroughly rotten night's sleep, Bunny rolled his head around his neck in a futile effort to magic away some of the pain. By the time he'd got into central London the previous evening, it had been nine o'clock and he'd needed to find a hotel. The Heathrow Express had whisked him into London Paddington. Anywhere would have done but, like Mary, Joseph and the baby Jesus, he'd found all the hotels were full, although the Saviour hadn't cried his first cry while being breathed on by a donkey because Robbie Williams, the Champions League and a packaging convention had been in town. Even more annoyingly, Bunny found that his Irish mobile wouldn't make outgoing calls.

Eventually, he thought to ask a cabbie where there might be a bed for the night and an extremely helpful Cockney with a preternaturally cheerful disposition directed him up Edgware Road to a place called the Angel's Rest. Bunny now strongly suspected that the Cockney had been so full of the joys of life because his favourite thing in the world was to direct unsuspecting idiots to the worst hotel in London.

The bed was supposedly a double, but Bunny's feet stuck out the bottom of it. It also took up all the available space in the room bar a six-inch gap just wide enough to shuffle around it and wallop your toes against its legs, twice. It was a warning to put your shoes back on, as if the patches of stickiness on the carpet weren't enough of one. There was a wardrobe in the corner that looked entirely unopenable to Bunny, who didn't bother trying, seeing as he'd nothing to put in it. And the water in the bathroom had two settings – Arctic blast or liquid lava. Regardless of what you did with the taps, the temperature seemed to oscillate wildly between the two. He decided to forgo the pleasures of the shower, as sometimes you just need to learn when to cut your losses and avoid having your face melted off.

As Bunny had tried to get his head down, he'd found the mattress managed to be both hard and soft, and was each of those things in exactly the spot where you'd have preferred it to be the other. After attempting to sleep on it, Bunny could have done with a spa day to recover, which seemed deeply ironic. Tired as he was, he'd been kept up half the night by groaning noises from the pipes, or that might have just been the Angel's Rest's other patrons.

On his way out the following morning, the fresh-faced and remarkably cheery girl on reception had asked him how he'd enjoyed his stay. He resisted the temptation to send that conversational serve howling back over the net with some real vigour, and instead assured her that it was top of his list of places to stay the next time his preferred park bench was being refurbished. She even tried to talk him into the breakfast. Bunny was tempted to order it out of a morbid curiosity, but he had places to be and, ideally, didn't want to have to contend with a severe case of the trots while on his way there, so he passed. He promised himself that, later on, he'd find a greasy spoon and indulge in a full Irish breakfast or, failing that, the lesser English equivalent. Opinions varied on what was in each, or whether they were, in fact, different at all, but in Bunny's experience, the English had a criminally insufficient respect for black and white pudding.

He checked his watch again – three minutes past nine. Finally, the guy in the phone box in front of him finished his call and skulked out, giving Bunny a shifty look as he did so. Bunny, twenty-pence coins at the ready, fed a couple in and dialled the number. In an ever-changing world, there were some things you could always rely on – Christmas starting earlier every year, toast landing butter-side down ninety-eight percent of the time and, come rain or shine, Garda Detective Pamela "Butch" Cassidy being at her desk at 9am sharp.

"Major Crimes, Detective Cassidy speaking."

"Jesus," said Bunny, "I love it when you talk all professional."

"Bunny," she said, the all-business tone dropping. "Where the hell are you? I tried to ring you back last night but I couldn't reach you. Did you forget to charge your phone again?"

"No," he responded defiantly. As it happened, his phone was also now out of charge, but it wasn't because he'd forgotten to plug it in. "As it happens, through no fault of my own, my charger is in a different country to me."

"I thought you weren't flying out until the weekend. Oh," she said, lowering her voice and whispering excitedly, "is it wall-to-wall with sultry beauties offering to slather suntan lotion over your alabaster Irish skin?"

"You can keep your fantasies to yourself there, Detective. I'm not in Mauritius, I'm in London."

"What? Why?"

"It's a long story."

"And seeing as you're ringing me to ask for stuff, you're going to tell it to me now."

Bunny gave her a brief overview and, when he'd finished, Butch tutted. "Damn, you must owe that crazy nun a seriously big favour."

"Actually, I was thinking about it all last night, while watching a spider trying to hang itself with its own web on the ceiling of my cesspit of a hotel, and, by my maths, I don't. If anything, she owes me one."

"Ah, but you're using conventional mathematics. Nun maths is very different. Whichever way you add things up, you end up owing them. They're like morality loan sharks."

Bunny fed the phone another twenty pence to stop it from beeping. "You might have a point there. Not to rush you, but I've only got a few coins left and, among other things, I've to report in to the aforementioned merciless sister of mercy after this, so we'd better move this along."

"You're in a phone box? I didn't think anyone used those any more."

"Oh, they do. I'm pretty sure the guy before me was ringing his dealer" – Bunny looked around him – "and, judging from the smell, before that somebody inexplicably confused it with a public convenience."

"I'll say this for you, McGarry, you certainly do know how to paint a picture."

"Speaking of which, would you mind filling me in on a few things?"

"Alright," said Butch. "To be honest, when you left a message asking about Stevie Brandon, I thought you were looking for a tip for Saturday."

"Saturday?"

"Seriously?" asked Butch, incredulous. "Don't you know he's got the big fight coming up? Unification of the belts against your man, Ricky Drake. The American lad who does all the talking. It's in Wembley or somewhere."

Bunny hadn't been aware of that. No doubt lots of people were, but Butch was an avid boxing fan who would probably reel off the undercard if given the chance. While diminutive in stature, she was also a black belt in judo and a couple of other disciplines Bunny couldn't even remember the names of, as well as being an avid enthusiast of all forms of hand-to-hand combat.

"I must ask him for a ticket when I meet him."

"How are you going to do that?"

"Well, to start with, you're going to tell me where I can find him."

29

"And how would I know that?"

"Butch, remember the bit about how I'm on a payphone?"

She tsked. "You're a lot grumpier in London than you are over here."

"You would be too if you'd seen how much I'd to spend to get a lukewarm cup of tea this morning."

"Alright," she said, suddenly all business. "Seeing as you asked, I did some checks. Firstly …"

Bunny pinned the receiver to his ear with his shoulder as he scribbled the address she gave him on the remainder of his boarding pass from the night before. Somewhere called Stripes Gym on Uxbridge Road in Shepherd's Bush.

"Apparently, it's where he first learned to box," Butch continued. "There was an article in the paper about it. Him going back to his roots to prepare for the big fight and all that."

"What else can you tell me about him?"

"Brandon? Tough upbringing. Was in trouble with the law a few times before boxing saved him."

"'Tis a tale as old as time."

"There's also that story about his father, which is almost certainly nonsense."

"Oh, yeah, I've already heard that one – that he killed him when he was thirteen."

"That's the one. People love crap like that. Aside from anything else, how many fully grown adults have we come across that have the wherewithal to get away with murder? The idea that a young kid could is bonkers."

"Amen. We're essentially kept in a job because people are idiots. So, what's this Stevie Brandon supposed to be like?"

"His fighting style is a mix of defensiveness with occasional flurries of brutality. He's pretty much the anti-Muhammad Ali. No showmanship. Grinds people down and has a jaw made of iron. Never hit the canvas once in his entire career. He's not exactly box-office gold, though. Hardly ever talks, owing to a stutter. Every weigh-in he just stands there looking pissed off, like his bus hasn't shown up. Doesn't seem interested in winning people over, either."

"Sounds like a right hoot."

"Yeah. Even in London I wouldn't expect him to have much support. Supposed to be the fight of the decade and they're struggling to shift tickets. He's had some bad press recently, too. He looks overweight and the tabloids are full of stories of his drinking. And then there was the thing with the sparring partner."

"As in?"

"Jesus, you really know nothing."

"Not all of us draw enjoyment from watching people batter each other around the head."

"This was all over the papers. He put one of his training partners in the hospital a couple of weeks ago. His camp described it as a freak accident, but the poor lad was in a medically induced coma, last I heard. Between that and the other stuff ... Well, let me put it this way: his management clearly thought this might be the fight where the British public finally take him to their hearts, but the tabloids have decided there's more mileage in making him into a monster."

"Oh, dear."

"And then there's his management situation, which doesn't help much."

"Go on."

"He's the jewel in the crown of Inevitable Management's stable of fighters, which is run by one Sparky Theakston, real name Alex."

"Hang on," said Bunny. "As in that big dealer?"

"No. Son of. Alex Theakston Senior was a big noise a few years ago, linked to the Callaghans over here. He disappeared a while back. He's either gone to ground or is actually in the ground. Last I heard, nobody had a solid case against him, despite dogs on the street knowing he was bringing a lot of product into Europe. So, if he is on the run, it isn't from the law."

"Do we know which of his business associates he may've pissed off?"

"We could draw names from a hat and it'd be as good as anyone's guess. You know what these international dealers of death are like, always falling out with one another. They're like teenage girls. Odds on, old Alex is deep-sea diving somewhere without the proper equipment."

"Which leaves ... What was he called again?"

"The son? Sparky. He's always gone to great lengths to distance himself from his dad. Says they've not spoken in years and all that. Outside of a couple of naughty-boy moments as a teenager, he's kept his nose clean, too. Still, the stink has hung around Inevitable, deserved or not."

"Sound like a fun bunch."

"Yeah." Butch hesitated slightly. "Seriously, Bunny, tread carefully here. These are some awkward customers, and you're not in Kansas – or Dublin – any more, Toto."

"I'm just here to find a missing young fella whose mother is worried about him."

"Exactly," said Butch. "And I know better than anybody how you get when you think a kid might be in trouble."

"Ah, he's probably not in trouble. This is just a find-and-return-to-sender job. Sean's likely just mooching around London. All I need to do is stick the lad on a flight home and I'll be drinking funny-coloured booze out of a coconut before you know it."

"There's one problem with that theory," said Butch.

"What?"

"If it was just a case of finding a kid and packing him off home, Sister Bernadette wouldn't have sent you."

The phone started beeping again and Bunny checked the coins he had left. He still had other calls to make. "I need to go."

"Like I said, Bunny, tread carefully."

"I'm beginning to think the whole lesbian thing is a ruse to hide the fact you're in love with me."

"And I'm beginning to think you should—"

Butch's riposte was lost as the line went dead.

Chapter Five

Shepherd's Bush was a hive of activity, in an angry-anthill-a-kid-has-just-rammed-a-stick-into kind of way. Mid-morning traffic honked and howled, and the pavements were thronged with humanity rushing about. The only people who looked relaxed were the homeless men huddled around a couple of benches in the middle of the green, sharing a large two-litre bottle of something between themselves while casually shooting the breeze.

Finding his way around had not been easy, but with the aid of the A–Z and the help of an older woman who didn't seem that inclined to offer assistance but who was walking too slowly for her refusal to be an option, Bunny eventually orientated himself. Whoever decided to have two separate tube stations on different lines, both called Shepherd's Bush, needed a clatter around the earhole.

His distracted internal musings on the subject meant that he was taken by surprise when he found himself standing in front of the Shepherd's Bush Empire. Bowie, the Rolling Stones, Johnny Cash, Jeff Buckley and Elvis Costello, to name a few, had all played legendary gigs there. The sign outside showed that this evening, West

London would be treated to a performance by the American band the Bloodhound Gang. Oh, well, they couldn't all be winners.

Uxbridge Road was one of the main thoroughfares that shot off each corner of the roughly triangular green. As he'd turned onto it, a woman on a mountain bike had ridden through a red light and, as the traffic camera had flashed, taken the time to toss a casual two fingers to the Man. Bunny couldn't help but smile. Even though he was a member of law enforcement, he could appreciate an act of well-executed civil disobedience as well as the next person.

As he turned around and retraced his steps north, he noticed the sign pointing people in the direction of the BBC's Television Centre, and then he remembered why the name Uxbridge Road had rung a bell. It had been bothering him ever since he'd taken down the address.

Up this way, the pace and intensity of the pedestrian traffic eased. It was still a couple of hours until lunch, but enticing smells were already drifting out of the various global fast-food joints. Bunny still hadn't had breakfast. He decided that after this, he'd resolve that issue emphatically. Sister Bernadette's wad of cash was tucked in the inside pocket of his coat and she could definitely stand him a solid breakfast, not to mention a better hotel, which he was determined to get for himself that night, should it be required. He was holding out hope that he might strike it lucky first time and Sean Malone would be at Stripes Gym. Then they could both be on an afternoon flight home.

Stripes Gym looked more like a builder's yard than it did a sporting facility, so much so that he almost walked past it. Large metal electronic gates stood closed at the entrance. The only indication of what lay behind them was a battered sign featuring a pair of boxing gloves, which could just about be seen through the bars, and the pale, acne-scarred man standing in front of them. He looked as if he was hit in the face on a regular basis, and as soon as Bunny entered into his first exchange with him, he felt inclined to join that particular club.

He'd say this for the man – normally, the kind of guys you find doing "unofficial security" are the sort who need to get their clothes from specialist shops and who can block out the sun while leering down at you. This fella, Bunny reckoned, was light middleweight at best, and while he had the muscle-bound build, he'd be suffering when it came to reach. He was no more than five foot ten with long blond hair that flowed majestically in the light breeze. He must have been using all kinds of conditioners and whatnot. As his mane of hair cascaded around a face that appeared to be fixed in a perpetual sneer, backed up by its owner's permanent bad mood, the overall effect was that of an Afghan hound that had been given too many steroids.

"I don't give a fuck who you fucking are or who the fuck you're fucking looking for," the guy snarled in a rapid-fire London accent, "nobody gets fucking in no matter fucking what."

"I appreciate that," said Bunny, trying to find a different way of phrasing his opening request. "I'm just here looking for a missing teenage boy as there's a family emergency and we think he might work here."

"What the fucking fuck is it that you're not getting? Fuck the fuck off!"

Bunny decided to abandon the charm offensive in the light of the offensive offensive. "Seriously? Are you on some kind of sponsored swear or something? I like a bit of effing and jeffing as much as the next man, but you appear to be making a run at getting into the *Guinness Book of Records.*"

The man pulled a face that was no improvement on the one he already had. "Oh, well, excuse me, Your fucking Highness. I wouldn't wish to offend your fucking ears." He jabbed a finger in the direction from which Bunny had come. "This is private fucking property, so why don't you fucking fuck the fuck off, fucker."

"Firstly, well done. I reckon that last sentence might be your personal best. Secondly," Bunny gestured at the pavement they were both standing on, "this isn't private property. It's a footpath."

He nodded to the closed gates behind Sweary. "*That* is private property, and normally, people leave their guard dogs inside the gate."

"Are you fucking calling me a fucking dog?"

"I would never do that," said Bunny. He mentally added that he would never be so rude to dogs as to lump this gobshite in with them.

Oddly, this seemed to mollify Sweary slightly, who mistakenly took it as some sort of victory. "Yeah. That's what I thought."

Bunny decided to take another shot at appealing to the guy's better angels. "Look, I'm not trying to cause hassle but I'm here on behalf of the kid's mother. She's really not well and she's desperate to find her son so he can come home to see her."

"Ahhh," said Sweary, dripping with insincerity, "that's touching. The journalist yesterday had an important message for the champ, and one last week had just found his wallet and was trying to return it to him."

"I'm not a journalist," protested Bunny.

"Exactly what one of you fucking parasites would say."

"If you must know, I'm a member of the Garda Síochána."

"The what now?"

"It's the Irish police force."

"Bollocks."

Bunny pulled his ID from his pocket and held it out. The man reached for it, but Bunny drew it back. Some tricks you don't get caught on twice. Once you've retrieved your badge from a canal in the dark the first time, that lesson stays with you. "Look with your eyes."

The man waved a hand. "Fuck off. What the fuck is that? Could be fucking anything. My mate Andy got a fucking card says he's an official boob inspector. Don't fucking mean he is one."

"I can think of at least one massive tit of his acquaintance."

"I'm not even sure you're fucking Irish. That accent sounds fucking fake and all."

Bunny could feel his eye starting to twitch. Something about that comment struck deep in his soul and made his knuckles itch. "What did you say?"

"You heard me."

"Do you realise you forgot to swear in that last sentence?"

The man's eyes narrowed. "I'll swear at you in a fucking minute."

"Now, that's an example of a redundant fecking statement."

"Ha," said the man triumphantly. "You ain't fucking Irish. The word "feck" was invented for that fucking *Father Ted* programme. Everybody fucking knows that."

Bunny threw out his hands. "Sweet baby Jesus on a fecking skateboard, give me strength. Is there any chance there's an eejit I could speak to, because it'd be a massive upgrade on what I'm currently dealing with?"

"You can—"

While Bunny had a very strong theory on where the rest of that sentence was heading, he never found out, as Sweary was interrupted by a blaring car horn that made them both jump.

He turned to see a brunette woman at the wheel of a silver BMW. She leaned out of the window, looking irritated. "Is there a problem, Sebastian?"

"No, Ms Theakston. Sorry, Ms Theakston."

Theakston. As in Sparky Theakston, presumably. A wife, sister, possibly daughter? Seizing the opportunity, Bunny stepped towards the road to address the woman directly.

"Madam, my name is Bernard McGarry. I'm a detective in the Irish police force and I'm here looking for a young lad called Sean Malone. His mother is ill, and we desperately need to find him. The last correspondence anyone got from him was a letter with a picture of him standing with Mr Brandon. The letter said he was working here." Bunny produced the photograph and held it out to back up his story.

The woman studied the photo for a long moment then said, in a softer voice, "OK, stay here, I'll be out in a couple of minutes and we'll see what we can do."

"Thank you," said Bunny.

"Sebastian?" she said expectantly.

Sweary stepped meekly to one side and pressed a button on a remote to open the gates.

As the car passed by and pulled into the yard, Bunny said under his breath, "Sebastian? No wonder you're so angry."

"Fuck off."

Bunny watched through the closing gates as the woman got out of the car. After a last look in his direction, she made her way inside.

He and Sweary stood there for a full minute until Bunny decided to break the frosty silence. He needed to tell somebody. "Interesting fact about Uxbridge Road. It was somewhere along here that *The Goon Show* team got themselves an apartment to work in so that BBC executives wouldn't keep popping by and bothering them while they were writing their scripts."

"What the fuck are you talking about?"

"The Goons?" he said to an expression of blank aggression. "Peter Sellers. Spike Milligan. Michael Bentine. That fella from *Songs of Praise*. Revolutionised British comedy. Precursor to Monty Python. The Goons?"

"Are you fucking drunk?"

"No," said Bunny, "but I think I'd have to be to enjoy this conversation."

Thankfully, the exchange didn't go any further as the gates behind Sweary started to open. Through them, Bunny could see the woman returning. Now that he had a better look at her, Bunny could see her dark-red suit was finely cut, and everything about her appearance evidenced a combination of taste and money. The man trailing in her wake gave off a decidedly different vibe. Broad-shouldered and dark-skinned, with neatly trimmed locs and a goatee, he wore a suit and moved with an easy grace. What struck Bunny first, though, were the guy's piercing brown eyes, which assessed him as he approached from across the yard. It was like being in an aquarium and experiencing the unnerving sensation that the resident shark was focusing its attention solely on you.

"Now," said the woman, "let's see if we can help resolve this situation." She threw a glance at Sweary. "Thank you, Sebastian."

Sweary nodded. "No problem, Ms Theakston."

The big guy gave an almost imperceptible eye-roll then jerked his head towards the building. Only then did Sweary Sebastian finally take the hint and skulk off with his tail between his legs. After he'd left, the woman favoured Bunny with a smile that was all business.

"Now, I'm Charlotte Theakston," she said. "And this gentleman is Lawrence Cooper, who oversees Mr Brandon's security, amongst other things. And remind me, please, you are?"

"Bernard McGarry."

"An Irish police officer?"

"Yes. I'm here as a friend of the family, though. Orla Malone, Sean's mother, is sadly terminally ill. Cancer."

"Oh, that's awful."

"Yes," agreed Bunny. "Her son came over to London looking for work and all that, but they've lost contact with him and they're desperate to let him know."

"Sorry, just so I understand," she said, tilting her head, "he's a runaway?"

"I wouldn't say that. 'Tis a complicated family situation. He had a rough childhood and he's come here looking for the father he hasn't seen since he was very young. He has a good relationship with his mother, though." Bunny produced the picture of Sean standing beside Stevie Brandon again. "He sent this to her. I just need to find him so I can tell him the bad news and bring him home."

Charlotte motioned for the picture and Bunny handed it to her. After studying it, she passed it to Cooper. "Do you remember this boy, Lawrence?"

The big man spoke for the first time, his voice a low rumble. "I think he was one of the drop-ins. Maybe here only once or twice. Never worked here, though."

39

He held out the picture for Bunny to take back.

"You have to understand," said Charlotte, "Stevie had a tough upbringing himself, and so he's always trying to be a positive influence on the youth. Kids regularly drop by the gym and he personally makes sure they get a good meal. He's always encouraging them in his way to make good choices. Of course, that side of him, the British press, in their infinite wisdom, has no interest in." There was an unmistakable undercurrent of bitterness to her last words. "They do so love to stereotype."

"Right," said Bunny, before turning his attention to Cooper. "Do you have any idea when Sean was last here?"

The guy shrugged. "Maybe last week. Like I said, a lot of kids come through here."

"Do you know anyone who might be able to tell me where he could be?"

Cooper just shrugged again.

Bunny nodded. "Could I have a quick chat with Stevie – see if he remembers anything?"

Charlotte shook her head firmly. "I'm afraid that's absolutely impossible."

"Just a couple of minutes."

"No. As I'm sure you're aware, this week is the biggest fight of Stevie's career and we cannot afford to have him distracted, even for a second."

"I appreciate that, and I wouldn't ask, only—"

"It's a hard no," she said, cutting him off.

"Is there anyone else I could—"

"Mr McGarry, while we are, of course, sympathetic to your situation, I don't think there is anything we can do to assist you. If you leave your contact details with Lawrence, we will definitely contact you should ... what was the name again?"

"Sean," supplied Bunny.

"Should we see Sean again," Charlotte finished. "But I highly doubt it. Besides, in the final week it's a completely closed camp, and after that, Stevie will be on holiday, and my brother and I are relocating to Las Vegas on a permanent basis. I'm sure you understand. The very best of luck to you."

And with that, she turned and walked back through the gates, leaving Bunny with Cooper, who folded his arms.

"Look—"

"You heard the lady. You want to give me a number?"

Sensing that there was no point pleading his case further, Bunny ripped off part of his boarding card and scribbled his Irish mobile number on it.

"If you think of anything, or anyone knows where—"

Cooper took the number, turned and walked back inside, the gates closing behind him. Bunny didn't have the chance to tell him he'd need to charge his phone first, but he had the strong feeling his number was going to find its way into a bin in about five seconds tops anyway.

As the gates clanged shut, Cooper stopped at the main door to the gym and gave Bunny one last long look before heading inside.

Something about the whole conversation had been off, but Bunny couldn't quite put his finger on it. He looked down at the picture he was still holding and the beaming grin on Sean Malone's face. He had to find the lad, and the one and only lead he had was the other person in the picture, Stevie Brandon. He needed to talk to the boxer, and nothing and nobody was going to stop him from doing so. He'd taken the sensible steps open to him, and that had left him standing here with nothing but a promise that was an obvious fob-off. He glanced to his left. If the mountain wasn't going to come to Muhammad, then Muhammad was going to drop by, regardless of how welcome he was going to be. In less biblical terms – sensible hadn't worked, it was time to get stupid.

Chapter Six

The thing about acting casual is that anyone attempting to do so is one of the most conspicuous sights known to mankind. It's like when somebody asks you to walk normally – suddenly, your legs feel as if you just got a lend of them from two different people and you've put them on the wrong way round.

This was why, as Bunny walked down the street to the side of Stripes Gym, he concentrated on scratching his armpit vigorously. In his experience, nobody wanted to spend their time looking at a man rummaging around in his own armpit. It was a judiciously selected bodily location. Picking at your nose or ear was gross enough for people to be drawn to look at you – much how people slow down to gawp at a car crash on a motorway. Similarly, if you were adjusting your underwear, then you'd be the focus of much attention because there was the possibility you might need to be burned at the stake for being a wrong 'un. Scratching your armpit, though? It spoke of questionable hygiene without being a public health hazard or a danger to the kiddies. Crucially, nobody looked at a man rummaging around in his own sweaty armpit and thought, *There's a man casing the joint in order to get up to nefarious activities.*

And casing the joint was exactly what Bunny was up to. He currently had precisely nothing to go on in his search for Sean Malone, and waiting around for that situation to change wasn't his style. Earlier, after he'd got off the phone with Butch, he'd rung the number Bernadette had given him that was supposedly for a contact at the Met Police, but all it had resulted in was the chance to speak to a voicemail using the standard network message. He'd said who he was, dropped Bernadette's name and mentioned that he was looking for Sean Malone or Sean's father, Daniel. He'd also said he'd call back later, assuming that whoever picked up the message hadn't immediately deleted it after dismissing it as the ramblings of a random nutter.

Now his options were trying to get into Stripes Gym where, presumably, Stevie Brandon was currently training, or spending most of his day sightseeing. He'd seen an advert on the tube for Madame Tussauds, but it hadn't grabbed him. For the life of him he couldn't understand why anyone would want to see good waxworks. The whole point was to go and view the ones that had got it hilariously, badly wrong. If you wanted to see what a famous person looked like, you could consult any of the hundreds of pictures of said celebrity available everywhere. That was the definition of a celebrity, someone you could identify on sight. As far as Bunny was concerned, the art form of wax-working existed only so you could stare in wonder at a Madonna who looked like she'd been captured mid-fight outside a kebab shop, or a Michael Jackson where the sculptor had, incredibly, failed to capture any of his multiple incarnations.

The threatening dark clouds from that morning were now releasing a drizzle that was striving to get upgraded to a full-on shower, which helped keep foot traffic in the area light. The side street, which comprised mostly terraced housing, was being used by a few pedestrians and even less vehicular traffic. Plus, it was bin day, so anyone out walking was primarily focused on dodging around the assault course that bin men see it as their duty to leave in their wake. A mother pushing a pram marched by, careful not to make eye contact. A postman went about his business. A woman sat parked up in her car, arguing with somebody on her mobile phone.

Bunny took a right turn and, after walking a few yards, found what he'd been looking for – a laneway. Disciplining himself not to look around first – a sure signal on the same list as shouting "I'm about to do something illegal" – he headed straight down the path. Back gates leading into postage-stamp-sized gardens lined either side of the alley, but straight ahead was the rear of a three-storey building with the functionality of a place of business rather than the warmer touches of a homestead. Its metal gate had the kind of chunky chain and padlock that screamed "seriously, don't bother" but, thankfully, there was a considerably easier option. A ten-foot wall stood between the building and the laneway, but there was also currently a large skip bin covered with a lid sitting flush against it, allowing easy access for the intruder on a tight schedule. God bless bin day.

As a rule, Bunny didn't break into places. As a law, in fact – given that it was an illegal activity pretty much everywhere in the world. Still, he was also aware that if he gained entry to the building without doing any breaking, and it was the middle of the day, the local boys in blue were unlikely to get exercised about it beyond a slap on the wrist and a firm reminder not to go anywhere near the place again. He was unarmed, not nicking anything and, ideally, looking to talk to the heavyweight champion of the world, to whom, Bunny assumed, he would safely be considered as posing no threat, unless the sport had taken an unexpected touchy-feely turn since he'd last watched a fight. It didn't feel like a great plan, but it benefited from being the only one he had.

He bent down to tie his laces and managed a surreptitious glance to confirm that nobody was watching him from the back windows of any of the surrounding houses. Then, in one fluid motion, he straightened up, hauled himself onto the skip bin, grabbed the top of the wall and slid over it. Bunny had always prided himself on being considerably more catlike than he appeared. When Butch took the piss out of the paunch he was developing, she was missing a crucial point: being a few pounds overweight simply allowed him to lull people into a false sense of security. It was his very own form of urban camouflage.

He landed on the other side of the wall in a yard where crates, a discarded sink and other detritus lay scattered about the place. He risked another scan of his surroundings to confirm he remained unobserved and, once satisfied, he paused to consider his next move. A few steps led down to a basement door that seemed well secured, judging by its three padlocks and the bars on its window. More promisingly, a metal staircase led to a fire escape that looked as if it was in regular use. Bunny climbed its steps and tried the door but found it firmly locked. It did reveal to him a more promising consolation prize, though. On the wall to the left of the door, about five feet up, was the frosted glazing of what looked like a bathroom window. The top of the casement was ajar, and it'd be a tight squeeze, but Bunny reckoned he might just be able to make it through.

Wedging his right foot onto a solid-looking clamp fixing a drainpipe to the wall to the right of the window, he gave it a little test. Reassured that it seemed as secure as it looked, he grabbed the pipe above and hoisted himself up until he could get his left foot onto the windowsill. Catlike. He didn't bother checking if he could hear anyone inside the bathroom as anyone in there would have already noticed him. He prised the top window open as far as it would go, before shoving his head inside. As expected, a bathroom – albeit one that could do with a deep clean. It'd be tight but Bunny reckoned he could make it.

Putting his arms through first, he braced himself on either side of the window frame and started to drag himself inside. He hauled almost half of his body in before hitting trouble, some of it impending, some of it immediate. His "urban camouflage", along with the bulk of his sheepskin overcoat, which he now realised he should've taken off before attempting this venture, were causing his midriff to get caught on the frame. Then there was the issue he'd not given enough contemplation to previously – namely, how he was going to get down to the floor. Entering feet first hadn't been an option, but it now seemed like head first shouldn't have been one either. At the moment, his best choice appeared to be falling in, and in doing so, he'd be doing well to avoid the sink almost directly below the window. Now he had a better view, he could see that in contrast to the rest of the bathroom, it was almost brand new. The one in the yard outside must have been its predecessor.

Bunny tried easing himself back, but it appeared he was too far in to extract himself. The only way out was forward. Or at least it would be, if the belt of his trousers wasn't caught on the lock of the window. As he tried to move his hands around to free it, he lost his balance and started tipping forward. He managed to get his hands down just in time to grasp either side of the sink, which prevented him going head first into it, but he was now utterly, completely and irreversibly stuck, mostly upside down, half in and half out of the window. This was not his most catlike of moments.

The thought that maybe he could free himself by opening his trousers had just occurred to him when the door to the bathroom opened. He couldn't see who it was, just a pair of trainer-clad feet.

"Thank God you're here," he said. "I'm having the weirdest shit imaginable."

The last thing he remembered was the dull thud of something hitting him hard in the back of the head, and then he blacked out.

Chapter Seven

The first time Bunny came to, someone was putting the boot into him and he could taste unwashed linoleum squashed against his mouth. His body clearly decided he didn't need to be there for that bit and he lost consciousness again.

The second time, he was flying. Or at least the ground was trundling by a few feet beneath him. Hands were on him. Two – no, three – people carrying him. Blood was dripping onto the oil-stained concrete. Some part of his brain that was mid-reboot took the time to inform him it was his. Whoever was carrying him came to a stop. Voices he couldn't make out through his mental fog had a brief discussion above his head. A bang followed and then, suddenly, he was flying upwards, a moment of weightlessness, swiftly followed by a painful landing inside a freshly emptied skip bin, which meant there was no cushion between him and its metal bottom. Bloody bin day. He waxed and waned between consciousness and unconsciousness again. Somebody barked something that he didn't catch, but he felt he'd probably got the gist of it given the context. The skip bin lid slammed shut with a deafening roll of thunder and total darkness enveloped him. The fetid stench should've made it hard to breathe, but the blood gushing from his nose was making any use of that part of his body a challenge. He could taste it, though. He lost consciousness once more for somewhere between seconds and days, then his head jerked backwards, and its additional collision with the metal wall was one he could have done without.

Bunny tried to gather himself together and take an inventory of his current condition. His nose was a bloody mess but from a tentative examination it seemed not to be broken. His ears were ringing and an impressive bump was already forming on the crown of his head. He guessed that might've been the sink. The pain in his ribs was all thanks to the welcoming committee, though. He'd lay good money on Sweary Sebastian having been involved. He felt around some more – a cut above his right eye was adding to the blood flowing down his face. Unbidden, five words bounced around his battered head – drinks with little umbrellas in.

The small part of his mind that was still functional was debating the merits of trying to get up versus staying where he was and spending the remainder of his days living in a bin, like a modern-day Oscar the Grouch, when the decision was made for him. A pounding on the side of the skip bin started up a steady rhythm, making it feel like he was in the innards of a metal monster, adjacent to its thumping heart. Finding enough anger to rouse his battered carcass into action, he struggled into a crouched position before getting to his feet, throwing open the large bin's lid and emerging, fists at the ready.

"What in the fecking—"

His brain hadn't had the capacity to expect anything, but if it had, the sight that greeted him would not have been it. A man in a crumpled white linen suit complete with a jauntily angled fedora was standing in front of him, a cane paused mid whack in one hand, a lit cigar in the other. His skin had the look of leather that'd been left out in the sun too long, but he wore a smile under his lively eyes. He was seventy if he was a day, and some of those days looked as if they'd been action packed.

"And he's back with us!" said the man in a breezy American

accent. "You're awake. Standing eight count. Life in the old dog yet, et cetera, as y'all like to say."

Bunny blinked a few times in order to focus his eyes. He hadn't hallucinated when taking wallops to the head in the past but there was a first time for everything. "What the hell have you come as? The Man from Del Monte?"

"People keep shouting that at me. Gotta say, I don't get the reference."

"You've not exactly dressed for the season."

"And you're in a dumpster covered in your own blood," said the man. "We've all made questionable life choices."

"You should see the other guy," said Bunny, placing his hands on the bin's metal rim as he tried to let his sense of balance sort itself out now that it looked as if he'd be staying alive – for a while, at least.

"I did," countered the man. "Three of them, in fact. Completely unscathed and in the full bloom of violent health as they tossed you into that receptacle in an incident eerily reminiscent of how my fourth wife left me."

"You've had four wives?"

"I've had seven."

"How've you had seven?"

"The trick is to keep getting divorced, or you could always convert to one of the wackier religions, but no woman worth having is happy to play second banana to anybody. Mind you, number five is now shacked up with a female deep-sea diver from Portugal, but I get the impression there's definitely no room in that particular rowboat for a man. More's the pity – she was a knockout. Still, that's me – I've got a lot of love to give."

"Apparently," said Bunny. "Between you and Liz Taylor, I'm amazed anyone is still single."

"Those who live in glasshouses shouldn't throw stones, and those who live in dumpsters ... Well, you can finish that one for yourself."

Bunny shook his head. "Sorry, who the hell are you?"

"Milton Fisk, lowly scribbler, highly regarded, dishonourable discharge national guard, two-time recipient of the LaBroxi award, barred from entering Colombia the country, honours degree from Columbia the university, and once called the greatest living boxing writer by Don King who, coincidentally, also has a restraining order out against me. Oh, and last time I checked there were two contracts out on my life, and I'm a more than adequate ballroom dancer."

Bunny attempted to take in at least some of that information. "Right," he said, because nothing else came to mind. Milton Fisk spoke like life was a horse race he was commenting on, and Bunny had a fair idea that even when at his best he'd probably have a hard time keeping up.

"And you are?"

"Bernard McGarry, but everyone calls me Bunny."

"Really? And you let them?"

"I do." Bunny normally got very defensive about remarks such as this, but given how his morning was going, it wasn't a fight he had the energy for right then.

"Well, we all have our crosses to bear. Anyway, how about you get out of the dumpster and I'll buy you a drink. I'll even see about getting you some complimentary ice and sympathy."

Bunny nodded. "One second." He bent over and vomited in the skip bin before straightening back up.

"There goes breakfast."

"Actually, that was what was left of last night's dinner. I've not managed to have breakfast yet."

"Just as well. It'd have been a waste. You can get out of there unassisted?"

It was phrased more or less as a question, but intoned in such a way that any answer other than yes would not be welcome. In response, Bunny gracelessly hoicked himself over the side of the skip bin, landing unsteadily on his feet and narrowly avoiding pulling the whole thing over on top of him.

"Can't keep a good man down," said Fisk cheerfully, in between puffs on his cigar.

"What gives you the impression I'm a good man?"

"Mainly the quality of the people who threw you in the dumpster. They haven't endeared themselves to me with the standard of their hospitality, although seeing how they treated you, I'm starting to think I got off lightly. My enemy's enemy and all that jazz." He did some kind of soft-shoe shuffle then extended a hand which was holding a handkerchief. "Speaking of which, you might want to clean off some of the ... everything."

Bunny took the handkerchief with a nod. "Thanks." He glanced down at the blood on his coat and shirt, not to mention the other less easily identifiable stains he'd picked up, because an empty skip bin is never truly empty.

As he started wiping some of the blood off his face, Bunny followed Fisk's eyes. The man was looking up at the rear window of one of the nearby houses, where an older woman in a housecoat was watching them, holding a phone to her ear.

"Would I be right in assuming you don't want to discuss this matter with the local constabulary?" asked Fisk.

"Best not," confirmed Bunny.

"I don't blame you. Never been in a situation that law enforcement sticking its oar in didn't make worse."

Fisk started walking down the alleyway and Bunny followed, his legs in surprisingly good working order, all things considered.

"Should now be the point at which I mention I'm a policeman?"

Fisk turned and raised an eyebrow at him. "Ideally, I think you should start all conversations with that piece of information."

"I'm not one here," clarified Bunny. "Back home in Ireland."

"I see. Do the locals over there ever throw you out with the trash?"

Bunny spat some blood on the ground as they turned back onto the street. "Not twice they don't."

"I bet." He gave a cheery wave of his cane. "Now, let's see about getting you that drink."

Chapter Eight

Bunny looked at the sign above the establishment they were walking towards. "The Duck and Trumpet?" he read. "What is it with the English and these mental pub names?"

"I like to think there's a story behind it and I don't want to ask for fear of being disappointed," replied Milton Fisk. "Guess I'm a romantic at heart."

"I'm sure all the wives would agree."

"Actually," said Fisk, favouring him with a grin, "I think they would. Only a true romantic is willing to hop back on the merry-go-round as many times as I have. Life is nothing but the pursuit of moments of pure unadulterated beauty, and I'm proud to say I've seen my fair share. Death is merely life's crescendo, we all just have to make sure we've put in enough notes to make it worth building up to."

"Did you just come up with that?" asked Bunny.

"What?"

"All that crescendo stuff?"

Fisk shrugged. "I don't know. To be honest, I don't really listen to what I'm saying half the time. I just let it flow." He clicked his fingers as he took a few quick puffs on the butt of his cigar before stubbing it out on a standing ashtray under the pub's awning.

Bunny paused. "Much as I'd love a drink right now, I'm not sure anywhere is letting me inside in this state."

Milton waved away his concerns. "No hostelry worthy of the name would turn away a valiant soldier wounded while fighting the good fight." He turned around and started to push his way through the pub's door backwards. "Besides – they love me here."

Bunny heard the voice before he saw its owner. It chimed as soon as Milton Fisk made it through the door of the Duck and Trumpet. "Oh shit, he's back!" It belonged to a female and was so husky it sounded as if it could be used to sand wood.

Fisk took a bow. "My darling, Barbara. I told you I would return to you."

"Yeah, like crabs."

Bunny came in behind Fisk and the owner of the voice, an attractive woman of around fifty with freckles and an impressive perm of dyed cherry-red hair, frowned at him.

"Christ, look what the Yank dragged in," she said. "No offence, love, but Milton, we ain't taking in waifs and strays now." She wrinkled her nose. "Especially ones I can smell from here."

"Don't be too hasty to judge, my darling Barbara. This poor soul is the one and only Bernard McGarry." Fisk waved his hands at Bunny like a magician performing the grand reveal at the end of a trick. "A brave knight who got waylaid on his noble mission by a gang of vagabonds and miscreants. He fought them off valiantly before being overwhelmed by their sheer number and thrown into an accumulation of refuse by said horde of villainy."

Barbara pursed her cherry-red lips and glanced at the two men sat at the bar, one in a flat cap and the other in a woollen beanie, both of whom were seemingly engrossed in their respective copies of the *Racing Post*. "Now, let me see if I can translate that from Milton speak to English – this poor bastard got mugged and dumped in a bin. Am I right?"

Bunny gave a sigh. "That's it, more or less."

She tilted her head. "You Irish?"

"I am."

She nodded her approval. "I like the Irish. Good drinkers."

Bunny returned her nod. Some stereotypes he could live with.

"You live over here?" she asked.

"No. I'm here looking for a young fella. His ma is seriously ill, and we need to find him."

"I see. And you're a friend of Milton's?"

"A fast friend," interjected Fisk. "In that we only met fifteen minutes ago, but I am an impeccable judge of character."

"Says the man who's been married seven times," replied Barbara.

"And each was a woman of impeccable character. I don't marry just anyone."

"Really?" said Bunny. "It sounds like you marry damn near everyone."

This elicited a deep and dirty laugh from Barbara. "Good one. Alright, he seems on the up and up, but we still got standards to maintain in this here establishment. You can use the shower in Milton's room. And you look about the size of my late husband, so I reckon we can find a change of clothes for you."

"That'd be very kind of you," said Bunny.

"You're an angel, Barbara," added Fisk.

"One who will be adding all this to your tab."

"I was about to insist," said Fisk with a flourish. "I and the good readers of *Cigar Aficionado Monthly* are delighted to assist this fine gentleman in his hour of need."

"You're staying here?" asked Bunny, surprised.

"Of course. Excellent location, top-notch facilities and convivial company," he said, indicating the two gents at the bar. The one in the woolly hat gave a huffed laugh in response. "What else could a man ask for?"

Barbara turned around and pointed at a door beside the bar. "Come on, then, Bernard. Let's get you sorted out."

"Thanks very much," he said, following her lead. "By the way, everyone calls me Bunny."

"Really?" she said, pushing through the door. "Takes all sorts, I suppose. I'm Babs."

"Thanks again for this, Babs," Bunny said, as she led him up the stairs. "And sorry to hear about your husband."

"What? Oh, I don't know for sure he's dead, I just like to think he is."

Behind the door, the walls were festooned with framed portraits of horses and dogs. From what Bunny could see, the whole place had a homely if rather dated feel. When Babs reached the top of the stairs, she turned to face him. They'd come to a stop on a landing with three doors leading off it and another set of stairs heading up to a third floor.

"Now," she began, "I'm happy to go along with that getting-mugged story because I keep my nose out of other people's business, but just so you know, I didn't come down in the last shower. I run a respectable establishment. You bring trouble to my door and you and I are gonna fall out fast." She wagged a red-nailed finger in his face. "And you'd better have nothing to do with drugs. I have no truck with the filth."

"A woman after my own heart," said Bunny. "Couldn't agree more." He didn't need it pointing out to him that, given the circumstances, revealing his profession was probably unwise. Besides, he wasn't a copper here. Over here, he was just another bloke who'd been thrown in a bin.

"Right, then," she said. "Seems we understand each other. Milton's room is through there, bathroom is on the left. I'll leave fresh towels and a change of clothes on the bed. Dump your things in the linen basket and I'll wash the lot." She grabbed Bunny's chin and moved his head about in an assessing manner. "Your nose ain't bust but I'll need to put a stitch in that cut."

"You can do that?" asked Bunny.

"Oh, yes." She let go of his chin. "You got a nasty bump coming up too, so I'll get you some ice, for all the good it'll do. Plenty of folk had a low opinion of my hopefully dead ex long before I did, so I got to learn some field medicine. Serves me right for not reading the signs. When people are frequently inclined to punch a man in the head, at a certain point you should take it as a sign. Give the water a minute to heat up."

* * *

Half an hour later, Bunny was back downstairs, clean, in fresh clothes, with a couple of stitches and a bandage around his head wound, and ice on the bump. Babs had indeed proved to be a gifted nurse, and she'd sewn him up with remarkable speed. He'd sat there, gritting his teeth through the pain, enveloped in a cloud of her sweet-scented perfume and trying to show a gentlemanly disregard for the eyeful of cleavage he was unable to avoid. She was good at the hard-as-nails act, but most people wouldn't put themselves out like this for someone they didn't know, and Bunny truly appreciated the kindness. The clothes were a decent fit too, and she'd even thrown in an anorak that would keep him warm against the biting winter wind.

Given how his trip had started, it felt as if things had finally taken a distinct turn for the better. This notion was confirmed when he re-entered the bar to find Fisk sitting in the corner booth, cigar on the go, a large whiskey in front of him and a pint of Guinness waiting on the far side of the table.

Fisk waved a hand at the pint glass. "I decided to take a chance on lazy assumptions. Apologies if I've committed an unwitting act of racism."

Bunny sat down and picked up the pint with a look of reverence.

"Forget what I just said," intoned Fisk. "I know the look of true love when I see it."

Bunny took a large sip without saying anything, before setting the pint down, smacking his lips appreciatively and looking over at Babs, who was back behind the bar.

"That's as fine as any pint you'll get on either side of the Liffey," he said.

Babs shrugged in response but failed to hide a little smile.

Fisk lowered his voice. "You've made a friend for life there. And speaking of making friends," he continued, shifting forward in his seat, "it seems you and I share an interest in one Stevie Brandon, and have both drawn the ire of his entourage. How about you fill me in on your exact interest here?"

Bunny brought Fisk up to speed and, seeing as he couldn't think of a reason not to do so, he didn't leave anything out, except the exact nature of his relationship with Sister Bernadette. The Sisters of the Saint took a hell of a lot of explaining, and it wasn't relevant to the task in hand.

Fisk listened intently as Bunny spoke. When he'd finished, Fisk flicked some ash from his ever-present cigar into the ashtray and said, "This picture, may I see it?"

Bunny fished the photo of Sean Malone and Stevie Brandon out of his pocket and showed it to the American.

"That's what I thought. I've been hanging around for a couple of weeks like a dog waiting for scraps. Hence, I've seen a lot of comings and goings. For what it's worth, I'm pretty sure I've seen that kid a few times."

"Really?" said Bunny, feeling a sudden upswell of hope.

"But not in the last few days."

"Oh."

"Just one of the many things that smells off about that place."

"How do you mean?" asked Bunny.

"Cards on the table," said Fisk, sitting back. "I've been in the boxing writing game a long time. Ali kissed me on the cheek and threatened to knock my block off. Frazier once called me a son of a bitch. I can't repeat what Tyson called me as there's a lady within fifty yards. My point is, I've seen them all, written about them all, and been fired from more publications than there are currently publications left. For all that, work has been a little slow recently." He tapped a finger on the tabletop. "This here is my last roll of the dice. I'm a dying breed. Nobody wants writers any more – they want automatons with typewriters, only the typewriter has gone the way of old war horses like me. It's all email and regurgitated press releases these days; the appreciation of depth has been lost."

As Fisk talked, Bunny was struck by his sincerity. The man had a showman's proclivities but there was an earnestness there too.

"All I was finding was closed doors," Fisk continued, "but then I was introduced to Edgar Pegg, publisher of *Cigar Aficionado Monthly*. More money than he knows what to do with. He got into the magazine game because he thinks it'll help him gain a certain standing in society – or, in other words, help him meet a higher class of lady."

"How's that working out for him?"

"To be honest, I think his money would be far better spent getting doctors to figure out why he spits so much when he talks, but that isn't my concern."

"Let me guess," said Bunny, "he's a big boxing fan?"

"No. But what hooked his interest is that the famously reticent heavyweight champion of the world has an insatiable love of a fine cigar."

"Does he?"

This earned Bunny a sheepish grin. "He might. Stranger things have been known to happen. More importantly, the gold-plated truth is that I have an 'in' nobody else does. Gabriel Fuentes, a middling bantam weight I met for the first time back in the sixties when dinosaurs still roamed the Earth, went on to become a damn fine trainer for near forty years. He's been in Stevie Brandon's corner for his last three fights. Me and Gabby, we go all the way back. I even introduced him to his wife. In fact, she was my wife first."

Fisk caught Bunny's raised eyebrows and waved away his concern. "Not like that. We were on our way out at the time and we both knew it. I gave Laura away at her wedding to Gabby and I spoke at her funeral forty-four years later. In between, you've never seen a more perfect couple than them. My point is, if anyone can get the champ to talk to anybody, Gabby can get him to talk to me, and when we spoke a few weeks ago, he said he'd make it happen."

"But?" said Bunny.

Fisk puffed on his cigar. "In what seems to be a recurring theme, I can't find Gabby. I've not seen him for near a week and nobody is giving me answers as to where the hell he is. Not Brandon's snake of a manager, Theakston; not the sister; not the police. Nobody. Forget the story, I want to find out where the hell my friend is."

"What did the police say?"

"They bought the bullshit story Theakston gave them – that Gabby left the camp. Said he had to go home and deal with a personal matter, and they don't know where he is."

"And you don't believe that?"

Fisk gave a dismissive shake of his head. "The hell I do. Laura is dead and they were never blessed with children. The only family he's got is his sister and she hasn't heard from him; he doesn't have any personal matters. Only boxing. And a lifer like him? There's no way he's walking out on a fighter prior to a big bout. Just no way."

Bunny ran a finger around the rim of his pint glass. "That does sound unlikely alright."

"You're damn right it does," said Fisk firmly. "We're days away from the biggest fight of Stevie Brandon's career and people around him keep disappearing. Something, my friend, smells very rotten in the state of Denmark."

Bunny chewed on his lip and looked around the pub. The same two men were sitting at the bar reading the *Racing Post*. Much like the upstairs, the place was well kept and scrupulously maintained, if a little last century. He spotted what he was looking for in the far corner of the room.

"Sounds like we might be able to help each other," agreed Bunny, getting to his feet. "If I may take advantage of your kindness a little further, any chance you've got some change, please? I need to make a phone call."

Chapter Nine

Misdirection. That's what magicians call it – when you're expecting one thing and then they pull the rug from under you by presenting you with something else.

When Bunny rang the number of the police contact Bernadette had given him for the second time, he got exactly what he expected – the same voicemail with the same standard network message. This time he could at least leave the number of the payphone at the Duck and Trumpet for the person to ring him back. Half an hour later, when the payphone trilled, Bunny narrowly beat the woolly-hatted horse-racing enthusiast to answering it.

"You think I got nothing better to do than deal with your crap all day?" snapped the voice on the other end. It was a hell of an opener. Of course, it could have been Woolly Hat's proctologist calling him back, but Bunny decided to go with the assumption that the voice belonged to his contact.

"Sorry," said Bunny, trying to be conciliatory, "I wouldn't be ringing if it wasn't important."

"Important?" barked the man. "Everybody thinks their crap is important. I've got a hundred different important pieces of crap on my plate. What's so important about your important crap, then?"

Bunny decided to ignore the weirdly scatological bent of the conversation and instead focus on what he needed to find out. First and foremost, anything in the system about Sean Malone. Failing that, a last known address for his father, Daniel Martin. Luckily, Bernadette had thought to provide dates of birth for both. Pushing his luck, he also said it'd be handy if he could find out if there was any intel on Alex Theakston, Stripes Gym, or Gabriel Fuentes.

"Fucking hell," said the voice. "Do you mind if I do my job at any point today or do you need me working for you twenty-four hours of the day? Talk about taking liberties. That bloody nun. One time you ..."

Bunny guessed the man was about to explain how he'd ended up in Bernadette's debt but clearly thought better of it.

"Anyway," the voice continued, "the Three Rings, Blake Street, Soho – five pm. You're a second late and I'm out of there."

"Thanks, I—"

Bunny's appreciations were lost as the connection went dead.

He spent the next few hours enjoying a hearty fry-up provided by the saintly Babs and being regaled by Milton Fisk's tall tales. The man was certainly entertaining company. Bunny's highlight of the time he spent waiting for his meeting in Soho was Fisk's explanation of what happened with wife number four.

"Cheryl-Lee, exotic dancer, and I don't mean some mere stripper. This woman was a true artist. Mesmerising to watch. Her signature routine featured a boa constrictor. I loved her. She loved me. But damn it, that snake had it in for me. There's only so many times you can wake with an eight-foot-long reptile trying to squeeze the life out of you before you start to take it personally. The thing could get out of any enclosure – was like a slithering Houdini. I said to her, 'Honey, I love you, but it's me or that damned snake.' Lesson learned – never try and come between a woman and her career. It'll end badly for you."

The man was full of such stories. Bunny wouldn't have bet the farm on any of it being entirely true, but he'd much rather be told entertaining lies than boring truths. Or at least, in the pub. In other areas, the truth was a more valuable commodity. He also didn't doubt the man's sincere concern for the whereabouts of Gabriel Fuentes. Bunny had no idea what Fuentes' disappearance could mean, or if it was connected to Sean Malone in any way, but it added to the sense he'd got this morning that all was not well in Stripes Gym.

After his ample meal, Bunny's spirits had soared to the point where the pain in his ribs had stopped bothering him that much. He reckoned that, at worst, there might be a cracked one or two in there, amongst all the bruising. Similarly, the bump on the head was painful to touch but fine if he just left it alone. His face, on the other hand – well, the terrified look of the woman opposite him on the tube as he travelled to his meeting told a tale. As soon as Bunny reached Piccadilly Circus, he splurged some of Bernadette's money on a pay-as-you-go mobile and a pair of sunglasses, in an effort to hide the effects of what trying to break into a boxing gym got you.

The Three Rings on Blake Street was not the pub he'd been expecting, but rather a magic shop. Misdirection. As he was a little early, he walked around the block first and entered the shop at a couple of minutes to five. There were only two other people in there: one was a short customer with his face pressed up against the glass of a display cabinet in one corner; the other was the guy behind the counter.

Bunny considered the shopkeeper briefly but dismissed him from the running. It was possible that a police officer could have a second job, of course – he knew many that did – but he doubted any serving copper in the history of time would voluntarily wear a spinning bow-tie. Police were fundamentally the same the world over, and you'd have to leave the country, never mind the force, if anyone ever found out about such a thing. Which left the short man staring intently into the display cabinet. The brown mac he was wearing reminded Bunny of a bloke he'd once arrested for flashing, but he tried to put that memory out of his mind. He stopped beside the cabinet, not sure what to do next. Up close the man stank of cigarettes and his skin had an unhealthy yellow pallor to it. Soho was well known for people sidling up to strangers for all manner of reasons, so if this wasn't the guy, the situation could turn awkward very quickly.

Thankfully, the need to make introductions was taken out of Bunny's hands.

"You must be the Irish wanker?" said the man, without looking round.

"Well, I wouldn't put it quite like that, but yes. Bunny McGarry, pleased—"

"I don't want to know your name," hissed the man, "and I'm sure as shit not going to tell you mine. For fuck's sake, you just come over on the last potato boat?"

"Alright. Calm down."

"Calm down, he says. Calm down. Do you've any idea the risk I'm taking helping you out?"

Actually, Bunny did, but he decided the guy seemed jumpy enough already without Bunny identifying himself as a fellow member of law enforcement. Instead, he went with "We appreciate your help."

"Fat lot of good that does me. I rang Shepherd's Bush nick to see if there was anything fishy about that bloody gym and fifteen minutes later got dragged into the chief's office to get my arse handed to me."

"Really?"

"Yes. Really. Had to make up some bullshit about being a big boxing fan and give a grovelling apology for over-stepping the mark. Last thing I needed."

Interesting, thought Bunny. Somebody somewhere was keeping an eye on the goings-on at Stripes Gym. "Very sorry about that."

"So you should be."

The man seemed permanently annoyed. Bunny decided to try to get him onside. "Big fan of magic, are you?"

The man made eye contact with him for the first time. His face was shadowed by two days of stubble. George Michael could work that look, but this guy couldn't. It just made him seem in need of a shave, a shower and a good night's sleep. A darkness around his eyes emphasised the last of those three things.

"I am, as it happens. And what the hell happened to your face?"

Bunny began to answer but the man quickly cut him off.

"Forget I asked. I don't want to know."

"Fair enough."

Bunny focused on the contents of the cabinet.

"Jesus!" he said, honestly taken aback. "Five hundred quid for that box. What's in it?"

"Nothing – that's the whole point. That's the haunted box. Incredible trick. Can do so much with it." The man paused for a second, then continued, his voice suddenly softening. "Thing is, you need to invest in some top-notch tricks these days, if you're serious about becoming a magician. Wanted to be one since I was a kid. Never got the opportunity, did I? Nobody round my way became an entertainer."

"'Tis never too late," said Bunny, still trying to win the man over.

"That's what I'm thinking," he agreed. "I bloody hate my job. Do you have any idea what it's like to be surrounded by the dregs of humanity every day?"

Bunny wasn't sure if the reference was to criminals or to other members of the force. He decided to interpret the question as a rhetorical one.

"I've nearly got my act worked out. Just needs a bit of investment."

A prickly feeling in the back of Bunny's mind suddenly gave him a premonition of where this conversation was heading. His suspicions were confirmed a few seconds later as the man licked his lips and made a little slobbery noise. "Maybe in exchange for all this information I got you, at great personal risk to my career" – *the one you hate*, thought Bunny – "maybe you can buy me the haunted box."

And there it was. Bunny might not play by the rules when it

came to being a copper, but not even his worst enemy would ever accuse him of being dirty. That was the lowest of the low in his book.

"I thought you owed Sister Bernadette a favour."

"Yeah – a favour. A. You've asked for a lot more than one favour's worth. Fair is fair. You gotta make up the difference." He nodded at the cabinet. "I reckon that should cover it."

Bunny considered his options – not that he had many. His only lead was whatever this guy had, and he'd no other way of getting this information. Assuming, of course, that the guy had information.

"How about you tell me what you found out, and then, if it's worth it to me, I'll buy the box for you after."

The man turned and sneered at Bunny. "Do I look like a virgin waiting to get boned? Do me a favour. I'll be outside having a cig. You want to know what I know, you'll be out there, haunted box in hand, before I finish it, or else you'll never see me again." And with that, he pushed past Bunny and out of the shop door.

Bunny could see him through the window display, lighting up a cigarette. He made his way to the counter, mumbling obscenities under his breath. He did consider trying to beat the information out of the little toad, but this wasn't his town, and he'd already been in one scrap that day. Sure, he was fairly confident he could take the odious little cretin, but then he'd have to explain to Bernadette how he'd burned one of her bridges, and he'd rather do a lot of things than have that disapproving stare of hers boring into him.

So it was that, three minutes later and five hundred quid of Bernadette's money lighter, Bunny emerged from the Three Rings with the haunted box in a small plastic bag, feeling like it was very little for the money.

The man tossed his cigarette and snatched the bag out of Bunny's hand. "Took your time about it."

He pulled out the box and, as he pawed at it, he allowed the bag to flutter away on the breeze. Bunny stamped on the bag to pin it in place, then bent down and snatched it up before it could fly away. He really didn't like this guy, and the reasons why were starting to mount up.

Seemingly satisfied that Bunny hadn't pulled a fast one, Toady slipped the box into the pocket of his raincoat.

"Alright,' said Bunny, "you'd better have something worthwhile. Start talking."

"Sure," said the man, a sneer on his lips. "Seeing as you asked nicely." He pulled a piece of ripped notepaper out of his inside pocket and read from it. "Sean Malone, seventeen, no fixed abode – got done for solicitation five weeks ago around King's Cross."

"Really?"

"Yeah. Looks like he's using what the good Lord gave him to feed his habit."

Bunny really wanted to punch this man in the head. Hard. "Was he definitely using?"

"Arresting officer noted needle marks."

"Any—"

"No idea where he is now."

That was nothing but bad news.

"As for daddy – Daniel Martin, he's got a sheet too. Quite the family. Mostly non-violent deception. Theft stuff. Conned a few grannies out of their pensions. Did some time but no big stretches. Real prince amongst men. Him, we do have a last known address for."

The man handed Bunny the piece of paper. There was an address in Kilburn on it.

"OK," said Bunny. "What about Stevie Brandon and his management – the Theakstons."

"That question got me in the shit," said the man. "I've a good mind to send you back in—"

Bunny, at the end of his patience, took a half-step forward.

"Alright, alright," said Toady, holding up a hand and trying to laugh it off. "Just a joke. Thought you Irish were supposed to have a sense of humour."

"The Theakstons?" repeated Bunny, by way of reply.

"That father was another peach. Vice reckon he's in the foundations of a Spanish hotel somewhere like Torremolinos. The two kids, Alex and Charlotte, have kept their noses clean but there've always been rumours. Having said that, I did get a bollocking for asking, so who knows."

"And Gabriel Fuentes?"

"My mate says they had him getting on a plane, so whoever went asking about that was just a time waster."

"Was that confirmed?"

The man drew his head back, showing off a collection of double chins. "You want to come over here and tell us how to do our jobs now, is that it?"

"I just asked a question."

"I've told you all I know."

"And we're saying that was all value for money, are we?"

"Don't shoot the messenger," said Toady, with a shrug. "Sounds like your lost boy doesn't want to be found."

"Anything else?" asked Bunny.

"Not unless you want to see me guess the card you're thinking of."

Without another word, Bunny started to walk down the street, shouldering the man as he passed.

"Oi!" cried Toady in his wake. "Not even a thank-you. Rude."

Bunny continued on his way for a couple of minutes then stopped by a homeless man who was sitting in the doorway of a closed sandwich shop reading a book. Bunny reached into his inside pocket, pulled out a twenty from his now rather depleted roll of spending money, and wrapped it around the innocuous wooden box that he'd lifted from Toady's pocket as they'd parted company. What kind of a magician couldn't spot when they were being pickpocketed?

Bunny bent down and handed the man the money and the box. "There you go, fella. Get yourself a hot meal, and then you can spend the evening amazing and amusing your friends."

Chapter Ten

B unny had never been to Allsopp Gardens before, but he knew the kind of place it was all too well. It was located on a council estate that had the look of being at tipping point. While appearances could be deceiving, they could also tell you a lot if you knew what to look for. Butch, Bunny's sometime partner, called it the fridge theory. In any residential area, the state of the properties' gardens could provide you with more information than a sociologist doing a week-long analysis. If the gardens were mostly neat and tidy, then enough of the residents gave a shit that they managed to drag the rest of their neighbours up with them. All but the most thick-headed of people didn't want to be the only household on the street with an overgrown jungle where their garden should be. The true tipping point, though, was the fridge. If someone had a fridge, or any other domestic appliance, sitting out in the garden – because it'd presumably broken down and been replaced – then that was the surest of sure signs that the area was on a downward slope.

As Bunny walked along the road looking for number 27, he passed a fridge, a washing machine, and what looked like a clothes horse that had been the victim of a violent altercation. None of this spoke well for the prospects of Allsopp Gardens. Mind you, the fact that three kids were using an abandoned car as a trampoline was another fairly good indication. Bunny resisted the urge to say anything. This was not his manor and the last thing he needed was more trouble.

The garden of number 27 was appliance-free, and the small lawn had been recently mown. The front door was even sporting a fresh coat of paint, in a pleasing blue. He rang the doorbell and waited. Inside, a dog barked and he could hear a female voice saying, "Shut up, Caesar. I won't tell you again."

A brunette woman of about forty opened the door with a smile. She was dressed in a spangly silver top and looked as if she was about to head out for the night. The speed at which her smile dropped from her lips made it very clear that Bunny was not who she had been expecting and his arrival was not a welcome development.

"Hello," said Bunny. "Sorry to bother you, but I'm looking for—"

"Danny bloody Martin," finished the woman. "Same as every other fucker. I'll tell you exactly what I told them. He ain't lived here for almost a year and I haven't seen him. If I had, I'd be up on a murder charge. He ripped me off on his way out the door, the thieving toerag, so whoever you're collecting for, you can tell 'em I got nothing to do with him. In fact, when you catch up with the human skidmark, feel free to break a couple more bones for me." Before Bunny could say anything else, she slammed the door so hard that it rattled. "Now piss off!" she shouted from inside.

Bunny looked around. Nobody seemed to be paying him any mind. He scratched his head, unsure how to proceed after that diatribe. Lacking any better options, he decided to give the truth a crack.

"OK," he said, raising his voice, in the hope that the woman was standing in the hallway and could still hear him. "I'm not here to cause trouble, I promise."

"You'd better not be," she said, "or I'll have my Caesar rip off something memorable. He's vicious."

"I'm sure he is, but neither himself nor yourself have anything to fear from me. I'm not here collecting for anyone and I'm also no friend of Daniel Martin."

"He don't have friends. Just people he hasn't fucked over yet."

"I can believe it. I'm here because his son, Sean, came to London looking for him, and it's him I'm trying to find."

"What's he done?"

"Nothing," said Bunny quickly. "He's not in any trouble. Well, at least not anything criminal. His mother, who's back in Dublin, she's ill, really ill, and she wants to see him while she still can. They lost touch and he doesn't know she's sick. Any help you could give me to find his father would be appreciated, as Sean might have managed to find him and, to be honest with you, I've not got much to go on. You're sort of my last hope."

Bunny's truth bomb was followed by a silence. One long enough that he wondered if the woman was ignoring him. Finally, he heard the click of the lock being disengaged. The door opened a crack and he could see one half of the woman's face eyeing him suspiciously. "How do I know all that's true?"

"It'd be a terrible thing to make up," said Bunny.

"I've seen people do a lot worse. How do I know you're not just hunting this poor kid over something he's done?"

"I'm ... Hang on." Bunny slapped the pockets of the unfamiliar anorak and eventually found what he was looking for. He took out the photographs and held out the one of Sean and his mother, arm in arm, beaming at the camera. "Look, that's Sean and his ma."

She studied the picture carefully. "She's Danny's ex?"

"You could say that. I don't think her opinion of him is any higher than yours."

This earned Bunny a mirthless laugh in response. "I'll bet. That bastard leaves a trail of destruction in his wake, make no mistake."

The woman eyed Bunny again before glancing back at the photograph and then, apparently, deciding something. "He was here," she admitted.

"Sean?"

She nodded. "Few weeks back. Him and his mate. Looking for his dad. Seemed like a nice kid."

"He is," said Bunny. "I've not met him, but I've heard good things. Think he might have gone off the rails a bit while he's been over here, but he's a good lad. His ma is mad about him."

"Yeah. Didn't think much of his friend, though."

"Friend?"

"Girl – maybe a year or two older than him. Had one of them whatchamacallits – like Mr T?" She waved her hand over her head.

"Mohawk?" said Bunny.

"That's the one. All this metal in her face, too. Disgusting." She pulled a face like she'd just been force-fed prunes. "Why do people do that? She'd probably be alright-looking if she didn't have half a toolbox hanging off her. Sean was polite and all that, but I didn't like her attitude."

"Did you get her name?" asked Bunny.

"No. I didn't invite them in for tea and biscuits or nothing. He – Sean – explained who he was. Told me he was looking for his dad. For what it's worth, I tried to tell him that he wasn't worth finding, but he didn't seem interested."

"So what did you tell him?"

She paused, gave Bunny another long look and said, "If I find out you're bullshitting me ... awful thing to lie about."

Bunny crossed his heart. "God as my witness. Lying about something like this and I'd be punching my own ticket for hell."

"Walthamstow greyhound track. Danny, piece of shit that he is, is a compulsive gambler, and dogs are his thing. Well, losing appears to be his main thing, but that seems to be the way he likes most. You want to find him, hang around there long enough and he'll show up. At least, assuming he ain't banned yet. Wears his welcome out everywhere eventually."

"Thank you. Is there anything else you can tell me?"

"That's all I got," she said firmly. "Probably shouldn't have even said that, but he seemed like a nice kid. Mother must be lovely because he sure as hell doesn't get that from his father."

"Thank you for your help," said Bunny. He was about to leave but stopped. "One last thing – you said other people had come around looking for him?"

The woman shook her head. "I ain't getting involved. Hope you find him."

And with that, she slammed the door.

Bunny looked down at the picture he still held in his hands. The two happy smiling faces.

"Well, looks like I'm going to the dogs."

Chapter Eleven

Bunny jumped up from his seat on the tube and darted out of the closing doors, having very nearly missed his stop. He'd been dozing off, a long day after a terrible night's sleep catching up with him. As he walked down the steps at Shepherd's Bush tube station – the right one this time, delivering him directly onto Uxbridge Road – he tried to run through everything he'd learned so far about Sean Malone. Frustratingly, it didn't take long. The young lad had clearly fallen in with a bad crowd, which made it all the more important to find him. Too many times Bunny had seen the effect drugs had on people, and he knew it could do long-lasting damage if help didn't arrive in time. He was also aware that telling a drug addict that their beloved mother was dying was not a recipe for bringing somebody back on the straight and narrow. He'd cross that bridge when he came to it, though, assuming he ever found a road that reached it.

Right now, he was heading back to the Duck and Trumpet, and it was past ten. Late enough that he'd have to hope he could infringe on Babs's charity again and see if she could offer him a bed for the night. He could pay, but a pub with room for one lodger was surprising enough – room for two would be all the more so. Ideally, he'd not like to join the extensive list of people who'd shared a bed with Milton Fisk, but he was so tired that he'd certainly consider it if it was the only available option.

The earlier rain had thankfully stopped, but as Bunny walked along, a biting winter wind tugged at the anorak he'd borrowed. He felt weird in the thing. His sheepskin coat had become like a second skin to him and he didn't feel like himself without it. He also didn't feel like himself on these streets that weren't "his", like Dublin's were. Over there, even with his eyes closed, he could sense danger coming his way long before it reached him. Over here, with his eyes open – though admittedly weighted down with tiredness – he was nowhere near as sharp. He only noticed the vehicle slowing down to match his pace at the same time as he clocked the man heading towards him along the pavement.

The guy was of slim build, with tightly cropped brown hair, and was wearing a nondescript denim jacket and jeans under a light-blue raincoat. Not dressed to impress, more the opposite – dressed to blend into the background. Bunny had seen him before. That day. He couldn't say where, exactly – in the street, perhaps, or on a tube platform – but somewhere. What's more, he was looking directly at Bunny, making no effort to hide his interest. The pair made eye contact and he stopped a few feet in front of Bunny, glancing around as he reached under his jacket, a smile playing across his lips.

He expected Bunny to stop, but if there was one thing Bunny had learned in life, it was never to do the expected. Instead, he rushed forward and ate up the ground between them, then unleashed a right hook straight into the man's jaw, catching him off guard and sending him sprawling backwards onto the damp pavement. The gun he'd been reaching for crashed onto the tarmac a couple of feet away. Bunny was reaching down to pick it up when he felt the barrel of the second gun being pushed into the back of his neck.

"Don't," ordered a female voice from behind him. "Hands in the air or I shoot you in the leg."

Bunny didn't know who these people were, but judging by the man currently staring daggers at him from his spot on the pavement, he didn't think they were "the criminal element". There was something too neat and proper about them. There was also something in the woman's tone. Calm. Professional. Trained.

Bunny raised his hands. The thing about the element of surprise was that you didn't get it twice, and whether or not you believed you did was the difference between a gambler and a corpse. He glanced to his right where the nearside rear door of the vehicle, which he now realised was a black Hackney cab, had opened. The female voice said calmly, "The gentleman would like a chat. Just a chat."

It wasn't as if Bunny had options. "Ah, sure," he said, shrugging his shoulders. "I'm always up for a good chinwag."

* * *

Bunny had to wait until the man on the ground had got back on his feet, retrieved his gun and, after glaring at Bunny like he'd give his left nut to spend some quality time introducing him to a baseball bat, settled into the fold-down seat on the far side of the back of the cab. He then covered Bunny as Bunny made his way inside the vehicle. As the woman climbed in behind him, Bunny took a moment to consider the man sitting opposite. He, in contrast to his two colleagues, was not dressed to blend in – he boasted a bowler hat that matched his finely tailored three-piece pinstripe suit. Rakishly thin, he also wore a pair of thin-rimmed round glasses that balanced on the end of his nose as he peered at Bunny.

"Ah, our esteemed guest," he said, his plummy accent entirely matching his look. "So kind of you to join us."

"I apologise," replied Bunny. "I didn't know it was a fancy-dress party."

"How droll," said the man.

"Seriously, I didn't think ye could still get them kind of hats. Are you trying to be Mr Benn or that fella from that old telly series *The Avengers*?"

The man ignored the question entirely. Instead, he raised his voice slightly to address the driver. "Off we go, James."

Once the taxi started moving, the man returned his gaze to Bunny. "I am Mr Smith."

"Right," said Bunny. "That's believable."

"You of all people shouldn't judge the proprietary nature of other people's monikers, Bunny." The last word was uttered like he'd just been assailed by a particularly nasty smell.

"You know, people have been taking shots at my name all day and I'm getting a bit sick of it."

"My apologies," said Mr Smith.

"And where exactly are we going?" asked Bunny.

"Why, where you were heading, of course."

"And how would you know where that is?"

"You'd be surprised what we know about you, Detective McGarry. But relax, I just wanted to welcome you to our fair city."

"Do you normally do that by pulling a gun on somebody?"

Mr Smith glanced at the person who'd done precisely that and who was still covering Bunny with said firearm. "And do you normally punch armed opponents, Mr McGarry?"

"Only if they fail the Chekhov test."

"Excuse me?"

"Chekhov said don't put a gun on the stage unless somebody is going to fire it. I judged your boy here wasn't intending to use it, just wave it about."

"And if you'd been wrong?"

Bunny glanced at the man beside him. "If I was so inclined, I could show you what would happen in that situation, because right now he looks like a man who'd be very happy to shoot me."

"Indeed," said Smith. "I very much imagine that Gareth here would agree. What a smart fellow Chekhov was."

"Oh, yeah," agreed Bunny. "He had to be in order to navigate the *Enterprise* for all them years."

The confused expression on Smith's face indicated he was not a *Star Trek* fan. The merest hint of a smirk on the lips of the woman beside him showed that the reference hadn't gone entirely over her head, at least. Bunny turned to her. "My compliments to the lady, by the way. She got the drop on me just now, and I saw her earlier on, behind the wheel of a car, pretending to have an argument on the phone, but it never dawned on me she could be surveillance. Gareth here could learn a thing or two."

The jibe elicited the beginnings of a low growl from Gareth.

"Yes," said Smith, "my people are normally excellent at their job."

"Ouch," said Bunny, looking at Gareth. "Got to feel there's a bit of a dig in there, fella."

"My name isn't Gareth, it's—"

"Irrelevant," finished Smith. "After all, we're here to talk about you, Mr McGarry. What are you doing in London?"

"Sightseeing, mainly."

The man's face tightened. "I have limited patience for tomfoolery."

"Tomfoolery? Seriously, have you travelled here from 1870 or something?"

Smith nodded at the man who wasn't called Gareth, who delivered a swift jab to Bunny's ribs.

"Something I said?" Bunny groaned when he regained the power of speech. At least this new injury was on the opposite side to where he'd been kicked earlier.

"Do I need to repeat the question?"

"If you must know, I'm here to find a lad called Sean McGrath. He's missing and his mother wants to find him."

"So, you are here in an unofficial capacity?"

"If I was here in an official one, would MI5 be assaulting a member of the Irish police force?"

"I didn't say we were from that organisation."

"No," said Bunny, "just a working theory."

"You're not as clever as you think you are, Mr McGarry."

"You're probably right. Still, why has MI5 got Stripes Gym under surveillance?"

"Who said we did?"

"Oh, so you *are* MI5?"

For the first time the man showed a hint of irritation. "I was merely going along with your hypothesis. What is your interest in it?"

"It's the last place Sean was seen. That's all."

"Very well," said Smith. "In which case, I believe I can be of assistance. Sean Malone has not been around there for quite some time, and so you have no need to go back there or have any further contact with anyone associated with it."

Bunny nodded. "Thing is, though, 'tis pretty much my only lead."

"Then, since you do not have one, perhaps it is time you returned home?"

"But I only just got here."

Smith leaned forward. "Why do I feel you are not taking me seriously?"

"If we're being one hundred percent honest with each other, I think it might be the hat."

Bunny had known another blow was coming and braced himself for it, but Not Gareth still delivered his shot with plenty of vigour.

Bunny drew a few deep breaths before looking up again. "I made a promise to a dying woman and I don't take that kind of thing lightly. Believe me, I don't want to be here any more than you want me to be, but facts are facts."

"And do you think that allows you to blunder into a sensitive situation, just because you have nothing else to go on?"

"I'm not trying to mess up anyone's investigation," said Bunny, "nor could I give two shits about Stevie Brandon or the Theakston family or anything else. But a kid is in trouble and I need to help him."

"And what makes you think this boy is in trouble?"

"A few things," said Bunny, "but mainly the fact that I called him McGrath just now, and you then correctly said his second name as Malone."

Smith's calm veneer finally cracked. "Consider this your one and only warning. You are messing with things far bigger than you or some runaway junkie. If you get in my way, I will do everything in my considerable power to remove you from it. Is that clear?"

Before Bunny could answer, his breath was taken away by a third blow being delivered to his ribs in the exact same spot as the first two.

* * *

Milton Fisk was standing outside the Duck and Trumpet, staring up at the sky and enjoying the evening air while taking intermittent puffs on his cigar. He was distracted only when the passing taxi slowed marginally, opened its rear passenger door and sent a man tumbling out and into the gutter before driving off. He looked down to where Bunny McGarry was now sprawled in a puddle in front of him.

Bunny groaned. "'Tis my own fault. I said drop me anywhere."

Fisk nodded. "Not for nothing, McGarry, but I'm starting to think you may need to work on your people skills."

Chapter Twelve

D espite having been in London for only slightly longer than twenty-four hours, in which time he'd been beaten up twice, thrown into a skip bin and thrown out of a moving vehicle, Bunny could feel his spirits starting to lift. It was amazing what the offer of a decent bed for the night and a plate of hot stew could do for you. Babs had played down the meal as reheated leftovers, but it tasted like manna from heaven to him. Between that, a very decent pint and a room upstairs for as long as he needed it if he "didn't cause any trouble", he decided that things could have been decidedly worse.

Across the table, he could feel Milton Fisk percolating with questions, but the American restrained himself while Bunny ate. Instead, for reasons Bunny couldn't entirely fathom, Fisk had somehow got himself onto an anecdote about touring Japan with Elton John.

"It was sometime in the early eighties – I was there covering Tadashi Mihara, a feisty light middleweight, superb technician, fighting for the world title. Elton was there being Elton John. Touring or what have you. It was back in his crazy days and the Japanese love a costume. So, we're at this shindig, and this flame-eater from a circus, total jackass, puts something in this sumo wrestler's drink, and it's going all kinds of bad. The big guy is losing it big time. Out of nowhere, he charges across the room, picks up Elton and is going to slam him into the wall. He thinks Elton said something about his momma, which is unlikely as the man has no English and Elton doesn't speak Japanese.

"Anyway – I see what's happening, and old Milton has always been good in a crisis, if I do say so myself. There's no taking the guy down, he's the size of a truck, but I throw my entire body into him and divert him just enough that all three of us go sprawling into the pool. I even drag Elton out, coughing and spluttering, and then me and six other people get the big guy, who, it turns out, can't swim. When this sumo wrestler comes round and realises what he's done, I swear to God, we had to make sure he wasn't going to hara-kiri himself from the shame, and Elton says I saved his life and he owes me big time." Fisk finally paused to take a puff on his cigar. "Never did take him up on that."

At this climax, the pub experienced a moment of near perfect silence, save for the annoying quiz machine trilling in the corner. Bunny had already realised that this was a common occurrence whenever Fisk came in for a landing. Anyone within hearing distance couldn't help but get drawn in. It was the closest thing Bunny had ever seen to actual hypnotism.

Fisk jabbed his cigar at Bunny's now empty plate. "So, seeing as you've been fed and watered, how's about you fill me in on how your evening went."

The rest of the pub turned its attention back to other things as Bunny did precisely that. He told Fisk about his meeting with the miserable magician and the info he'd provided on Sean and his father, followed by his trip to Daniel Martin's last known address, and then his unexpected meeting with what he was still assuming was MI5, or something similar.

"Well, well, well," said Fisk, when Bunny had finished. "I'll say this for you, McGarry – you certainly know how to poke the hornets' nest."

"'Tis a gift," Bunny replied, as he shifted in his seat in an attempt to lessen the pain in his ribs. "Although if I keep it up, I might not make it through tomorrow."

"Agreed. I think you should maybe stay away from Stripes Gym for a while. They know me too. We need to find some other way of keeping an eye on the comings and goings there. I don't suppose you know any cheeky street urchins?"

"Actually, I do. Pretty much an unlimited supply of them. Unfortunately, they're all in Ireland."

"Never mind. We'll come back to it." He raised his voice. "Hey, Daves."

Woolly Hat and his companion, by some miracle still perusing copies of the *Racing Post* at the bar, looked up.

"Yeah," said Fisk, in an aside to Bunny, "they're both called Dave." He raised his voice again. "When's the next meet and where is it?"

"Walthamstow," replied Woolly Hat. "Tomorrow night."

"Thank you." Fisk paused. "Would I be right in saying there's a bookies just opposite Stripes Gym on Uxbridge Road?"

"Might be," said the other Dave.

Standing behind the bar, Babs rolled her eyes. "Oh, good God, how is that not a yes-or-no answer, Dave?"

"Depends who's asking," the other Dave responded defensively.

"He is," said Barbara, waving her bar-polishing cloth in Fisk's direction. "Who else do you think was asking? You reckon we got a rogue ventriloquist in tonight?"

Dave glanced around at the other half-dozen or so patrons of the Duck and Trumpet, finding nobody in possession of a creepy wooden dummy.

"The person who is asking, my dear Dave, is a man who is willing to offer some enterprising gentlemen one hundred pounds cash, if they'd be willing to sit in the aforementioned bookmaking establishment and report back on the comings and goings at Stripes Gym."

Dave nodded. "And who is this man?"

The other Dave raised his hand. "Just ... stop talking." He turned to Fisk. "One fifty."

"Done. From opening to closing and I'm trusting you to fill me in on every detail."

"What about pee breaks?" asked the other Dave, still determined to somehow have some kind of input.

"There's two of us," said his companion.

"Ah," said flat-capped Dave triumphantly, "but there's only one toilet."

"Please, I'm begging you, shut up."

Fisk turned back to Bunny. "Well, that's that taken care of. You and I can make a trip to Walthamstow tomorrow evening and hope we get lucky on more than a dog."

Bunny nodded. "Sounds like a plan. Come to think of it"– something that had been pecking away at the back of Bunny's brain finally made itself known – "tell me more about this sparring partner of Brandon's."

"OK."

"Hang on," said Bunny, "hold that thought. There's something I need to do first." He stood up. "Got to go talk to a nun."

Fisk crinkled his brow. "Is that a euphemism?"

"I wish."

Chapter Thirteen

Bunny fed the payphone some change and dialled the number. It was picked up on the third ring.

"Yes?"

"Yes?" repeated Bunny. "What kind of a way is that to start a civilised conversation?"

"I'm a bit busy," said Bernadette.

"Too busy to say hello? It's only two more letters than yes. In fact, you could've gone with hi – that's one letter less. Could have saved yourself a bit of time there."

"Did you ring up to give me a lesson in etiquette or does this phone call have a point?"

"A point? You told me to ring in with daily updates, and need I remind you that *you* asked me to go to London in the first place. Begged me, in fact."

"I definitely did not beg. I do not beg."

As soon as the words had left his mouth, Bunny realised how ridiculous they'd sounded, but he was not in a conciliatory mood. "Maybe I'm remembering it wrong. I got a bump on the head when the heavyweight champion's entourage threw me into a skip bin, so it could be from that, or it's possibly a side effect of MI5 having just chucked me out of a moving vehicle."

"What?"

Bunny gave Bernadette a brief recap of his day while she listened in silence.

"What interest would MI5 have in Sean Malone?" she asked when he'd finished.

"I was about to ask you that. Is there something you're not telling me?"

"You know everything I know."

"Really?"

"About this. Obviously, there are many things I know a lot more about than you, but none of them are pertinent to this conversation. I assume you've dealt with your phone?"

"I got a pay as you go," said Bunny.

"Not that. If MI5 are interested in you then I presume you've had the common sense to turn off your Irish mobile in case they try to use it to track you?"

"Obviously," lied Bunny. "I'm not an eejit. Of course I've done that." Well, he could now save himself the trouble of charging the thing up at least.

"Alright, then—"

Bernadette was interrupted by a shriek of pain on her end of the call, which was not from her.

"What the feck was that?" said Bunny.

"Nothing."

"Nothing? It didn't sound like nothing."

"Of course it isn't nothing. By nothing, I mean it's one of those things I need to know about and you don't. Suffice to say it's not what you think."

"It sounds like something illegal that I really don't want to know about," replied Bunny.

"In that case, it is exactly what you think. Ring me tomorrow with better news."

"Oh, sure, I'll ..." The rest of his sarcastic response died in his mouth as the phone went dead.

Chapter Fourteen

The next morning Bunny found himself at Charing Cross Hospital. He wasn't there for himself, although God knew the bump on his head would suggest that perhaps he should be, or if not for that, then for the pain in his ribs or the bruising around his eyes. He'd not been a massive fan of London before this trip, and his first full day in the city had done nothing to improve his opinion of the place. Instead of waiting for medical attention, he was sitting outside on a bench, with a takeaway cup of tea, just waiting. Not for a particular someone. He was waiting for something and he'd just have to hope he'd know it when he saw it.

The night before, he had possibly been guilty of over "self-medicating", in that he'd stayed up drinking with Fisk and Babs to an inadvisable hour. He could kid himself that the Guinness had aided the pain in his ribs, or that the whiskey that had followed it had helped him get a good night's sleep, but he knew that was nonsense. Still, after a day of being kicked around by all and sundry, it'd felt good to feel like a human being again. Besides, Milton Fisk was many things, but damn good company was right near the top of the list. The man was a bona fide raconteur, the last of a dying breed, and time spent with him was a worthwhile experience.

Bunny and Babs had spent the night laughing at the tales Fisk recounted, and Bunny had fallen fast asleep as soon as his head had hit the pillow. The second spare room above the Duck and Trumpet was nothing fancy, but it had a homeliness to it that made it better than any hotel. He'd slept the sleep of the just, the well-fed and the intoxicated. That morning, he'd awoken refreshed and surprisingly early. Bunny didn't consider himself any great shakes in the detecting stakes, that wasn't really what he did, but it turned out that if he left his subconscious alone for long enough, it might string together a few things all on its own. He'd rushed from the room, pounded on Fisk's door and entered to find his new acquaintance unsurprisingly still in bed, if surprisingly wearing a silk smoking jacket and reading a copy of *The Great Gatsby*.

"The sparring partner," Bunny said. "The one he put in the hospital?"

"Good morning," said Fisk, placing a bookmark between the pages of his book and closing it. "And yes, I believe his name is Marcus Phillips. He and Stevie Brandon are supposedly tight."

"You're sure?"

"Gabby said so, and he'd know. That's not unexpected. You don't spar every day with someone you don't like. There's a mutual respect there. It's why whatever happened was such a freak occurrence."

Bunny nodded. "That's what I thought. I knew a lad in Dublin, Dinny Gilfoyle. Daft sod got into a fight with his best friend when they were both hammered – over a packet of cigarettes, of all the stupid things. He put him in a coma and then went on the run. Guess where we found him?"

Fisk shrugged.

"Sitting at his buddy's bedside in the hospital. He'd snuck in. Wanted to see if he was OK."

"You think Brandon might be going to visit Marcus?"

"Makes sense to me."

"Alright, but what good does that do us? How are we going to know when he's there? And hospitals don't let just anybody wander in."

"Ah," said Bunny, "but where there's a will there's a way."

"I'm glad to hear it," said Fisk. "And not to put a dampener on the mood, but would you consider putting some pants on? As a rule, I like the first genitalia I see of a morning to be my own."

"Oh, right. Sorry."

Once Bunny was decent and Fisk was dressed, they'd taken their lives in their hands and woken Babs. Bunny hadn't wanted to do it, but he needed her help, and for some things you need a woman's touch. In particular, people are far more likely to trust a female voice on the other end of the phone so, after a considerable amount of grumbling, groaning plus two cigarettes and a cup of coffee, Babs had indeed delivered the goods.

And so it was that Bunny was outside the staff entrance of Charing Cross Hospital at 8am sharp, just as the majority of the nurses on the night shift were finishing up. This whole plan was a long shot, but given all he currently had was the name of a dog track, it was worth taking a punt. He sat there feeling like an idiot for wearing dark glasses in the middle of winter, watching the group of men and women as they filtered out in ones, twos and threes, coats on over uniforms, yawning in the early morning sun.

It was an odd thing. As far as Bunny was aware, there were no physical features that distinguished an Irish person from an English, Scottish or Welsh one, and yet, somehow, you could spot your own. Not just the Irish either – he was sure it worked the same for different nationalities all over the world. Right at that moment, in Japan, two Swiss strangers were probably nodding to each other as they passed in the street. It was some weird little sense that worked on a subatomic level that the brain wasn't consciously aware of. He'd homed in on the brown-haired girl with pale skin and freckles as soon as he'd seen her come out of the door. She was chatting animatedly with a brown-skinned woman whose dark hair was tied up in a large bun. It was the laugh he'd heard as he'd casually made his way into her path that had let him know he was right. He only caught the accent that confirmed his suspicions when he was a couple of feet away.

"Am I going mad," said Bunny, "or is that a Tipperary accent I'm hearing?"

The duo stopped and the voice's owner gave him a wary smile. "Might be. Cork, is it?"

"'Tis indeed."

She nodded. "I can smell you lot a ways off."

"To be fair, I've been in Dublin a while now, so you might be picking up their stink."

"Oh, dear," she said with a laugh. "Sorry for your trouble."

"Ah, it's not so bad. I'm a guard, so I get to lock them up."

"Best place for them."

Bunny chuckled too, then pointed behind her. "Are you working in the hospital?"

"I am."

It was one of the safer bets Bunny had taken in his life. You could be sure to find Irish nurses in every country on the planet. That wasn't to say that this girl couldn't have been a doctor of course, but she looked a tad too young to be qualified. Besides, this was the exit usually used by the nurses. Babs, who'd rung the hospital earlier, pretending to be an auntie back in the country for a couple of days, hoping to find out how she could surprise her niece who was on nights this week, had extracted that information from the nice lady on the switchboard.

"Is there any chance you could help me with something?"

His request earned him a suspicious look from both the Irish girl and her friend.

"It's nothing dodgy," he said, "I promise." That wasn't technically true, but he needed to get through his pitch without them making a run for it. He'd been giving it a lot of thought on the tube ride over and he'd settled on the approach he thought gave him the best chance of a fair hearing, or not getting maced, at least.

He pulled out the photograph of Sean and his mother, and held it out to them. "I'm over here looking for the lad in this picture. Unfortunately, his ma – that's her with him – has cancer. Stage four. She's not got much time and she wants him to come home."

The girl took the picture out of his hands and gave it a long look. "That's awful, but I'm afraid I don't recognise him. If you think he's been treated here, you'll be hard pressed to find someone who remembers him. We get a lot of people coming in and out. Busiest hospital in London, and that's really saying something."

"Right," said Bunny, taking the picture back. "Actually, I've got another possible way of finding him." He showed them both the next photo. "This is the last picture we have of him."

The girl's friend leaned in. "Isn't that the boxer guy?"

"Stevie Brandon," confirmed Bunny. "It is, yeah.' Sean – that's the young fella's name – we think he was working at the gym this guy trains at, but they won't talk to us. I can't get in to see him and he's our only lead. His management are a right shower of ballbags, but I think he might be coming here to visit a friend of his that's in a coma."

It was all Bunny could do not to wince as the duo drew back from him, suddenly aware of where he was heading.

"We can't help you," said the Irish girl.

"Look," said Bunny, putting out his hands in a placatory gesture. "I wouldn't be asking if I'd any other way. I just need someone to tip me off when he's here and—"

"That's not something we can do," said the friend firmly. "C'mon, Sharon. We should go."

Bunny took a step back, careful not to block their path. "Hand on heart, I think this kid could be in a lot of trouble. I just want to get him home to his ma."

Sharon hesitated, brushing her hair back over her ear. When she spoke again her tone was notably less friendly. "And how do I know this isn't all bullshit you're making up because you're, I dunno, some journalist looking for a story, or maybe you're the trouble this kid is in?"

"Fair point," said Bunny. "That's a very fair point. I bet you know at least one guard at home?"

Her friend tried to pull her away but Sharon indicated she should wait. "I might do."

"If you don't," said Bunny, "you'd be the first Irish person who doesn't. Give 'em a ring and ask about me."

Sharon scoffed. "Right, because every guard in Ireland knows who you are?"

"No, not at all. But they'll know somebody who knows somebody. I'm Bernard McGarry, but everyone calls me Bunny. I mostly work out of Sheriff Street and Pearse Street stations, and I graduated from Templemore in eighty-six."

"And how do I know you're really this 'Bunny' fella?"

"I've got my Garda ID," he said, slapping his pockets.

She waved him away before he could take it out. "Right, because anyone over here would know what one of them is supposed to look like. I sure as shite don't."

Bunny hesitated. "I ..."

The friend tugged at Sharon's arm again and the young nurse really looked like she was about to go this time.

"The eye," he blurted.

"What?" said Sharon.

Bunny pulled off his dark glasses.

"Fucking hell," said the friend. "Someone smacked the shit out of you."

Bunny shrugged. "The joys of trying to get answers out of a boxing gym. But look ..." He pointed to his left eye. "I've got a lazy eye. Anyone who knows me knows that. Between that and the Cork accent, I'm hard to fake."

Sharon still seemed unsure.

"How about this," said Bunny. "There's one of them Pret a Manger places over there. I'll grab myself a bit of breakfast and I'll be there until ten o'clock. You head off, make a call or two, and if you decide you want to help, you know where I am. I swear, everything I've told you is true, and you'd be helping out a sick woman and her son massively. Don't take my word for it, though – ask around."

Sharon eyed him warily one last time, nodded and then headed off, she and her friend in deep conversation.

* * *

It took forty-three minutes for Sharon to sit down opposite Bunny at the Formica table in the corner of the sandwich shop. She opened with, "So help me, if you make me regret doing this, I will hunt you down and make you feel pain like you've never experienced. I'm a nurse – we know how to do that."

"I don't doubt it, and thank you."

"Yeah," she said. "Don't get too excited, I'm not promising anything."

"Fair enough. Can I treat you to a sandwich or a cup of tea?"

"No, thanks. I'm full to the brim with caffeine already and I've had my breakfast."

"Just as well," said Bunny, indicating the nearly finished sandwich and cup of tea he'd been making last for the preceding forty-three minutes. "I got a cuppa and a sandwich for as much as I think my da paid for his first house. I must be a shareholder in this place now."

Sharon gave a brief laugh. "Welcome to London. The streets are paved with gold, but you have to dig it out with your bare hands. How long have you been over here?"

"I arrived Tuesday night."

"Jesus, from the look of your face, you know how to make friends fast. By the way, if you'd like my professional opinion, you really should get yourself seen to. Looks like you've taken a fair battering."

"I'll be fine."

93

"Ah, the last words of many a stubborn Irish male. Have it your way. I'm not your mammy."

"I take it you made a couple of phone calls?"

"I did. My cousin rang a guy he trained with. He knows you."

"Good."

"Said you were a massive pain in the arse."

"Oh."

"But he also said you'd not lie about something like this, and while you're a lot of things, you're at least honest."

"Not the best reference I've ever had but I'll take it."

"Beside the point, but I've spent years getting annoyed at English people thinking that all Irish people know each other. Feels like this morning is setting the cause back on that one. Oh, and while I think of it, it's 'Manger' as in the French word with a silent 'r', and not like where the baby Jesus was born." She gave a slight smile. "You're showing up the nation."

"*Excusez-moi, madame. Je suis très gêné.*"

She drew back in surprise.

He shrugged in response. "I might well be honest, but I've found there's an advantage to letting people think you're the big Cork lummox they're expecting. Force of habit."

"Well, now, aren't you the cute hoor – and Jesus, haven't I had a hard time explaining that phrase since I've been over here." She glanced around then lowered her voice. "Alright, if – and I emphasise if – I were to help you, what would you need me to do?"

"Well," said Bunny, "I'm guessing that Stevie Brandon might be nipping in here to see his unfortunate friend, and I'm guessing, seeing as he'd not be keen on people knowing it, he's probably doing it in the evenings?"

She considered him for a long time before replying. "I've not read through the small print of the Hippocratic oath recently, but seeing as he's not actually the patient, I believe I'm allowed to say that, as it happens, he has been in. I mainly work in paediatrics, but the girls talk, and the heavyweight champion of the world sitting there talking

94

to the unconscious bloke he put in a coma is the kind of thing that gets a mention at three in the morning when the coffee machine is broken again."

Bunny nodded. "I thought as much."

"Why is it I get the feeling that isn't going to be all you're going to ask me?"

"I need to talk to him, so I need to find out when he's next in."

Sharon leaned back in her chair. "And how exactly would you hope to achieve that?"

Bunny winced. This woman was nobody's fool. "I'd need you to get me into the hospital."

She shook her head. "And that last bit would be the difference between a stern talking-to and an immediate dismissal."

"I'd never tell anyone your name, whatever happens."

She leaned forward again. "We're a modern hospital. They have cameras."

"Oh, right."

She turned towards the window and her gaze settled on the early morning commuters rushing past. The silence stretched out between them and Bunny decided that giving her space was the best option. Eventually, she said softly, "This woman, the mother?"

"Her name is Orla."

"You're telling me the truth?"

"I am."

"And you want me to risk my job to help this woman I've never met?"

"If it's any consolation," said Bunny, "I'm doing the same."

At this, her head snapped back to meet his gaze. "What?"

"A friend – or at least someone I trust completely – asked me to do this, and told me exactly what I'm telling you. Forty-eight hours ago, I didn't know who Orla or Sean Malone were, and I could barely pick out Stevie Brandon in a line-up."

"You got the crap kicked out of you to help someone you've never even met?"

"I did. Also got thrown into a skip bin and out of a moving car."

"You're joking?"

"No. And in the interest of full transparency, like I said, Orla asked my friend to find Sean – all that is just like I told you. Since I've been looking for him, though, it seems there's some bad shit swirling around Brandon, or his management at least, and somehow I think Sean is involved. I know that because I'm pretty sure the people who threw me out of the car were MI5."

"Good Christ, man," said Sharon, leaning further forward. "Why would you even tell me that?"

"Because I'm being honest with you."

"Given my dating history, I can't believe I'm saying this to a man, but you might want to try a little less honesty."

Bunny shrugged. "Too late now. That's all of it."

"Oh, good," she said sarcastically. "I'm glad it's all so straight-forward."

Bunny left another gap in the conversation and when it became clear that Sharon had no further questions, he decided he'd better ask one of his own. "These cameras?"

"Yeah," she replied. "Like I said, we're a modern, state-of-the-art medical facility, so of course there are cameras, but we're also a hospital in the criminally underfunded National Health Service so I didn't say they were all working. Assuming the lads in Facilities don't get their arses in gear, there might be an uncovered fire exit where the camera is banjaxed that allows a cheeky fag break to go unobserved."

He nodded. "OK."

"They don't give us our own smoking area, which is daft. Nobody wants to be having a fag beside a member of the medical staff – doesn't inspire confidence." She looked at him again and drummed her fingers on the tabletop, making a decision. Finally, she said, "Ah, shite, give me a phone number I can reach you at."

"Thank you."

"I'm not promising you anything, just give me the number. I'll need to ask around and see if I can get someone to let me know when he's in. This is very shift-rota dependent."

"There's a place in heaven set aside for good Samaritans like yourself," said Bunny, scribbling down his pay-as-you-go number on a napkin.

"Yeah, and a place in the dole queue, assuming I don't end up in prison."

"That won't—"

"Don't make any promises you can't keep," she said. "Now, that is something I've said to a couple of men before." She took the napkin. "Like I said, no promises."

"Understood. One last thing before you go."

"For feck's sake, man—"

Bunny held up his hands. "This is an easy thing, I promise." He lifted the top off what remained of his sandwich. "What do you reckon that green stuff is?"

"Avocado."

"Oh, right," he said. "Is that new?"

She got to her feet, shaking her head. "Is that new," she repeated. "Irish men. God save us all from Irish men."

Chapter Fifteen

Detective Inspector Fintan O'Rourke heard Commissioner Gareth Ferguson before he saw him. By all accounts the man was a gifted baritone who had sung in a well-known Dublin choir for many years, only leaving when a soprano and an alto got busted running a money laundering ring and tried to use their supposed relationship with him to have the arresting officers look the other way. After their unsubtle attempts to sully his good name, Ferguson made very sure that the Mountjoy Prison Choral Society received a serious boost for a few years. Three to five, if O'Rourke recalled correctly.

The commissioner was not singing now, though. He was shouting down the phone at someone and, given that O'Rourke could hear the noise from the hall outside, he couldn't help but feel sorry for whoever the poor bastard on the other end of the line was.

"... and I do not care what their plans are. I want them standing in my office by the end of today, and if they'd like to bring a rep, a lawyer, a priest, or indeed their entire houses on their backs, that is entirely their prerogative, but rest assured, either they will be standing here or you will, and if it ends up being you, it won't be for long owing to the application of my boot up your arse!"

As O'Rourke opened the door to the outer office where Ferguson's assistant, Carol, was sitting, she winced at the sound of a phone being slammed down before being picked up and slammed down again repeatedly.

"Carol!" came the holler.

In response, Carol pressed a button on the intercom on her desk and spoke into it. "Detective Inspector O'Rourke is here, sir."

"Send him in." Ferguson's tone took on a sheepish quality. "Oh, and code orange again, I'm afraid."

"Understood. That's—"

"I know. Twice today. I apologise."

"Yes, sir."

Carol clicked off the intercom and only then did she look up properly at O'Rourke, who threw a furtive glance at the doors to the inner office.

"I would ask about his mood, but ..." O'Rourke began.

In response, Carol opened the bottom drawer of her desk and took out an object wrapped in white tissue paper, which she held out to him. "Could you please give him this and inform him it's the last one I have."

O'Rourke took the item, a bemused expression on his face. "Right. I don't suppose you could give me a hint at what he wants to see me about?"

"I honestly have no idea."

Something about that chilled him to the bone. Carol was the most well-informed person in the world of Irish policing, seeing as it was her job to remind the most important person in the world of Irish policing of anything he might forget. If she didn't know ...

He pointed at the door. "Is it whatever that call was about?"

"No. Whatever you're here for was our first code orange of the day. It's been quite the morning."

"What's a—"

O'Rourke jumped at the roar that came from behind the door. "Fintan! Are you waiting for an engraved invitation or would you like to get your posterior into my office this instant?"

In response, O'Rourke hurried towards the door and knocked briefly before entering. As he closed it behind him, he could have sworn he heard Carol utter the words "good luck".

Commissioner Ferguson was behind his desk, picking up piles of paperwork and setting them back down again, seemingly at random, so O'Rourke stood to attention, his thoughts racing as he attempted to figure out one last time what the hell this was about. It had occupied his mind for the whole drive back here from the site of the botched gangland shooting in Rathfarnham, but nothing sparked the cerebral cortex quite like looking down the nostrils of the proverbial dragon. Eventually, Ferguson gave up on whatever he was doing, made a grumbling noise and turned his attention to O'Rourke.

"Fintan. And I see you brought me a present. You shouldn't have."

O'Rourke stood there dumbly for a couple of seconds before remembering the object in his hands. He held it out. "Carol gave me this for you, sir."

"Oh, right, yes."

Ferguson snatched the article out of his hand and tore off the tissue paper, revealing a plastic handset for one of the desk phones. He unplugged the smashed receiver from his desk and tossed it in the wastepaper basket, which O'Rourke could see held another similarly shattered one, before replacing it.

"Don't make them like they used to," mumbled the commissioner, before eyeballing O'Rourke, almost daring him to react. O'Rourke gave his best motionless mid-distance stare at nothing.

Repairs complete, Ferguson waved a hand at the chair on the far side of his desk. "Sit down, Fintan."

The DI did as he was told.

"Before we get to why you are here," the Commissioner began, "did you hear about the three guards from Letterkenny racing snails?"

O'Rourke found himself wrong-footed. "I ... This isn't a joke, sir, is it?"

"No, although also, very much, yes. Three members of this police force, God give me strength, have been racing snails. They haven't been racing against them directly, you understand, although given the mental capacity of these dim-witted dullards I wouldn't put it past them, but no, worse yet, they have been racing them against each other."

"I see," said O'Rourke. Who couldn't yet see the whole picture, but had a fair idea where the thing was going.

"Indeed, and, unbelievable as it sounds, this has grown into an illegal betting ring where, reportedly, sums reaching five figures are changing hands at these so-called meets."

"Really?" said O'Rourke, who couldn't hide his surprise.

"Yes. Turns out there's not much to do in Letterkenny on a Friday night. So this little enterprise took flight with the local sergeant acting as head bookie, with his two cretinous assistants along for the ride. Would you care to guess how all of this came to light?"

O'Rourke thought for a moment. "I can't even begin to—"

"Race-fixing allegations."

O'Rourke laughed then, seeing the facial expression of the highest-ranking member of An Garda Síochána, immediately regretted it. "You're serious, sir?"

"As a heart attack. A disgruntled punter went to the local press."

"Oh, dear."

"Yes," said Ferguson, giving a deeply exaggerated nod of his head. "If only it had been horses or dogs or, I don't know, a fight club. But no, snails. Bloody snails! There's going to be cartoons in the newspaper, you see if there isn't. This is the kind of grist that keeps that unfunny doodling mill going. There'll be comedy sketches too, on that damnable TV show. A snail's shell with a siren on it. I'll bet your life on it. Why on earth can't the dimmer lights in our firmament get it through their imbecilic brains that if you're going in for corruption, at least have the sense to do it in a way that doesn't get the RTÉ costume department all a-flutter?" He picked up a pile of paperwork and slammed it back down again, his face an indication that the action had done nothing to assist in the venting of his volcanically bubbling temper.

Given the context, O'Rourke was stunned to find three words coming out of his own mouth before he could stop them. What was it they said about curiosity and cats? Yet there he was, taking his life in his hands because his curiosity got the better of him. "Can I ask—"

"No, Fintan," said the commissioner, cutting him off, "I have no idea how someone would go about fixing a snail race, or running one for that matter, but rest assured, that will be one of the many questions I shall be asking in a few short hours. I will of course keep you updated in our next little gossip session, but sadly, I have not brought you here this afternoon for a casual chinwag."

O'Rourke nodded. "Yes, sir."

Ferguson leaned back in his chair, which groaned a little under the man's considerable weight. "If I were to ask you the current whereabouts of one Bernard McGarry of this parish, what would your response be?"

O'Rourke's heart sank, even as his confusion grew. "He's in Mauritius on holiday, sir. I'm sure of it." A lot of people knew about McGarry's plans, mainly because a pool was going that involved a Dulux colour chart so that people could wager what colour sunburn he'd return with. O'Rourke hadn't partaken himself, but the concept was an amusing one. The force loved nothing more than an office pool and, as three poor bastards from Letterkenny were about to find out, the commissioner was unofficially fine with some but crucially not all forms of gambling. Given how, despite O'Rourke's protestations to the contrary, the commissioner insisted on viewing him as some kind of unofficial handler for McGarry, he'd even made a call on the way over to be doubly sure he was on holiday.

"You're sure of it?" echoed the commissioner, leading O'Rourke to instantly regret his choice of words. "Would you therefore be surprised to find out that I have it on very good authority that he is, in fact, contrary to popular belief, in London?"

"Oh."

"Oh, indeed," said Ferguson. "Would you like to guess how I know that?"

O'Rourke held his tongue.

"I received a phone call earlier on from an assistant commissioner of the Met Police."

"Was it—"

"Yes, *that* assistant commissioner. The odious little toad. It was a serious call, too – the smug bastard couldn't even find a way to shoehorn in a mention of the size of their budget before getting to the meat and potatoes."

A couple of years ago, there had been what could be loosely called a "diplomatic incident" at a symposium, which, ironically, had been put on to foster improved co-operation between the Irish, English and Welsh police forces. The assistant commissioner of London's Metropolitan Police had decided it was appropriate to refer to the Provisional IRA as "your boys". The subsequent eruption and paint-stripping dressing-down was a large part of the Gareth Ferguson legend, which made him both feared and adored in equal measure by the rank and file. Meetings were held on a ministerial level and it was a sign of the severity of the fallout that a cross-border golf day was cancelled.

"And do you know what the rodential little so-and-so said to me?"

O'Rourke again refrained from comment. If you were to survive in this office for any length of time, you needed to develop an awareness of the commissioner's rhetorical flourishes.

"Nothing," continued the commissioner.

"I'm sorry?" said O'Rourke. "I don't think I understand, sir."

"Then let me explain it to you, Fintan. As a matter of course, all calls in and out of this office are logged. I've no doubt a similar practice exists at their end. Hard as it is to believe, not just anyone can ring the commissioner of An Garda Síochána." He raised his eyes to the ceiling. "Oh, Christ, that reminds me. Carol!" He shouted his assistant's name before remembering himself and hitting the button on the intercom on the desk in front of him instead. "Sorry, Carol. Make sure I return the call from the head of the ISPCA straight after this."

"Yes, sir," came the voice on the other end.

"The Irish Society for the Prevention of Cruelty to Animals. I mean, are snails even classed as animals? Aren't they insects or something?"

"They're actually members of the phylum Mollusca and are more closely related to the octopus than they are to any insect."

This gem earned O'Rourke a raised eyebrow from the commissioner.

"Sorry, sir. I did that quiz team thing a few years ago. Some random facts stick in the brain."

"I see. I'll run that by the ISPCA chap, see if he shares your penchant for pedantry. Now, where was I?"

O'Rourke cleared his throat. "You were saying about the call from ..."

"Yes. The point is all of our calls are logged. Can you therefore guess why the aforementioned waste of oxygen would ring me only to hand the phone to someone else?"

O'Rourke once again chose to remain silent.

"This is an actual question, Fintan. Given your barely concealed lust to sit on this side of the desk one day, you should probably test out your deductive reasoning on something beyond locking up villains. Well?"

O'Rourke paused before venturing, "He passed the phone to someone else because that someone else isn't allowed to call you?"

"Very good," he said. "Big gold star for Fintan. Now for a bonus question. The individual in question didn't even identify themselves, which means ..."

"Security services?"

"Ding, ding, ding," said the commissioner, before turning to an imaginary assistant. "Tina, let's show the detective inspector what he's won." He swivelled his chair back towards O'Rourke. "Yes, that's right. MI5, MI6, MFI – I don't know who, but they asked me very directly why one of my serving officers is apparently attempting to harass the heavyweight champion of the world."

"I'm sorry, what?" said O'Rourke.

"Yes, you heard that correctly. The heavyweight champion of the world."

"Boxing?"

"Is there another one?"

"Actually—"

"Let me assure you, Fintan, this is not a good time for you to share another factoid from your quizzing days."

"Right. Why is—"

Ferguson finished the detective inspector's thought. "Why is Bernard 'Bunny' McGarry in London, annoying not only the boxing heavyweight champion of the world but also Her Majesty's brotherhood of James Bonds? I don't know, so that is very much what I'd like you to find out."

"Again, sir, I'm—"

"Not McGarry's commanding officer any more. Yes, yes, yes. I am well aware. I'm also aware that I am both yours, his and, not to toot my own horn, but everybody else in this country's commanding officer. However, were I to take an official interest in this, then I have to be officially interested, if you take my meaning, and I very definitely don't want to be that. So, if, say, you were to find out what the hell he is up to and casually mention it in our next gossipy little chat, which will occur, oh, I don't know, let's go with as soon as you find out what the hell is going on, then that would be greatly appreciated by me, in an entirely unofficial capacity."

"And what will we do if you don't like the answer?"

"If?" barked Ferguson. "If? Not to be a pessimist, but unless you all chipped in to get him to pick me up a prized scalp for the autograph collection I don't possess for the birthday I don't have coming up, let's go with *when* I don't like the answer. At that point, I would imagine you and I will, unofficially of course, put our heads together and figure out how we can stop your buddy from putting us on a full war footing with our friends across the water."

"Yes, sir," said O'Rourke. "Understood, sir."

"Excellent. One final question, Fintan," said the commissioner. "What the hell are you still doing here?"

Chapter Sixteen

Bunny looked at the gobshite standing in front of him and instantly disliked what he saw. He was wearing a charcoal suit with one of those godawful waistcoats that snooker players seem to love so much. The outfit was completed by a pair of black patent leather shoes you could see your face in and a paisley tie that might have been shat out by a unicorn in a trippy sequence from a bad sixties movie. The thing that Bunny hated most about the individual standing in front of him was that it was his own reflection.

"What do you think?" asked Fisk from his seat in the corner, where he was entertaining himself by twirling his fedora on the tip of his walking cane.

"I fecking hate it," said Bunny with real feeling. The obsequious Italian man who'd been attending to him for the last half an hour looked horrified by the assessment of the outfit. "No offence," Bunny added, waving at the ship that had long since sailed off into the distance.

"That's the spirit," said Fisk cheerfully. "Don't look a gift horse in the mouth if you can kick it right in the wild oats."

"If the gentleman likes," began the Italian fella, as if he were pleading for his life, "we could perhaps try the dickie bow again?"

"Not while the gentleman is still breathing," said Bunny.

"It's absolutely perfect, Anton," said Fisk with a breezy flick of his hand. "So wonderful, in fact, that the gentleman shall leave it on. If you would be so kind, please pack up the clothes he came in with, resist the urge to incinerate them, and take comfort in the knowledge that you have done an impossible job to an impeccable standard."

The little fella nodded as he stepped backwards gingerly then scuttled away, patting his sweaty brow with a handkerchief.

"Is all of this really necessary?" asked Bunny.

"Necessary? Good God, man, it's compulsory. We're going to the Dorchester for lunch. You can't walk in there wearing the same outfit you were tossed in a dumpster in."

"It's been washed."

"Nothing is ever that washed," countered Fisk. "If we had the time, you'd be getting a fully tailored Savile Row suit but, sadly, the starters are being served in less than an hour's time. We're turning up to an event we haven't been invited to. Hence, it is of paramount importance that you look the part."

"But I look like a fecking clown."

"Precisely. This is a luncheon and award ceremony for the best and brightest of the boxing world. It will ergo consist almost entirely of clowns, charlatans and the dregs of society, all of whom will be overcompensating dreadfully for their shortcomings by dressing to the nines."

Bunny pointed at his forehead. "Even if I wear the stupid dark glasses, I've still got the gash on my forehead."

Fisk waved away this concern. "These people are in the fight game. Blood and money are its two major products. Don't worry about it. If anything, along with the outfit it makes you look even more the part."

"How come I'm getting *My Fair Lady*-ed," protested Bunny, "whereas you're wearing the only suit I've ever seen you in?"

Fisk glanced down briefly at his creased and crinkled linen suit. "Ah, this is the thing. I've spent my entire life looking like I don't belong anywhere, which, paradoxically, means I look like I belong everywhere. It's a ridiculous phenomenon I've long since given up wondering about. It's as if I've been gifted with a backstage pass since birth."

"Ask me hole," said Bunny.

Fisk pulled a face. "I'm going to assume that one got lost in translation."

"So, you've been to the Dorchester before, have you?"

"Several times, in fact. Indeed, if memory serves, it was there that I once got slapped in the face by the seventeenth in line to the throne of Sweden."

"Who gives a shit who's seventeenth in line in Sweden?"

Fisk hopped to his feet with a sprightliness that entirely belied his age. "Funnily enough, it was me making that very point that resulted in the slap."

"Clearly your charms don't work on the Swedes."

"On the contrary. I could regale you with what happened later that same evening with the aforementioned seventeenth in line, but a gentleman never tells." He wiggled his eyebrows. "And if that were the case, I'd be telling three times."

Anton reappeared with what was, presumably, Bunny's clothes, tied up in brown paper and string. He held the parcel out in front of him as if either it or its owner were liable to explode.

Fisk patted him amiably on the shoulder. "Thank you as always, Anton. Please put everything on the account." He proffered a piece of paper to the outfitter. "And if you could have those clothes delivered to this address where both Mr McGarry here and I are staying, I would be greatly obliged."

Anton took the note and bowed so low that Bunny wondered how the man didn't headbutt the plush carpet.

Fisk grabbed Bunny's elbow and guided him towards the shop

door. "Come, Miss Doolittle. Time and overgilded food waits for no man."

"You have an account here?" whispered Bunny.

"Not as such."

"Jesus. We're not nicking this?"

"Heavens, no," said Fisk. "The account belongs to a friend of mine. Well, her husband, to be exact."

"And he lets you use it?"

"She does, and if he has enough money not to notice, then he clearly has too much money."

"I'm going to need my coat back."

"No, you won't. It's only a short walk to the hotel, but nobody turns up to these things on foot, so we're going to have to over-tip a taxi driver obscenely for five minutes' work."

* * *

The Dorchester was exactly as Bunny had dreaded. A man in a green tailcoat and a top hat opened the door of their taxi. The gesture was one of the many rich-people things he'd never understood. Who the hell didn't want to open their own door and get out? A steady stream of guests was arriving along with them, joining those already milling about in the lobby. As Bunny exited the cab, he felt like everyone was looking at him but, after a few seconds, he realised they were mostly looking at his companion.

Fisk clapped his hands together. "What a lovely day for it. Off we go."

As they walked into the lobby together, Fisk waved at people left and right. Many of the guests didn't seem too happy to see him and very few waved back. Bunny had to concede that Fisk's assessment of the kind of people in attendance had been bang on. No expense had been spared on outfits, or indeed wives, unless they'd all brought their daughters – in at least one case, granddaughter – with them. Waiting staff glided silently through the crowds with trays of champagne and orange juice.

They were there because Fisk was certain that Sparky Theakston would be, and Fisk had questions regarding Gabriel Fuentes that he wanted answers to. Bunny had a few questions of his own, as well as feeling obliged to tag along and make sure Fisk didn't end up next on the worryingly growing list of people that couldn't be located.

"I probably should have asked this before," said Bunny quietly as they joined the short queue of people waiting to talk to the hostess, "but you've got a plan, right?"

"You are correct," said Fisk through a grin of gritted teeth. "You should have asked that earlier."

No follow-up questions were possible as the group in front of them moved off, leaving Fisk and Bunny next in line. The hostess wore a dazzling smile that was all business. "Good afternoon, gentlemen. May I have your names?"

"Of course," said Fisk cheerfully. "Milton Fisk plus one."

The woman continued to beam as she ran her finger down the list. Her expression faded a little as she consulted it again. "I ... I'm afraid I don't seem to have you here."

"I'm sorry?"

"On the list. Your name. Would you be under anything else?" She turned her attention to Bunny. "Perhaps the other gentleman's name?"

"No," said Fisk cheerfully, "there's only one Milton Fisk, and he does not go by any other name, I assure you."

"Hmmmm." She checked the list for a third time, in the highly unlikely event that his name might suddenly have appeared.

"Try Fisk, Milton. People do occasionally get them in the wrong order."

"I've checked that already. Do you know who would have put you on the list?"

"Who?" Fisk laughed. "It could have been anyone. Everyone.

Someone who is going to be embarrassed when they realise they have made quite the booboo."

A man who looked like a human pencil materialised as if from nowhere. "Is there a problem, Monica?" he said in a voice like slippers on carpet.

"No," said Fisk. "It's just my name isn't on the list."

"I see," said the man.

Fisk leaned in. "To be honest, you're lucky this is happening with me. Between us, there are some sizeable egos attending this event, who would be throwing their toys out of their baby buggy right now. Histrionics. Alpha-male, tedious stuff. Luckily, Milton Fisk is a man of the people and I understand you folks have a job to do, so I'm going to wait while you go and check with whoever you need to in order to get this ironed out."

Bunny had to hand it to him. The way Fisk was speaking, even he was beginning to think that Fisk's name must be on the list.

"Yes, sir," said the man, exchanging a glance with Monica. "If you wouldn't mind, I'll go and speak with the committee chair and the secretary."

"No problem at all," said Fisk. "My friend and I are going to stand just over there, beside the vase full of rather fetching chrysanthemums, and you do what you need to do." He wagged a finger at Monica. "But you keep an eye on us, Monica. You've got to be on the lookout for gate-crashers."

They all smiled at the joke in the way people do when it isn't actually funny but they nevertheless appreciate the effort. Fisk and Bunny moved to the spot Fisk had indicated, and then the American pointed at the floor beneath their feet and gave Monica a big thumbs-up. She gave him a slight smile in return before moving on to dealing with the next guests.

"What exactly is the plan here, Fisk?" asked Bunny, trying to look relaxed while resisting the urge to readjust the trousers on his damnable suit.

"Evolving," he replied while nodding to passersby.

"Evolving?" repeated Bunny. "Jeeves is going to be back in about ninety seconds and we're getting thrown out on our—" On the far side of the lobby Bunny noticed a figure he recognised. "Crap," he said, ducking his head behind the vase of flowers as subtly as he could. "That's Lawrence Cooper, head of security for the Theakstons."

"I thought I recognised him," said Fisk. "Last time I saw him, he was throwing your ass in a dumpster."

Bunny noted Cooper was now glaring at them, and stopped his futile efforts to remain unseen. "He looks even less happy to see me this time." He gave the man a wave.

"Look lively," murmured Fisk. "The plan just showed up."

Before Bunny could ask what he meant by that, Fisk stepped forward into the path of a man who resembled Danny DeVito if he'd eaten another Danny DeVito. The man was accompanied by a woman wearing a jewellery store and a scowl, and a slightly taller version of himself around twenty years younger and sixty pounds lighter.

"There he is," proclaimed Fisk loudly, drawing the attention of most of the guests milling about in the lobby as he stretched out his hands. "Michael Bianchi, you old son of a bitch, have you lost weight?"

To say the man didn't share Fisk's bonhomie was an understatement. As soon as Bianchi laid eyes on the American, his lips formed into a snarl. "Fisk, you bastard. I said if I saw you again, I'd kill you." Nothing in his delivery made his statement sound anything less than heartfelt.

"Oh, come on, now, Micky – is this about that little misunderstanding in Vegas?"

"You had ten tons of horse shit delivered to my house," Bianchi hissed.

"A little joke."

"They put it in the window!"

"I know," said Fisk. "But in my defence, it would have taken them an age to put it through the letterbox. How's the ex-wife, by the way?"

Bianchi charged at Fisk, who, with a flourish, took a step to the side like a matador dodging a bull. His attacker stumbled past and clattered into the large vase of flowers, sending it crashing to the ground and attracting the attention of the last few members of the assembly who weren't already looking their way.

"I'll kill you, you motherfucker!"

Fisk stepped backwards into Bunny. "Hold me back," he instructed, while doing a more than adequate job of doing just that himself. "Hold me back."

Bianchi's son grabbed his father and tried to restrain him, before he was quickly joined by a couple of hotel doormen in their distinctive green coats. Between the three of them, they more or less kept a grip on the man, but it was a close-run thing. Other members of the hotel staff were running about like headless chickens, clearly unused to having to break up fistfights in the lobby.

Bunny, ostensibly holding onto Fisk, stood there, confused about what to do next.

"You're a disgrace to the fight game, Michael," Fisk shouted. "I know it. Annabelle knew it. Dogs on the street know it." He lowered his voice as he whispered to Bunny, "Back, back, back."

Bunny finally got the idea and started dragging Fisk away from his assailant.

"Put 'em up," Fisk challenged Bianchi in a passable impression of the cowardly lion from *The Wizard of Oz*. "Fight me like a man."

"You're dead, Fisk," roared Bianchi. "You hear me? Dead. They'll find you in the desert with your head in a bucket of crabs and your balls in your mouth. You understand me? I did it before. I'll do it again."

"My father's just joking," wailed the son plaintively. "None of this is admissible in court."

The last thing Bunny saw before he and Fisk disappeared through the doors at the side of the lobby and into the main part of the hotel was the scrum of individuals holding Bianchi back. They all collapsed to the floor as Bianchi made one last, desperate surge to get to Fisk while, in the background, his unfazed female companion took a glass of champagne from one of the circulating trays and calmly took a sip.

The doors closed behind them.

"OK, McGarry," said Fisk cheerfully. "You can let go of me now."

Bunny happily did just that. "That was your plan?" he asked, exasperated. "Waiting for the guy who wants you dead to wander in?"

"The guy?" repeated Fisk. "*The* guy? I've been writing about the fight game for nearly fifty years – I'm offended you think there's just one person here who wants me dead." He pointed down the hallway. "This way, I think."

And with that, he walked off briskly and Bunny had no choice but to follow in his wake.

"I'll tell you something, though," started Fisk conversationally. "Micky really has lost weight. He looks fantastic."

Chapter Seventeen

Bunny held the sheet of toilet tissue between his thumb and forefinger and rubbed them together inspecting it. "Jesus, that's magnificent," he said to himself. "Absolutely magnificent."

He almost fell off his perch atop a box of carpet squares when the storeroom door opened suddenly, but was relieved to see it was Milton Fisk, who stepped inside and closed the door behind him.

"Feck's sake, Fisk. You nearly gave me a heart attack."

"Apologies, I forgot which storage cupboard I left you in. I've just interrupted two members of staff who were running between bases, if you get my meaning."

"I don't, actually. I've never understood baseball, either in real life or as a sexual metaphor."

"You're missing out on both fronts. Anyway, we're all set. We need to wait five minutes, then you go into the gents down the hall and get in position. Sparky Theakston will be along presently. I'll do crowd control redirecting would be pee-ers, to get you some quality alone time, and then you ..." Fisk gave Bunny an expectant look.

"What?"

"How do you normally get information out of people?"

"I ask them questions."

Fisk pulled a face. "Yeah, but there is asking and there is *asking*."

"I don't go around roughing people up willy-nilly, Fisk."

"How about the boss of the guys who beat you up and threw you in a dumpster?"

Bunny considered this. "Well, when you put it that way …"

Fisk peered at Bunny closely. "Have you been … crying?"

"What? No. We're in a storage cupboard. 'Tis the fumes from all the disinfectant."

"It is pretty strong," conceded Fisk. "Although the base runners didn't seem to mind."

"While we're waiting," said Bunny, picking up one of the rolls of toilet paper he'd been fondling, "would you feel the softness of this?"

Fisk waved him away. "I don't believe in toilet paper."

"What do you mean you don't believe in toilet paper?" asked Bunny, genuinely outraged. "How can you not believe in toilet paper?"

"I'm not denying its existence, I just personally prefer not to use it as part of my process."

"But it's … How do you …?"

"There's more than one way to skin a cat," offered Fisk.

"Yeah, but you can't wipe your arse with it afterwards."

"Anyway," said Fisk, "not to change the subject, but do you know much about Sparky Theakston?"

"No. Come to think of it, I'm not even sure what he looks like."

Fisk turned his eyes to the ceiling. "Oh, boy."

"In my defence," said Bunny, "I wasn't expecting to be meeting him in a toilet today. This is all very short notice."

"Don't worry, you stay in the cubicle and I'll signal you."

"How?"

"It'll be obvious. Do you know what you're asking him?"

"Where the hell are Sean Malone and Gabriel Fuentes?"

"OK, at least we got that part down."

117

"Hang on," said Bunny. "How do you know precisely when he's going to be going to the bathroom?"

"Because we're doing the Milton Berle Fandango."

"The who, what now?"

"An old trick. I've bribed a waitress to drop a drink in his lap at precisely one thirty in the afternoon and then we meet him in the nearest bathroom. Henry Kissinger told me this was how the Cuban Missile Crisis was really resolved."

"Well, that's a terrifying thought. How much did you give her?"

"Who?"

"The waitress."

"Five hundred pounds."

"For spilling a drink!" exclaimed Bunny.

"Keep your voice down," hissed Fisk. "All the rooms in this place are supposedly soundproofed but I don't know if that includes the broom cupboards. And yes, five hundred English pounds, because I'm not paying her to spill a drink, I'm paying her to do it at a precise time, in a precise lap, and risk getting in all kinds of trouble for doing so. Never under-bribe – it's one of the golden rules."

"I shudder to think what the rest are."

Fisk checked his watch. "Still a little too early. Timing is everything." He rolled his neck around his shoulders. "Hey, while we're killing time, did you know that this place is owned by the Sultan of Somewhere, and a few years ago, during a court case, it was claimed his brother was keeping forty prostitutes at a time here."

"Really?" said Bunny. "Forty? As in four-zero?"

"Yeah. I mean, moral considerations aside, imagine the logistics involved in that? You'd have to start dishing out name badges."

"Or at the very least have a numbering system. I mean, forty – that's almost two entire rugby teams including subs, give or take." said Bunny.

"I doubt they were playing rugby."

"You say that," said Bunny, "but you'd need to entertain them all somehow."

"Yeah," agreed Fisk, "I'd imagine the board-game budget was through the roof." He checked his watch again. "OK, time successfully killed. Let's do this. You'd better get this bastard to talk."

"I'll do what I can," said Bunny, getting to his feet.

"Excellent. And McGarry?"

What?"

"Put down the roll of toilet paper. They have those in there."

* * *

Three minutes later, Bunny was sitting in a cubicle that was, well, all right. Nothing special. Pretty much standard, in fact. He'd been expecting something incredible, given it was the Dorchester, but he supposed there was only so much you could do with concept. He brushed his fingers against the toilet roll to his left. Damn it – it definitely wasn't the same stuff. That stash back in the cupboard must have been what they kept for the A-listers. He suddenly felt cheated. In truth, he was trying to distract himself from the horrible realisation that he was trapped in Milton Fisk's hare-brained scheme, which, with apologies to Milton Berle, didn't feel like it would work. It was as if his entire trip to London so far had been one long shot after another, and his luck wasn't in.

Before he could give it any more thought, he heard the main door of the bathroom slam open and someone came in, swearing to themselves. Bunny heard Fisk asking, "Can I assist you, sir?" And then a voice snapped, "How? You got a bloody dry cleaners on you? If not, piss off."

As signals went, it wasn't the most subtle, but it was effective. Since he'd been sitting in the cubicle, Bunny had been keeping track of, for want of a better phrase, the comings and goings in the bathroom. He reckoned someone was just finishing up at the urinals and one of the other stalls was occupied. He heard a flush and gave it a minute, listening to the swearer over by the sinks still hissing invectives at the world in general. Then he stepped out of the cubicle but quickly nipped back in again when he remembered to flush, if only for the look of the thing.

There were two other men in the bathroom, both standing at the sinks. Fisk was nowhere to be seen. One, an older man, was just finishing up washing his hands, while the other, a man in his thirties, was patting the crotch of his expensive-looking powder-blue suit with a handful of paper towels. The colour of the suit set off the guy's deep tan and it looked like he was fighting an expensive if futile battle with a receding hairline of black hair. He'd compensated for it in no way whatsoever by growing a ponytail. The stain on his lap was a big one – Fisk had at least got his money's worth.

"Stupid fucking bitch. Unbelievable. Un-be-fucking-lievable."

Bunny took up position at one of the unoccupied sinks and proceeded to start washing his hands thoroughly. He and the older gent exchanged a look of disapproval, although he doubted they were disapproving of the same thing. The old fella was probably outraged by the swearing, whereas Bunny had just noticed that the younger man, who was undoubtedly Alex "Sparky" Theakston, wasn't wearing any socks. What was the world coming to? Bunny had to wear a la-di-da suit in order to sit first in a storage cupboard and then in a toilet cubicle, and this dipshit wanders in not wearing any socks. He deserved the athlete's foot he had coming, and a lot more besides. The older gent did a fly-by of the hand dryer and then, with one last disapproving harrumph that went entirely unnoticed, made good his exit, leaving Bunny and Theakston alone.

Bunny dabbed at his hands with a paper towel then tossed it in the bin before turning to Theakston.

"Ye alright there, champ?"

Theakston glanced up. "Do I look all fucking right? Stupid question."

"There's that Sparky Theakston charm I've heard so much about."

Bunny's comment did the trick and earned him a slightly longer look.

"Do I know you?" Sparky asked him.

"No," replied Bunny, and something in his head clicked as he spoke. He didn't know what he was about to say until the words came out of his mouth. He didn't know this guy, but he knew his type. All bollocks and bluster. Someone who acted the hard man despite never having done a hard day's anything in their life. In that moment, Bunny was certain that this little shit wasn't going to answer any questions, so the trick would be to get answers by not asking anything. "I'm a friend of Sean Malone's and I know exactly what happened."

Now he had Sparky's undivided attention.

"Who?" the guy said, in a piss-poor attempt at a bluff, which Bunny took as confirmation that whatever instinct had just kicked in had been the right one.

Bunny laughed. "Don't bother lying. I think you just pissed yourself, but lucky for you it won't show."

For the first time since stepping off the plane, Bunny felt in his element. Squeezing some little scrote to get to the truth. Some things were universal and Sparky Theakston's sort were some of the easiest-to-predict creatures on the planet. Sure enough, here came the cornered animal lashing out as Sparky drew himself up to his full height, which was still a couple of inches shorter than Bunny.

"Do you have any idea who you're dealing with?"

"As it happens, I do, Sparky, and you're not anywhere near as intimidating as you think you are. You're not daddy, but then I'm guessing, deep down, you already knew that."

And now there was the flash of impotent rage in the eyes. Good, keep him off balance.

"I don't know what some worthless junkie told you he thought he saw, but nobody's going to believe a word he says."

It turned out Bunny was more unpredictable than Sparky. Before he knew what was happening, he had Sparky's lapels in his fists and was pinning him up against the wall, having slapped away the guy's feeble attempts at blocking him. He spoke with his face inches from

Sparky's. "You don't get to call junkies worthless when your family made its money peddling them misery, you entitled piece of shit. I think it's time we talked about Gabriel Fuentes."

"Get your hands off me!"

"Or what?"

Before the conversation could go much further, the "what" came crashing through the door behind them.

Bunny released Theakston from his grip and turned to see Lawrence Cooper standing in the doorway. The head of security's muscles were straining against the material of his tight shirt, rippling with power.

Theakston suddenly sounded a lot braver. "Have him, Lawrence. Show this prick how we deal with blackmailers."

In response, as Cooper strode towards them, a blade appeared in his right hand out of nowhere. A butterfly knife. Bunny was a big man, but Cooper was a giant, and between the cubicles and the sinks, even in this grandiose bathroom, there wasn't much room to work in. Bunny felt the air move behind him and instinctively threw his left elbow backwards. He caught Sparky, who'd sensed an opportunity to get a cheap shot in, with a satisfying blow under the chin that sent his head snapping up as he tumbled backwards. At least Bunny could now dedicate all his attention to the considerable problem of Cooper. He made the decision to drop into a crouched stance. Attempting to bob and weave would be a useless strategy – this fight might as well be taking place in a phone box, with the other guy having all the advantages. Bunny was just going to have to hope something would come to him.

Cooper feinted with the knife then threw a left hook. Bunny had been expecting the move but still only narrowly avoided it, then felt the blade brush past his cheek as Cooper followed up with the other fist. Lightning fast. Cooper must've had a glass jaw, because it sure as hell wasn't speed that must have derailed his boxing career. His footwork was good too, as Bunny's attempt to lash out with a kick to his knee was deftly avoided.

A scream that didn't come from either man ripped through the air, and they both turned to look back at the main door to the bathroom, the blade disappearing from Cooper's hand as quickly as it had appeared. Fisk, hand on chest like a scandalised maiden aunt, was standing beside a member of hotel staff dressed in a black suit.

"You see?" said Fisk. "Men engaging in sexual activity in the bathrooms of the Dorchester at lunchtime. Lunchtime!" he wailed. "What hope is there for us as a species when even lunchtime is no longer sacred?"

Five minutes later, Fisk and Bunny found themselves roughly escorted from the Dorchester by security, their undesirability having been made abundantly clear to them.

"To reiterate, you are banned from this establishment," said the Jeeves who they'd met briefly on their way in.

Fisk, picking up his fedora from the pavement, bristled as he brushed it off. "I've been banned from way better places than this, fella. In fact, I was banned from here over ten years ago when it was a much finer place than it is now."

"Yeah," agreed Bunny. "Youse are skimping on the bog roll in the toilets, and don't think people haven't noticed."

With that, the pair started to move off, just in case the hotel changed its mind about calling the police.

"Seriously," said Bunny, as they made their way down Park Lane, "why did you have to go shouting we were shagging in the bogs?"

"I didn't pick you for a homophobe, McGarry."

"Not at all, but ... it lacks a bit of class."

"If I yelled 'fight', the guy would've gone running for help. It's why they tell women if they're attacked to yell 'fire'."

"Come to that," responded Bunny, "why didn't you yell 'fire'?"

Fisk considered this. "Hmmm, you might actually have a point there. Anyway, how'd it go? Did you find out anything?"

"In a manner of speaking. I don't know what they're scared of, but they're really scared of something."

Chapter Eighteen

It took DI Fintan O'Rourke a couple of attempts to find the Jojo Dojo because its entrance was a stairwell between a Chinese takeaway and a carpet wholesaler. There was a sign, but it was only visible as you drove past from one direction, and even then it wasn't that easy to see. He might have missed it entirely had he not noticed the motorbike, which he happened to recognise. He'd always wanted one in his younger days, but his wife had made clear that his impending mid-life crisis would not be featuring such a thing. Besides, one of the many downsides of being a guard was that once you've inevitably had to deal with a motorbike accident, they quickly lose their appeal, although not to everyone, apparently. The bike didn't fit with his mental image of its owner at all, but he guessed that was rather the point.

He parked up and climbed the stairs to the dojo. Halfway up, the sound of the call-and-response chanting reached him.

"Right," shouted the leader. "What is the golden rule, ladies?"

"Get Ken," came the response.

"I'm sorry, ladies, but I can't hear you."

"Get Ken." Louder this time.

At the top of the stairs now, O'Rourke could hear the lead voice more clearly. It belonged to exactly who he'd expected it to.

"Nope. I'm still not getting it, ladies. I need to hear it like you mean it. Like you really fucking mean it! I want you all to picture some useless ex, some annoying co-worker or, if you must, your ma when she's saying something like, 'Oh, that's a brave outfit choice.'"

A chorus of laughter spilled into the stairwell. O'Rourke glanced around the door to see the diminutive figure of Detective Pamela Cassidy standing in the middle of a space that resembled a converted storage room with a few mats thrown down on the floor. Facing her was a line of tracksuit-clad women and girls of all ages, shapes and sizes. O'Rourke was fully aware that damn near everyone referred to Detective Cassidy as Butch, but as her commanding officer, he'd always refrained from doing so. He stood at the back of the room, out of the way, but she still clocked him.

"And give it to me one more time, like you mean it, ladies." She leaned back and roared at the ceiling. "What do we do?"

"GET KEN!" came the screamed response, followed by gales of laughter.

"That's more like it," said Cassidy, clapping her hands together. "Right, Debs," she said, pointing at a larger girl standing nervously to the side. "C'mon. Front and centre, missy. I need my best student for a demonstration."

As the girl stepped forward tentatively, with some encouragement from the others, Cassidy grabbed a life-sized dummy of a man that had been positioned in the corner, whose grey hoodie was emblazoned with the name KEN in black marker. She plonked the dummy in the middle of the floor and Debs took her place in front of it.

"Here we go, Debs. It's time that Ken here got a much-needed lesson in personal space. What do we do, ladies?"

"Get Ken," the ladies chimed again.

"Yes, we do." Cassidy wrangled the dummy into an upright position and smiled at the girl. "Go on, Debs. Just like we practised. Get Ken. G?"

"Groin," shouted the group with gusto.

Debs stepped forward and half-heartedly raised a knee in the general direction of Ken's hypothetical groin.

"C'mon," cajoled Cassidy. "Don't be shy. I want you to put a lump in Ken here's throat, Debs. One ... two ... three ..."

Laughing, this time Debs planted a knee firmly in Ken's nether region, a move which was cheered by the rest of the class.

"Yes, yes, yes!" roared Cassidy. "And now E?"

"Eyes," roared the group, as Debs, with considerably more confidence, poked Ken in the eye.

"T?"

"Throat." Debs delivered a chop.

"That's it. Right in the Adam's apple," shouted Butch. "K?"

"Knee!"

A blow to Ken's knee was duly delivered.

"E?"

"Ears."

Getting into it now, Debs delivered an open-handed slap to Ken's left ear that caused him to sway to the side.

"I love it!" shouted Cassidy. "And big finish – N?"

"Nose!"

Debs sent a flat-palmed jab to Ken's nose, after which Cassidy threw him to the floor and raised Debs's arm in triumph while the rest of the group cheered her uproariously.

"Excellent work. Excellent work," said Cassidy, breaking into a round of applause as a smiling Debs rejoined the line of students. "And now, before we finish for this week, we've got a special guest star joining us for a demonstration. Ladies, please give a warm welcome to Detective Inspector Fintan O'Rourke."

O'Rourke waved Butch away, but she was not to be dissuaded. As the group turned around to look at him, she crossed the room quickly and grabbed his arm to lead him into the centre. He noticed some of the women glancing at him nervously, so he tried to smile reassuringly, even though he himself wasn't feeling in the least bit reassured.

"Now," said Cassidy, "the DI is here to give a demonstration of a technique we are going to go into in a lot more detail next week."

"I'm not really dressed for it," protested O'Rourke, indicating his suit and tie.

"Nonsense. Blokes in suits can be arseholes too." Butch took up position with her back to him. "OK, Fintan, I want you to grab me from behind."

"Pamela—"

"Do it," she instructed, a firm edge to her voice.

O'Rourke took a step forward and cautiously put his arms around her.

She responded with an exaggerated sigh. "Jesus, Fintan, put your back into it. You're supposed to be an attacker. Grab me."

He tightened his grip.

"Harder."

He tightened it further.

"That's it! Now, as you can all see, seeing as I'm a short arse, the DI here has a good foot in height on me, and he's grabbed me from behind. First thing you do is lean forward as much as you can." She arched her body forward, pulling him down slightly.

"Then, hard as you can, throw your head back."

She did so with rather more speed than O'Rourke was expecting, but he managed to step back and move his face out of the way just in time.

"Now, if you're lucky, you might smash right into the prick's face, but even if you don't, I guarantee he'll change his footing to redistribute his weight, and then ..."

Before O'Rourke knew what was happening, Butch had bent forward quickly, seized his right leg that was now positioned between hers, and had wrenched it up, sending him crashing down onto his back and knocking the wind out of him.

"You can grab his leg, pull as hard as you can, and even a highly trained member of the Garda Síochána will lose his balance and end up flat on his arse," Butch concluded.

She looked down at him, a broad smile on her face. "Let's have a big round of applause for the detective inspector. Such a good sport."

* * *

O'Rourke stood there awkwardly as the students picked up their bags from the corner, trying to look like a man who hadn't just got body-slammed by a five-foot-nothing woman. He noticed Butch made sure to have a word with each of the girls and ladies before they headed down the stairs. Only when they'd all left did she turn her attention back his way.

"Thanks for your assistance, Inspector."

"Happy to help. I'll send you my chiropractor bill."

"It was worth it."

"I think so. You certainly look like you enjoyed it." He nodded towards the stairs. "Seems like a fun class."

"Has to be. Easiest way to get the information across and get around the inbuilt female fear of confrontation."

"Get Ken? Not heard that before."

"I came up with it. In a moment of crisis you need something that'll stick in the head. Might be the difference between freezing and fighting. Hence the repetition."

"I'm sure they'll all remember it should they ever get attacked."

Any trace of joviality left her tone entirely. "Too late. They've all been attacked already. That's why they're here."

O'Rourke was taken aback. "Oh. I ... Did we get the guys?"

She raised an eyebrow in his direction. "How many of them do you think we even went after?"

"I ..." O'Rourke didn't know what to say to that.

"And while we're on the subject, and I appreciate you meant no harm, Fintan, but if you ever walk uninvited into a female-only self-defence class again, you should expect a lot more than a little embar-rassment."

O'Rourke felt like he wanted the ground to open up and swallow him. "Shit. Sorry. I didn't think—"

She waved away the apology. "Anyway, not that I can't guess, but to what do I owe the visit?"

Feeling like a prize shit, O'Rourke puffed out his cheeks. "I don't want to be here any more than you want to be asked ..."

"Sure. I'll save us both some time. I don't know where he is, what he is doing or whether he's wearing clean underwear or not."

"This is an unofficial conversation, Pamela."

"My unofficial answer is the same as my official one."

"This time, I think he's got himself into more trouble than he realises."

"That doesn't sound like him," she said sarcastically. "Did he forget to take sunblock or something?"

"He's in London," O'Rourke said, "but I'm guessing you knew that."

"No offence, sir—"

"Unofficial."

"OK. No offence, Fintan, but you can keep guessing 'til the cows come home, and in case you're not picking up on it, I'm resenting the hell out of this conversation."

"I was getting that loud and clear."

"Good, I was worried I was being too subtle. Now, if you don't mind" – she waved a hand around – "hard as it is to believe, this state-of-the-art facility doesn't have showers, and I'm starting to smell myself."

She turned to grab her bag from the corner of the room.

"MI5 are asking about him."

The newsflash caused her to spin back around. "Bollocks!"

"I'm as surprised as you are," he said. "Actually, probably more so, seeing as I've no idea what he's up to, other than allegedly pissing off the great white hope of the boxing world."

"And Her Majesty's Secret Service care about crap like that, do they?" she asked.

"Apparently," said O'Rourke with a shrug. "They've been asking around at the highest level."

Butch furrowed her brow. "How high?"

O'Rourke neglected to give an answer beyond raising an eyebrow.

"You're kidding?"

He continued to keep quiet.

"Shit."

"Yes," he said finally. "Indeed. And whatever's going on, he's not answering his mobile, so I have no idea how to get a message to him. Or, to be exact, a warning."

Butch folded her arms. "And I'm supposed to believe whoever sent you is just looking out for Bunny's best interests, am I?"

"No, but given that none of us wants to see a serving member of the Garda Síochána getting himself into some serious trouble with the British authorities, I think we can all agree that, in this instance, his best interests might align with those of the powers that be."

"OK, even if all of that's true – and I'm not saying it is – what do you expect me to do about it? He's not answering his phone. I've been trying. And London's a big place."

"You're a very fine detective, Pamela."

She jabbed an angry finger at him. "If you're about to pull some crap where the idea of a promotion gets floated in exchange for me—"

O'Rourke held up his hands. "Relax. Not where I was going. I promise."

She nodded, looking at least partially mollified. "Alright. So?"

"So," said O'Rourke. "You work all kinds of hours ..." Butch let out a sarcastic bark of laughter at this. "... and it turns out you're owed a week's holiday that slipped through the system."

"No. I'm—"

"Bloody IT systems are a nightmare. Not fit for purpose."

Cassidy nodded again, catching the drift. "Yes. A disgrace."

"So, with apologies, the Garda Síochána—"

"Are you all of a sudden here in an official capacity again?" she asked, tilting her head.

"We were just wondering – and I've sorted cover, before you ask – but would you mind taking a week's leave from tomorrow as we need to get the system back in order as soon as possible."

Butch delivered a very long, piercing stare in O'Rourke's direction before eventually saying, "Even if I could find him, I'm not going to beg him to come home."

"Understood."

"And I'm not reporting in on him."

"Please don't," said O'Rourke. "I think I can confidently say that neither I nor anyone else on the force wants to officially know what either of you gets up to on your holidays. Unofficially? Well, let's just say that a certain someone isn't known for his diplomacy skills …"

"And I am?"

"Speaking as a man you just slammed to the floor, yes. Compared to him. And even if you can't convince him not to do something, I'd rather he had someone relatively sensible to bounce his bad ideas off first."

"I don't have—"

O'Rourke pulled a couple of sheets of paper out of the inside pocket of his suit jacket. "Someone apparently paid cash and got you on the six-thirty flight in the morning."

She pushed the tickets away. "They wasted a bit of cash there. There's a two am ferry tonight. I've been meaning to go on one of those biking holidays. Might as well start now."

He tucked the papers away. "Please yourself."

"I've always wanted to visit the Tower of London."

"I hear it's quite impressive."

"Yeah, fingers crossed we don't both end up locked up in it."

Chapter Nineteen

Bunny studied the race programme in front of him and tutted. In the seat beside him, Milton Fisk sighed.

"Are you going to mention your overcoat yet again, McGarry?"

"No," said Bunny. "As it happens, I wasn't going to mention that you took my overcoat off me, made me wear this ridiculous suit, and that's why I'm sitting in this stand in east London on a bitterly cold night, freezing my knackers off."

"Thanks. I appreciate you not bringing that up. Again."

"You're welcome. I was tutting at the fact that in the next race there's a greyhound called Mother Teresa."

"Clearly someone's a fan and wanted to do their own, I grant you, unusual form of tribute."

"That's the thing," said Bunny. "I don't think they've thought it through. Think about it – you'll find yourself saying things like, 'Mother Teresa, stop licking there,' or 'Give me a poo bag, Mother Teresa's just dropped a messy one on the foot-path.' I'd argue it's not the touching tribute they may have envisioned."

"Hmmm," mused Fisk. "And to add to your point, Mother Teresa hasn't done better than fourth in its last five races."

"So someone is screaming, 'Move your lazy arse, Mother Teresa' at her now, too? I mean, 'tis not dignified."

"You may have a point," conceded Fisk, "but ..." He paused.

Bunny, suddenly alert, scanned the crowd beneath them. They'd been at Walthamstow greyhound track for over two hours now, having headed straight there from the Dorchester, and so far there hadn't been any sign of Daniel Martin, aka Sean Malone's father. They'd got there when the gates had opened and racing started in the afternoon, and had watched as the place grew steadily more crowded as the evening drew in. They were seated out in the open air and although there was a restaurant area behind them that looked fancier and considerably warmer, it appeared to be the preserve of corporate groups on a company night out. All they knew of Daniel Martin was that he was an inveterate gambler and far more likely to be spotted milling around the "chicken in a basket" area, or around the half-dozen bookies with pitches in front of them on the concourse that sat a few feet below the track level to avoid blocking people's views.

"False alarm," said Fisk. "In fact, I think it might be the same guy I got excited about last time."

Bunny rubbed his hands up and down his arms. "I'm getting the distinct feeling that all we're going to catch tonight is pneumonia."

"Ye of little faith," said Fisk.

Above their heads, the Tannoy crackled into life at a volume Bunny had not been shy in postulating was significantly too loud. "Next race is the McNamara Sweepstakes. Get your bets in fast, folks. It's gonna be a barn burner!"

"We're in east London," said Bunny. "Why is that gobshite doing a Texas accent?"

"You think that's Texas?" replied Fisk.

"I think he thinks he's doing Texas."

"Maybe he's part of the line-dancing craze that's apparently sweeping the nation. I saw a flyer."

"I take it from your tone you're not a fan?" asked Bunny.

Fisk shrugged. "Once you've danced the tango with Raquel Welch, everything else is just rhythmic walking."

"Yeah," agreed Bunny, "that's definitely how I feel about it." It was an indication of just how grumpy he was feeling that he decided not to take the bait on that story. Not that it seemed to bother Fisk in the slightest.

"Oh, and to go back to your earlier point ..." said Fisk. "Teddy bears."

Bunny scrunched his brow. "What point was I making that involved teddies?"

"Strange things being named after famous people. The teddy bear is named after no less a man than President Theodore Roosevelt."

"Oh, right," said Bunny. "I'm trying to remember if I know what he looked like. He wasn't the guy with the hat, was he?"

"The hat?"

"Looked like a chimney."

"No," said Fisk. "I think you're referring to Honest Abe – Abraham Lincoln, the man who ended slavery and won the Civil War."

"Alright," said Bunny defensively. "How many Irish leaders from history can you name?"

"Point taken," conceded Fisk.

"So, did old Teddy look like a bear, then?"

"Not especially," said Fisk. "It was named after him because, apparently, on a hunting trip, he refused to shoot a bear that had been chased, clubbed and tied to a tree."

"That's an achievement, is it?"

"Seemingly."

"Personally, I'd have been more impressed if he'd shot the prick that tied the poor bear to the tree."

"There is that," said Fisk, standing up. "It's almost time for the next race and it's my turn to go down. Have you selected your hound yet?"

Bunny sighed. "Ah, I dunno. Haven't backed a single winner all night. Give me a fiver each way on whoever number three is."

Fisk consulted the programme in his hands. "Transcendental Meditation it is."

"Again, what kind of name is that for a dog? 'Transcendental Meditation, stop licking your arse.' People haven't thought this through."

"Be that as it may," said Fisk, "I'm backing Mother Teresa for the win and I'm rolling it over."

Fisk had now won four races in a row and was up nearly a hundred quid.

"At this rate, you'll be able to pay your own tab back at the pub."

"I think you've grossly underestimated how much I drink." With a salute, Fisk briskly turned and headed down the steps towards the bookies' enclosure.

"Two minutes to go, folks," came the slightly distorted voice over the Tannoy. "Just about two minutes. You've got to be in it to win it. Don't miss your chance to beat them there bookies."

"I'd fecking love a chance to beat you, ye yee-hawing jabbering jingoist," mumbled Bunny. "Should be somewhere running the fecking Waltzers."

"Excuse me?" came a voice from behind him.

Bunny turned to see an older woman in a thick fake-fur coat eyeing him suspiciously. "Sorry, was just talking to myself."

She didn't respond to this, maybe because she thought he was a lunatic. Given the way he was dressed, he couldn't blame her. He turned back towards the track and looked up at the darkening clouds overhead. Rain was on its way. Course it was. Perfect end to a perfect day.

All they'd been able to find out from his confrontation with Alex "Sparky" Theakston at the Dorchester earlier on was that a) the man was an arsehole, and b) Sean Malone was definitely in some kind of trouble, possibly because he'd seen or heard something he shouldn't have. Bunny hadn't even managed to broach the subject of Gabriel Fuentes before they'd been interrupted.

All of it smelled very off and Bunny was working on the assumption that whatever had happened with Gabby and Sean, the two disappearances must be related. They were still no closer to finding Sean, and seeing as it now seemed likely that they weren't the only ones looking for him, he was probably doing all he could not to be found.

As for MI5 – or whoever Mr Smith and his associates were, who'd had a little chat with Bunny the previous night before tossing him out the back of a taxi – he still had no idea what their involvement was in all of this. Theakston's dad had been an international drug dealer, so Bunny assumed it must be something related to that, but then again, was that something MI5 got involved in? It seemed like more of a policing matter. Bunny didn't know or particularly care. All he wanted to do was get hold of Sean Malone, take him home to his mother and, if possible, help Fisk out with the mystery of where the hell Gabriel Fuentes had gone.

Bunny was so lost in thought that it took him a while to notice that Fisk, standing in line at one of the bookies, was trying to get his attention. Judging by the frustration on his face, he had been doing so for some time. Once he finally caught Bunny's eye, Fisk removed his fedora and cocked an eyebrow subtly in the direction of the far end of the crowd. Bunny's eyes scanned the assembled spectators and fell on a man talking to two ladies from one of the corporate nights out.

Daniel Martin.

A little greyer on the temples than he was in the picture Bunny had, but it was him. He was even flashing the same smile and clearly doing his best to charm the women. To what ends, who could say? It could well be the normal ends that men endeavoured to do such things for, but given his rep as a low-level thief and conman, the options were wide open. Bunny nodded at Fisk and started to make his way down the stand, trying not to look too keen. At the same time,

Fisk broke off from the queue and started walking towards Martin, up the far side of the concourse near the railings.

As Bunny made his way forward, one of the city boys in a flash suit banged into him. Despite being the one doing the barging, he fronted up to Bunny. "Watch where you're fucking going."

Bunny gave him a quick glare before moving past.

"Hey," said the man, clearly pumped up on booze, or possibly something that explained the slight cold he seemed to have. He grabbed Bunny's arm and jerked him around. Two of the guy's friends flanked him on either side, both wearing amused smiles.

Bunny leaned in so that only the grabber and his chums could hear him. "Listen very carefully. Take your hand off me now, or I'll rip your whole arm off, shove it up the grinning blond idiot to your left, and then use him to beat the bald fella on your right around the head until he cries for his mammy."

Despite their superior number, Bunny could see the bolshy confidence drain out of the group, and he was able to pull his arm free, turn around and be on his way. Damn it! He'd lost sight of Daniel Martin. His eyes darted across the concourse and, through the crowd, he spied the distinctive fedora that was now moving parallel with him. Fisk gave him a nod in the direction of the stands. Bunny moved swiftly around another group of spectators and caught sight of Martin again to the side of a set of stairs. One of the women had made herself scarce while the other appeared to be giving him her number, giggling as she wrote it down on the back of a business card.

Martin looked up and the smile fell from his lips as he caught Bunny watching him. Bunny averted his gaze and slowed his pace but Martin stayed focused on him. From the corner of his eye, Bunny could see the woman was saying something, but Martin no longer appeared to be paying her any attention. As he took a couple of steps backwards, the woman gave him a confused look and held out the business card.

"Shite," said Bunny, he'd been made. While mentally admonishing himself, he clocked a secondary threat coming at him from the side.

He turned quickly to casually stick a fist into the nether regions of the city boy who thought he'd managed to sneak up on him, before using his other hand to clap the guy on the back. As he crumpled to the ground with a groan, Bunny loudly chided, "Bloody hell, James, pissed again." Having dispatched the scourge of Canary Wharf for a second time, he turned around to spot Martin hurrying away. His female companion was still standing there, business card in hand, watching him with a mix of confusion and humiliation.

Bunny made after him quickly. There was no point trying to be inconspicuous now. Martin glanced over his shoulder and broke into a run just as the Tannoy squalled into life. He pushed past a couple of punters and was sprinting by the time the traps were released and the crowd began to roar.

"And they're off."

Bunny took off in pursuit.

All pretence of looking casual gone, Martin was legging it towards the end of the stand as fast as his feet could carry him. Bunny was through the thickest part of the crowd now, and with everyone's attention on the race, it was easier to bob and weave around any spectators in his path.

"They're coming up to the first turn and it's Transcendental Meditation from Uncle Buck and Tyrannosaurus Dave ..."

Martin disappeared from view around the corner of the stand as Bunny finally hit some open ground and was able to build up a bit of speed. His ribs gave him a not so subtle reminder of how much they remained against any form of exercise in their current condition. He whirled into an involuntary pirouette to avoid crashing into a teenage kid rushing out of the gents to watch the race.

"... and round the turn it's Transcendental Meditation holding off Uncle Buck, and Salmon Chusty is coming up the outside ..."

Bunny rounded the corner of the stand just as Martin vanished behind it.

"And Uncle Buck passes now, and it's Uncle Buck from Salmon Chusty with Transcendental Meditation fading ..."

As Bunny turned the next corner and his new leather shoes slipped on the wet tarmac, he stumbled wildly. Ahead of him, Martin was sprinting towards the far end of the stadium and the entrance gates. Bunny realised his chances of catching him now were bad heading towards non-existent.

"I just want to talk to you," he roared.

"Piss off," came the response.

"But here comes Mother Teresa making a late run ..." screamed the PA.

"It's about S—"

Bunny's foot hit the rim of a drain he hadn't seen, and this time he lost his footing completely, falling forward and landing heavily on the ground. He cried out in pain and when he looked up, Martin was slowing his pace and turning to face him, a large smile back on his lips.

"Looks like—"

The rest of Martin's witty riposte was lost as the walking cane he hadn't seen coming caught between his legs and sent him sprawling to the ground.

Milton Fisk, having just appeared from behind some packing crates, stood over him.

"And it's Teresa by a nose. Mother Teresa wins it!"

Fisk grinned in Bunny's direction. "Looks like it's my lucky day."

Chapter Twenty

Bunny picked himself up off the ground and made his way to where Milton Fisk was standing over the supine figure of Daniel Martin. As he approached, the younger man shifted his position, as if considering trying to make another run for it. Bunny watched in amazement as Fisk flicked his wrist and a wickedly sharp-looking blade a couple of inches long popped out of the end of his walking cane.

"Jesus, Fisk. Let me guess – a present from James Bond?"

"Close. James Brown." He looked sideways at Bunny. "Why else do you think I'd be carrying a cane? Are you OK?"

"I'll live, which is more than can be said for these slippery bastard shoes that I'm going to burn at the first available opportunity."

"No offence, McGarry, but you're a nightmare to shop for."

"Look," said Daniel Martin from where he lay, "this has all been a big misunderstanding."

"Has it?" asked Bunny.

"Absolutely. I have Ivan's money. I actually came here to collect it, and then I was going to head straight over there with it. On my mother's life."

"Jesus, man. Don't fecking swear on your ma's life, even in the unlikely event you're not lying."

Martin changed tack. "You're Irish – hey, me too! Is that a Cork accent? I've lots of relatives from down that way."

"Please keep that to yourself."

"I didn't know Ivan had any Irish guys working for him. I thought the whole crew was Russian."

"I don't work for whoever the shitting hell Ivan is. I'm here on behalf of your ex."

"I'm going to return that money—"

"For Christ's sake," barked Bunny. "Stop guessing. Not that ex – or any of those exes. If you owe Orla any money, I imagine she gave up on the idea of seeing it a long time ago. I'm here looking for Sean."

"Whatever he's done," said Martin, "it's nothing to do with me."

"He hasn't done anything," snapped Bunny. "I'm just looking for him to take him home, wonderful as it is to see your protective paternal instincts in full flow." Bunny considered sharing the details of exactly why he was looking for Sean but decided against it. He'd only been close to Daniel Martin for about a minute, but he could already envisage the slimy little toad finding some kind of workable "angle" with that information.

"Look," said Martin, "Sean came to see me but, I dunno, I don't know what he's looking for, to be honest with you."

"Just a wild guess," said Bunny, "but I'd imagine a father."

"That ain't me. I'm a free spirit."

"No, I'm a free spirit," repeated Fisk. "I think you might be confusing the term with being an asshole, which is not the same thing."

"Where is Sean?" asked Bunny.

"How would I know?"

"Because you not knowing means I have no reason at all not to let Fisk here stab you."

"He's not going to stab me," said Martin, looking up at Fisk.

"You never know," said Fisk, raising an eyebrow, "Us free spirits are capable of anything."

"And if he doesn't," said Bunny, "I'm a Corkman who's been beaten, frozen, chucked in a skip bin and thrown out of a moving vehicle. Frankly, I'm looking for someone to take out my frustrations on, and you seem like a very good candidate."

"Relax," said Martin, raising his hands. "He came around to see me a couple of times. Y'know, it's a weird situation – I hadn't seen him since he was three."

"When you hightailed it out of there."

"Relationships are complicated. You've not heard my side of the story."

"I have," said Bunny. "A hundred times before. Just not told by you. Now, where is Sean?"

For good measure, Bunny gave Martin's foot a sharp kick because his annoyance levels were steadily rising.

"All I know is he said he was staying in some squat. I've not seen or heard from him since last week. He rang me in the middle of the night."

"Why?"

"He said he was in trouble."

Bunny's eyes narrowed. "And what did you do to help him?"

"What was I supposed to do? I've got enough problems of my own. He was probably just high or something. None of my business."

Bunny clenched his fists but looked down to see Fisk's hand appear on his arm. The older man gave him a brief nod and stepped forward.

"Sure," Fisk began, gently moving his cane to give Martin the slightest of jabs to remind him of its presence. "We get it. What we need to know is how we can find him. Tell me about this squat."

"Hammersmith," yelped Martin, like a burning man who'd just remembered the word for water. "Somewhere down in Hammersmith. I ..." He stopped. "Yeah, he mentioned something about it being near the Apollo. That's all I know."

"And do you have a number for him?" continued Fisk.

"No. He rings me. To be honest, I regret giving him my number, but that horse has bolted." He turned his attention to Bunny. "I've tried to help him any way I can. He's a good kid but, y'know, I got stuff I gotta deal with."

"Sure," said Fisk. He drew a card out of his jacket pocket and scribbled a number on the back of it. "Here's my UK cell phone number. If you see or hear from him again, give this to him or ring me."

"Absolutely."

Fisk extended the card between two fingers then pulled it back as Martin went to take it. "You help us find him, and there's a grand, cash, in it for you."

Martin's eyes lit up. "I'll let you know as soon as he gets in contact."

* * *

Fisk and Bunny didn't speak for a couple of minutes after leaving Daniel Martin. It was only once they'd walked beyond the gates of Walthamstow greyhound track that Fisk broke the silence.

"Do you want to talk about it?"

"What?"

"I mean, the guy is a piece of shit, no question, but it feels like Mr Martin stirred up a few things."

"It's been a long week."

"OK."

"Are you really going to give that waste of oxygen a grand?"

Fisk shrugged. "If it means finding the kid and, who knows, hopefully helping me figure out what happened to Gabby, then sure – why not?"

"That fella needs a boot in the head a lot more than he needs a grand."

"Nothing I said precludes him from receiving both." Fisk raised his cane. "Let's get back to the Duck and Trumpet. It's been quite the day."

Bunny put his hand on Fisk's arm. "Alright, but no black cabs. C'mon, I think I saw a taxi place around the corner."

Chapter Twenty-One

This time, the call was picked up on the second ring.

"Yes?"

"Yes?" repeated Bunny. "Seriously, do you start every phone conversation that way?"

"You're the only person who has this number, Detective McGarry," replied Bernadette.

"Oh. Thanks very much, I'm sure. Nice to know the level of civility I warrant. If anyone ever told you that you were a people person, I hope you realise they were taking the mickey."

"No one ever has. They've also never described me as a patient person. Now—"

She broke off at what sounded a lot like a chainsaw being started up on her end. Bunny listened as the nun pulled away from the phone and shouted something in what sounded to him like Mandarin. After a second, the chainsaw ceased. She then returned to the call.

"Have you found him?"

"What the hell was that?" asked Bunny, ignoring the question.

"That is yet again one of those things that you do not need, or want, to know about."

Bunny thought of the very short list of things a chainsaw could be used for. "I'll take your word for it."

"Now, have you found the boy?"

"No," said Bunny. "But on the upside, I've not been beaten up or thrown out of any moving vehicles by the security services today, so I'm taking that as a sign of progress."

"I wish I shared your enthusiasm. Are there any more tangible signs of progress? I went to see Orla earlier today – she is not a well woman."

Bunny didn't appreciate the unnecessary application of pressure invested in that statement, but he let it slide. Instead, he gave the nun an update on how his day had gone while she listened in silence.

"It appears Sean is definitely in some serious trouble, then," she said, once he'd finished.

"It certainly seems that way," agreed Bunny.

"So, get him out of it."

"Well, yes, that's the plan, I just—"

Bunny stopped talking as the line had gone dead.

"Preposterous," he said, staring at the receiver in his hand. "Absolutely preposterous."

Chapter Twenty-Two

Bunny stood under the borrowed umbrella as the heavy rain drummed down around him, so hard that the drops bounced when they hit the concrete. The dark clouds from earlier in the evening had finally stopped their ominous portent and got around to delivering a full deluge. Bunny had been sitting in the Duck and Trumpet, with a well-deserved pint in front of him, when his pay-as-you-go mobile had rung. Babs had given him a lift to the meeting place suggested by his contact – despite Fisk's protestations, Bunny had vetoed the idea of him coming along. His contact was already nervous enough about helping him, and the last thing he wanted to do was further impinge on their generosity.

He watched through the rain as a figure ran towards him, a coat held over their head. He was standing on the margins of the car park, trying to look inconspicuous, despite there not being many reasons for a man to be there at eleven o'clock at night in the middle of a biblical downpour. Sharon, the nurse from Tipperary, came to a halt in front of him, already soaked, despite her best efforts.

"Jesus Christ," she said. "It's like a bloody car wash out here."

Bunny moved the umbrella in an attempt to shelter her, but it was a largely futile gesture.

"I know," he said. "Passed a fella trying to round up two of every animal in London on the way in."

"He should try our A and E department – that's where most of them end up. Although the one advantage of this weather is the nutters generally stay home and we've a relatively quiet one. Turns out crazy is soluble."

Bunny nodded his head repeatedly. This was clearly the end of the small-talk section of the evening, but he wasn't quite sure how to move things on.

Sharon glanced around the car park then fixed him with a look. "Seriously, you'd better not fuck me over on this."

"I promise," said Bunny. "I'm not going to cause trouble for you or anybody else. I just need to find this young fella, Sean, and Mr Brandon might be the only person who can help with that. That's all."

"Is there nobody else you can ask? His management or something?"

"I tried. They're extremely unhelpful. To be completely honest with you, Sharon, they're a bunch of dodgy so-and-sos, and I'm beginning to think it might be them that Sean is hiding from."

"Great. That's really reassuring."

"I promised I'd tell you the whole truth. If there was another way, I'd not be here."

The young nurse bit her lip and gave him a long look before saying, "Ah, feck it. I asked around and, apparently, he's in pretty much every night, including tonight. He's up on the eighth floor, room eight-one-two. I'll leave the fire door open for you to get in, but after that, you're on your own. Just try and look like you're supposed to be there, and everyone will probably be too busy to question it."

"Is there security?"

"Down in A and E, but I doubt you'd see any elsewhere. And remember, whatever happens—"

"I don't know you. I've never met you. I couldn't pick you out of a line-up."

"Alright, then," she said. "Give it a minute then follow me back over. The door will be held open by a bit of wood. You should leave the same way, so try and remember where it is."

"Right," said Bunny. "I will. And Sharon, thanks again for doing this."

"Yeah," she replied. "Just don't make me regret it."

With that, Sharon took a deep breath and headed back the way she'd come. Bunny waited the full minute before following.

* * *

Thankfully, it proved remarkably easy to reach Marcus Phillips's bedside. Alarmingly easy, in truth, if you worried about such things as hospital security. He'd passed a couple of people in the hall but had managed to blend in by wishing them an enthusiastic hello. People didn't necessarily like cheerful people, but they also tended not to be suspicious of them either.

In less than five minutes, Bunny found himself at the door to room 812. A private room in a particularly quiet area of the hospital. Now that he was here, he wasn't quite sure what his approach was going to be. It did feel terribly invasive to intrude like this, but he hadn't been lying to Sharon when he'd said he really had very little choice. Still, barging in on someone visiting a sick friend was crass in normal circumstances – when the individual in question is a heavy-weight boxer with a renowned temper and a right hook that could take down walls, it could prove fatal. Nevertheless, while all that might be true, staring at a door handle wasn't going to make his job any easier. Bunny steeled himself. He'd just have to wing it and hope for the best.

The lights in the room were turned down low, meaning that Bunny needed a second for his eyes to adjust. A large window provided a view of a cloud-topped London skyline, and the heavy rhythms of the rain beat against the glass. In the hospital bed, Marcus Phillips lay silently, the machines keeping him alive making all the noise in the room. The *thunk-hiss* of air being pushed into his lungs, the beeping of a heart-rate monitor confirming his slow and steady pulse. Beside the bed, with his back to the door, sat the massive, hunched figure of Stevie Brandon.

"I'll be out of here in a m-m-minute," Brandon said softly.

Bunny closed the door behind him and remained silent. Brandon, sensing he was not a member of the regular medical staff turned his head and looked at him. "Get out."

"Sorry to bother you," Bunny began. "I was wondering if I could have a quick word?"

"No."

"I—"

"Get. Out."

"If you could just—"

The big man was already on his feet and heading towards Bunny. "Fucking vultures."

"I'm not press," said Bunny quickly, stepping away until his back was against the wall. "I'm a friend of Sean Malone."

"Bollocks," said Brandon.

The boxer's disbelief was palpable but at least it put enough doubt in his mind to stop Bunny from enjoying a record-breaking short journey to A&E. Instead, Stevie Brandon was now looming in front of Bunny. This close, the man was quite something. Bunny was a big man but Brandon was truly massive – it was like standing in the path of a rapidly approaching tank.

"Actually," said Bunny, "I've never met Sean. I've been sent over here to look for him by his mother."

"He's not here, is he?" As Brandon leaned in, Bunny caught the distinctive whiff of whiskey on the man's breath. "So, p-p-piss off."

"She's sick. Like, really sick. Stage four cancer, and she's desperate to see her son one last time. It's why I'm trying to find him."

Brandon leaned over Bunny for a long moment, his breathing

heavy and oddly in sync with the steady rhythm of the life-support machine behind him. Eventually, he moved back a little bit, only to suddenly lean in further. "If you're lying ..."

"I'm not," said Bunny. "Honestly, I wish I was, but I'm not. I've been sent over because she's no way of contacting him. He used to send letters, but she's not received them for a couple of weeks. The last one she did receive contained this, though ..."

Bunny reached into the pocket of his overcoat and withdrew the photograph of Sean standing beside Brandon. The boxing champ took the picture and gave it a cursory glance, suddenly looking tiny in his massive hands. "I've not seen him for a week. He was helping out at the gym."

"Do you've any idea where he is?"

"No."

"Or why he would have left?"

Brandon shrugged his immense shoulders. "Dunno. He's got some problems."

"I know," said Bunny. "Drugs."

"Nah. He's off them. Least he was. C-c-condition of him getting the job."

"Oh, well, that's good."

"Yeah, he left, though. So," – Brandon shoved the picture back towards Bunny – "don't know about now."

"His ma is very worried about him. She's desperate to see him again."

"He mentioned her. Said she was nice."

"She is," confirmed Bunny. "A good sight nicer than his shitheel of a father."

"F-fathers for you." Brandon thrust the picture towards Bunny again, who took it this time.

"I think he might be in trouble," said Bunny. "Sean, I mean. There seem to be people after him."

"Who?"

"Well, I think he might have pissed off your manager."

151

"Bollocks," said Brandon. He straightened his shoulders with the sudden effect of looming even larger. "Sparky's got nothing to do with Sean."

"I think he does. I think Sean saw or heard something he shouldn't and—"

"No," said Brandon, turning around. "Get out."

"What about Gabby? Gabriel Fuentes?"

"What about him?"

"He's disappeared too."

Brandon waved a massive mitt dismissively. "Not missing. Left. Buggered off home."

"But why would he leave?"

"Everybody leaves," said Brandon, his voice a rumble. "Everybody leaves." He turned and pointed to the door. "You should leave too."

"There's something wrong here," said Bunny. "Something's going on and I think you know it. Theakston—"

"S-Sparky takes care of me. Always has. Nobody else does."

"I appreciate that, but Sean is running from something and I need to—"

"Get out."

"His mother—"

Brandon's voice rose, buoyed by anger. "I said get out."

"I need your help."

Brandon moved swiftly back across the room and shoved Bunny against the wall. "I ain't helping nobody. I'm a monster, ain't you heard? Nearly killed my best mate. Killed my dad – d-d-didn't you hear? When I was twelve or ten or two. Lots of versions of that one. I don't help nobody." The whiff of whiskey was stronger this close and a noticeable slur had found its way into in his voice.

"Bullshit," said Bunny. "You helped Sean. And he needs your help now more than ever. Help me find him."

"Told you already," said Brandon, the anger no longer present in his voice. "Don't know where he is."

"Alright, but ..."

"Just go."

"That young lad is in trouble, and if anything happens to him, you're going to hate yourself for doing nothing to prevent it."

Brandon glared at Bunny then glanced over to the bed. "Got enough reasons for that. I'm a bad man."

"You can still be a good friend to Sean. If you just—"

The door to the room opened softly and a male, middle-aged nurse appeared in the doorway. He looked at Bunny in shock. "Who are you?"

"I'm—"

"He's leaving," said Brandon.

Bunny looked at the big man standing with his back to him then back at the nurse. He remembered his promise to Sharon. "I am."

"Yes," said the nurse. "I think you should. An exception has only been made for Mr Brandon," – his face flushed – "given the circumstances."

"Right," said Bunny, trying to sound conversational. He patted his pockets. "I'll leave my number if—"

"Don't bother," said Brandon.

Bunny glanced at the nurse again, who was eyeing him suspiciously. "OK. I'll be off, so."

The nurse turned and walked off briskly.

Bunny made his way out the door and was about to close it behind him when Brandon spoke again. "You know that story? The one about my d-d-dad?"

"Yes?"

"If that was true, how come I still sleep with the light on?"

Bunny didn't know what to say to that. Brandon stood there in silhouette against the rain-covered window, his head down, shoulders rounded.

"That's something you, me and Sean have in common."

"What's that?"

"Shitty fathers."

Brandon said nothing. The only sound in the room returning to the *thunk-hiss* of air being pushed into lungs and the beeping of a heart-rate monitor confirming a slow and steady pulse.

Bunny stole a glance at the nurse's station where the nurse who'd told him to get out was now on the phone. He took one last look at the hulking figure of Brandon, his eyes shining wetly in the low light as they caught his gaze, and then he turned and left.

Chapter Twenty-Three

Butch shrugged off her biker jacket, bundled it up and tried to use it as a pillow. She shoved it around a bit, punching it harder than necessary in a futile attempt to make it play ball. With a heavy sigh, she gave up on the idea completely. Again. Same result as on the previous three occasions. The leather wasn't a comfortable material to rest your head against, and no matter how she positioned the jacket, a zip always seemed to be sticking in her somewhere.

Not for the first time in the last hour, she cursed herself for not stumping up the extra cash to get a cabin when she'd booked. Despite it being a 2am sailing in the middle of winter, and the ferry being largely deserted beyond a few truckers and a smattering of other passengers, she'd been just too late to reserve the last cabin when she'd enquired at guest services after realising her mistake. Given the size of the communal areas and the dearth of other travellers, it should have been easy to find a quiet spot to grab a couple of hours' sleep.

Theoretically. In reality, the upgraded guest lounge she'd paid for had indeed contained reasonably nice sofas, but it also contained a man who was snoring so loudly he was drowning out the sound of the ship's engines. Unfortunately, he was an elderly gent whose wife was sitting beside him in a wheelchair, and none of the other passengers were prepared to let their grumpiness extend beyond pointed looks that went entirely unnoticed. The bar area was also a definite no, as the two men who'd taken up residence there were knocking back a few pints and regaling each other at volume with boring stories of other times they'd consumed alcohol of various types and quantities. It was none of Butch's business, but if you found yourself drinking on a ferry in the middle of a rocky sea at 3am and all you could talk about were the occasions when you'd done similar, you probably needed to have a serious word with yourself, or possibly a medical professional.

From there, Butch had tried a lounge area – one with an incredible sock-stench that was so bad it was almost impressive; a restaurant – home to a crying baby; another lounge – full of arguing football fans; and now she was on one of the sofas opposite the reception and guest services desk. The sofa in question was nothing short of a design phenomenon devised by someone with a magnificently evil eye for detail. Somehow, it had been manufactured in such a way that there didn't appear to be anywhere or any way to rest your head on it comfortably, and even someone as physically small as she was could not lie down on it without the boat's rocking motion causing that person to fall off, in the unlikely event they ever did achieve something approaching sleep.

All in all, it was not a great start to her not-a-holiday holiday. While she'd been telling herself that she was looking forward to getting out on the open road, it was possibly more of an enticing idea than a reality. She'd only had the bike a little while, and while it was certainly handy for getting through rush-hour Dublin traffic, deep down she knew that wasn't the reason she'd bought it. Her ex had made some remarks about her being boring, and she was overcompensating in a way normally only embraced by middle-aged men who, for whatever reasons, couldn't manage a gym membership or an affair. In her defence, she enjoyed the bike, but it was unlikely that anyone's idea of hitting the open road extended to doing it through rain-soaked Wales before negotiating motorways all the way down to London.

And then there was the open-ended question of what the hell she was going to do once she actually reached London. DI O'Rourke was clearly worried about Bunny, and that made her worried. Well, even more worried. She was one of life's worriers, but she went out of her way to attempt not to show it. More concerning than O'Rourke or MI5 was the fact that Bunny wasn't answering his phone. It had been almost three days since they'd last spoken. Even a caveman like Bunny could have found a phone charger by this point, and while he wouldn't admit it, under normal circumstances he'd never have it switched off for that long. On more than a few occasions he'd been the first port of call when one of "his boys" – meaning any past or present member of the St Jude's Under-12s hurling team – had found themselves in a spot of bother, and he prided himself on always being there for them. In the case of many of them, he was the only dependable rock they'd known, and under all the bullshit and bluster, she knew he took that seriously. He might be a ham-fisted muck-savage from the wilds of Cork, with all the social graces of a baboon who'd got hold of some whiskey, but the man had a heart the size of a continent. And that was why she was here in the middle of the Irish Sea, in the middle of the night, closing her eyes and attempting to sleep on an item of supposed soft furnishing she was fully convinced had been designed by a brilliant sadist.

Still, she must have managed to nod off somehow, as she awoke with a start at the sound of a voice.

"Unbelievable!"

Heart racing, her eyes flew open. Her fists were clenched, ready to defend herself against all threats. The "threat" in question appeared to be a middle-aged man who, on a boat full of other options, had inexplicably decided to plonk himself down right beside her. He also seemed entirely oblivious to the fact that in doing so, he'd very nearly received a probably non-fatal punch in the trachea.

"Unbelievable!" he repeated.

"What?" Butch asked, trying to catch up with what the hell was going on.

He waved in the direction of the reception desk. "The service here," he said. "Unbelievable. I've had quite the week already, let me tell you."

"Why?" said Butch, belatedly realising that the man was taking this as a request for further information and not in the way she had meant it, which had been in the why-would-I-let-you-tell-me sense.

"I'm glad you asked. I tried to fly over to London a couple of days ago, only the fascists at the airline wouldn't let me take my bag on the plane. I foiled them, though – I took all my clothes out and wore them. Ha! Let me tell you, the other passengers loved that. As people kept saying to me – it's a point of principle. You've got to stand up for the little guy."

Butch rubbed her eyes, already deeply regretting not punching this guy while she'd had plausible deniability.

"Anyway, I get to Customs at Heathrow, and they ask to see my passport. Turns out I left it in my bag back in Dublin, but I told the fella I don't need it anyway, because we're in the Common Travel Area. He says that's true but I have to produce some form of photo ID, if requested, and I says to him, no I don't – it's a matter of principle. We then start having some back and forth, and other passengers are getting annoyed because this jobsworth is holding up the queue, then, when his boss comes over and asks me why I'm wearing all those layers of clothes. I made a joke – just a joke, mind – that it was to keep the bomb safe, and Lord, God Almighty, it all kicked off then."

"Yeah," said Butch. "Anyway—"

"Long story short ..."

"That boat's already sailed."

"They sent me back! Can you believe that? They sent me home.

I've got to be in London for a very important stamp-collecting conference, and they sent me home."

"Shocking. I'm trying to sleep, so maybe you could—"

"So now," he continued, oblivious, "I'm on the ferry over, because I won't get on an aeroplane on point of principle. Well, that and they've banned me. But I wouldn't, even if I could."

Butch picked up her jacket. "I'm going to move, but feel free to keep talking ..."

"And I'm trying to sleep. Paid for a cabin and everything but it's impossible."

"I know the feeling," said Butch.

"I go to the reception and talk to the so-called lady, and all I said was, the engines are very loud, is there any chance you could turn them down? And do you know what she said to me?"

"No, obviously," said Butch, who, despite herself, was somehow not moving.

"That's right. Gives me all this about if we turn the engines off, you'll wake up in the morning and we'll still be in the middle of the Irish Sea. She was sarcastic to me, can you believe that? I've a finely tuned ear for these things."

"I can tell," said Butch. He nodded, proving conclusively how utterly wrong his last statement had been.

"So then," he continued, "trying to be reasonable, because I'm nothing if not reasonable ..."

"Clearly."

"I says, alright, then – my cabin is rocking back and forth a lot, can I get another one?"

"What?" Butch was starting to wonder if this was all a vivid stress dream.

"And she says to me, no. Gives me all this guff about how the whole boat is rocking and we're on the sea, blah, blah, blah. Well, I wasn't having it, so ..." He puffed out his chest dramatically. "I demanded a refund for my cabin. Got it too. It's a matter of principle."

Butch stood up. "Excellent."

"Thank you."

"Not you," she said. "You're an idiot, and an incredibly annoying one at that."

The man gasped, outraged. "You can't say that to me!"

"And yet I just did. I'm off."

"But ... You're not going anywhere, young lady, until I've received an apology."

Butch took a step back and pointed at him squarely. "Let me make myself very clear. If you do anything, and I mean anything, to prevent me from walking away, you're going to be walking funny for a very long time."

"That's it," he said, a model of indignation. "I'm going to talk to the crew. You cannot behave like this."

"Knock yourself out," said Butch. "I'm off to talk to the nice lady at reception. Turns out a cabin just became available. Bye!"

Chapter Twenty-Four

Bunny and Fisk sat side by side on the tube for the short trip to Hammersmith, takeaway cups of coffee in their hands. As a rule, Bunny wasn't much of a coffee guy, but after a terrible night's sleep, he needed the caffeine boost. Despite being exhausted, he'd lain awake for hours, running things over and over in his head. Every which way he turned looking for clarity, everything just got muddier, or perhaps the better word for it was dirtier.

Stevie Brandon was equal parts terrifying and pitiable – the heavyweight champion of the world who seemed steeped in his own misery. Daniel Martin was even more of a piece of shit than Bunny had been expecting, and, given he'd known he was an absent-father inveterate gambler with a side of conman and thievery, that was really saying something. Alex Theakston, Brandon's manager, was equally despicable in his own way, and the memory of Lawrence Cooper heading across that bathroom at him, knife in hand, had played across Bunny's mind several times. It wasn't like it was the first time someone had pulled a knife on him, far from it, but what worried him was the precedent it set. Cooper, under Theakston's instruction, was more than happy to resolve a problem with serious violence, even in the palatial surroundings of the Dorchester. It didn't bode well for how they'd deal with Sean if they found him and, given what Theakston had said about Sean seeing or knowing something he shouldn't, he'd no doubt they were looking. Then there was Smith and his crew, whether they were MI5 or some other amalgamation of letters and numbers. They added a whole other layer of complication to affairs – one Bunny couldn't begin to figure out.

"I just don't get it," said Fisk out of nowhere.

"What?"

"You're sure he was drunk?"

"Breath stank of whiskey, slurring his words. Sherlock Holmes I'm not, but the one thing I can do is spot a drunk and, given the size of the man, I'd say he must've been a good few in."

"But the biggest fight of his career is tomorrow. I mean, boxers like to blow off steam, do they ever – but only after the fight. This close in, after all the preparation and training, they should be a taut ball of nervous energy. Razor sharp. I thought I'd heard everything in the fight game but I'm telling you, I've never heard anything like that."

"'Tis possible the guy has a problem. He certainly seemed" – Bunny recalled some of the last words Brandon had said to him, about still sleeping with the light on – "like he was dealing with some stuff."

"That I believe. To do what they have got to do, some fighters need to go to some dark places. Sure, it's a cliché, but clichés end up being clichés for a reason. It's just—"

Bunny slapped him on the knee. "C'mon, this is Hammersmith."

"Oh, wow," said Fisk. "You weren't kidding. That really was quick."

* * *

Five minutes later, they were standing in front of the Hammersmith Apollo.

"Well," observed Bunny, "if nothing else, I'm getting to see a few of London's famous music venues."

"Yeah," said Fisk. "On one of my previous visits to jolly old England I saw Frank Zappa do a gig here. Not really my bag but he was one funny cat." He paused to take in all the traffic rushing past. "So, did he say whereabouts this squat might be?"

"He just said near the Hammersmith Apollo."

"Looks like a whole lot of places are near the Hammersmith Apollo."

"I know," said Bunny. "I told you, you didn't have to come."

"Easy there, McGarry. I'm just saying. Besides, I got nothing to do before the weigh-in this evening than sit in the pub and get my regular updates from the Daves."

"Do you think they're really keeping an eye on the gym?"

"Babs threatened to bar them from the pub if they didn't, so yes, I do. I mean, I think they're doing it as long as the bookies is open. I got a very thorough report yesterday, full of irrelevant information if you'd like to see it?"

"No, thanks. Wish you'd offered me that when I was having trouble sleeping." Bunny turned around on the spot. "Alright, Fisk, you're the lucky one here – pick a direction."

"At random?"

"Unless you know something I don't."

In response, Fisk licked his finger, held it aloft, then, after about ten seconds, he pointed in a direction. "Thataway!"

* * *

It turned out Fisk was considerably luckier in backing greyhounds than he was in the rather more niche area of attempting to locate a squat. Three hours later, the pair had nothing but sore feet to show for their efforts, and even Fisk looked in danger of finally running out of conversation. They were probably looking for a needle in a haystack, but Bunny couldn't help thinking that, in hindsight, it could have been a considerably more organised search, and that was on him. The relevant page in his *A–Z* was annoyingly small for the purpose of recording where they'd been. They'd also taken a rather higgledy-piggledy route for the first couple of hours rather than being systematic. They'd discussed splitting up, but the problem with that approach was that neither of them was sure precisely what they were looking for, given that squats probably didn't advertise their existence.

When they turned a corner onto yet another street, Fisk stopped. "We've been down this way before."

"No, we haven't," replied Bunny.

"We have. I recognise the stone lions on the pillars of that house. I remember thinking they were a little grand for a pretty ordinary-looking house."

"They aren't that grand. People have those all the time."

"Why?"

"You'd really have to ask them about that."

"Is it an English thing?"

"No, we have them in Ireland too."

A couple of years ago Timmy Gleeson from the St Jude's team also went by the nickname "the Lion King", which had confused Bunny. At least it had until it was discovered he'd been collecting ornamental stone lions from far and wide. They eventually found thirty-seven of them in his granny's shed. He was on an apprentice-ship scheme at Dublin Zoo these days, and doing alright by all accounts.

"I'm telling you," insisted Fisk, "we've been down this way before."

"We haven't because—"

Bunny grabbed Fisk abruptly and dragged him back around the corner.

"What in the …"

The two men hunched down behind a hedge.

"I recognise the man walking up the far side of the street there, with the plastic shopping bag in his hand." Bunny peeked back around the corner. "'Tis definitely him. He's getting into the blue Volkswagen Golf."

"You're sure?"

"Oh, I'm sure," said Bunny. "I never forget a face. At least not one that tried to pull a gun on me and then chucked me out of a moving vehicle."

"I take it he's one of this Smith person's crew?"

"Yep. Gareth. At least that's what his boss called him. I'm guessing this means they're here looking for Sean, just like us. And they're keeping an eye on a certain squat, which means it's on this street. That looked like a man coming back from the shop with supplies for his stake-out. I'd bet any money there's a bottle of Snapple in that bag."

"Do I want to know … Oh, wait, never mind, I think I just figured it out."

Bunny poked his head around the corner again, and tried to get a good look at the Volkswagen Golf. It was parked up about a hundred yards down the street, facing away from them. Then he scanned the buildings on the far side of the road from it. "Bingo! About halfway between us and him. I'm guessing that's our squat."

Bunny doubted they would have spotted the house had it not been for the rather big clue provided by Gareth. On the one hand, a couple of its windows were boarded up, but on the other, the front garden was an explosion of colourful, well-tended plants. It looked as if the Chelsea Flower Show had been shoved into an area six feet square.

"Our next problem," he announced, "is that we need to figure out a way to get in there."

"We could go round the back?" offered Fisk.

"That we could," said Bunny, "but I'm guessing there's more than just Gareth here, and they'll be on the lookout for me. I don't want to risk getting spotted, and he's got at least one colleague who's considerably sharper than he is."

"So?"

"So," said Bunny, "I think it's time you went for a little walk."

* * *

Garrett sat in his car shovelling Maltesers into his face. He was being punished – he knew that. They'd been staking out this place for two days now and he'd done twice as much as anyone else had as penance for messing up when they were scooping up the Irishman. He'd worked for Smith only once before, but the guy could be brutal if anyone earned his displeasure. Touch wood this would be the last time their paths crossed and he could go back to working for someone who didn't take some weird pleasure in calling him Gareth. At least he wouldn't be sitting here getting pins and needles in his arse for much longer – Smith had issued the instruction to "shake the hornets' nest". Fingers crossed for some actual action happening imminently.

He checked the shopping bag for the bottle of Snapple. He could do with using it right now. He might be able to hold out, but if he drank all the Snapple first, he'd definitely need it. His gaze fell on the passenger-side footwell, at the bottle he'd already filled over halfway. Theoretically, he could just use that, but what if he had more to go than he expected? He could find himself having to stop midstream and that wasn't a simple matter. Sure, in his younger years he could turn it on and off like a tap, but these days ...

His executive decision-making process was interrupted by someone whacking the front of his car with a walking stick. He looked up to see some old duffer in a white linen suit and fedora standing right in front of him.

"Frank, you old bastard," the man roared in a cheerful American accent. "Trying to surprise your old buddy!"

Garrett stared at him, assuming the guy would realise his mistake when he got a proper look at him. Undeterred, the man continued, "I thought you weren't getting in 'til the weekend, you old sly dog, you.

Get out here and give me a hug this minute, you sneaky son of a bitch."

This was the last thing Garrett needed – some mad old bastard blowing his cover. He waved him away angrily.

"What?" responded the Yank. "You're not still annoyed about that thing with the alligator, are you?"

Garrett wound down his window. "Mate, I'm not who you think I am."

"Don't be like that, Frank. Like I said before, if you want to play dress-up on weekends, that's your business. No skin off my nose."

"I'm not ..." started Garrett. "My name isn't Frank, now piss off."

"Frank!" the Yank boomed again, full of indignation. "I can't believe you're being like this. Like I said at the time, taking a baby alligator away from its mother would be cruel, and doing so to impress a cocktail waitress when you're only just married a year, that ain't the Frank I know."

Garrett tossed his shopping bag aside, climbed out of the car and approached the man. He glanced around to make sure nobody was looking at them then spoke in an angry hiss. "Look, you mad old fucker, I'm not Frank, you know. Now bugger off and leave me alone."

Somewhere nearby a dog barked vigorously.

"Never!" hollered the Yank, pointing a finger in the air. "Your friendship means too much to me, Frank. For heaven's sake, you're godfather to my daughter and you named a parakeet after me. Some bonds cannot be broken by a small falling-out."

"Get lost or I'm calling the police."

The Yank stepped back, clutching his chest in outrage. "Frank, I told you about that honest mistake involving Mrs Ranganathan's nest egg in privacy. I cannot believe you would use it to threaten me like this." He went back to finger-pointing. "I've done nothing wrong. It's all a big misunderstanding. I shall defend my good name vigorously in a court of law. You see if I don't."

"Just—"

The Yank held up a hand. "One moment." He pulled out his mobile phone and looked at it. "Well, that's odd." He answered the call. "Frank?" Then he glared at Garrett. "You're not going to believe this, *amigo*, but there's some crazy British guy here trying to pass himself off as you."

"I'm not!" said Garrett.

The Yank wagged a finger in Garrett's face. "Shame on you, sir. Shame. On. You!" Without further ado, he turned on his heel and started to walk off happily down the footpath, gabbing on his phone. "Frank, you old sea dog. I got us a crate of Schnapps, two jars of pickles and tickets for *Phantom of the Opera*. It's gonna be just like old times!"

Garrett, shaking his head, got back into his car, entirely unaware that he'd just screwed up again, and that, once again, it involved a certain Irishman. Bunny McGarry, having successfully traversed a road and hopped over ten garden walls, was now standing in the side passage of a large old house he very much hoped was a squat. Given that on closer inspection the front door, while painted in a friendly yellow, was clearly barricaded up, he reckoned he was in the right place.

Once he'd texted Fisk that he was in, he shoved his phone back into his pocket. He'd almost done himself a mischief while making his way through one garden, when a tiny dog had leaped at the window, utterly outraged at his presence. He'd also trampled a bit of the beautifully maintained foliage in the front garden of the squat, which he felt bad about. Down the passageway he found a metal door. This was the place alright.

Chapter Twenty-Five

Bunny glanced over his shoulder to make sure he wasn't being observed, then banged on the metal door. A grunt sounded from inside before a slot in the door flew open. It afforded him a view of hair. A lot of hair. Some of it belonged to a beard and some of it was just hair, but it was impossible to tell entirely where one ended and the other began. Somewhere in there was a pair of eyes.

"Yes?" As the male voice drifted out, so too did a wave of smoke that Bunny was pretty sure would give him a fit of the giggles and a case of the munchies if he stayed there breathing it in for long enough.

"Howerya. I'm here looking for a friend of mine."

"I see," said the voice, in an artificially high-pitched trill that resulted in a bout of coughing. When its owner had recovered, the mountain of hair didn't return to the slot but it did continue in a noticeably lower pitch. "I see. To enter here say thee to me, the answers to these questions three."

"What?"

"I said," repeated the voice, "to enter here I ask you ... No, wait.

169

You ask me ... Nope, hang on ... Yes!" he declared, like a man who'd suddenly relocated the mental thread he'd been looking for, quite possibly for decades. "To enter here say thee to me, the answers to these questions three." He giggled before adding proudly, "Nailed it. Absolutely nailed it."

"Look," said Bunny, "no offence, but I'm kind of in a hurry here."

"Then answer the question."

"What question?"

There came a pause, followed by, "Good point."

"I just need to get inside."

"Then you need to answer the three conundrumeses, condrumals, whatchamacallits."

"The plural of conundrum," said Bunny, "is actually conundra."

"Correct," said the voice. "You're doing very well, mate. Should feel proud of yourself."

"Could I not—"

"Question two: What has four legs in the morning, three in the afternoon, and two in the evening?"

"Ehm ..." said Bunny. "Do you mean three in the evening and two in the afternoon?"

"I mean exactly what I said."

"Only, four in the morning, two in the afternoon and three in the evening is a man."

"How would that be a man?"

"It's a whatchamacallit – a metaphor for life. Look, I just need to—"

"That doesn't work. How's he got three legs in the evening?"

"A walking stick."

"But he could walk in the afternoon? What happened? Did he fall over?"

"No, it's—"

"And why was he on all fours in the morning? Was he pissed or something?"

"No, it's ..." faltered Bunny, trying hard not to lose his temper. "It's a riddle."

"Alright," said the voice. "Ask me another one?"

"You're supposed to be asking me."

"Correct," said the voice. "That's two. You are absolutely smashing this. Seriously, give yourself a pat on the back."

"Thanks," said Bunny, giving up on trying to swim against the tide of the conversation.

"Third question," said the voice. "The big one." He began a drumroll on the steel plating of the door. "Now – what has four legs in the morning, three in the afternoon and two after tea?"

Bunny sighed. "We've been through this. You've got it the wrong way round."

"No, I don't."

"You do. It's supposed to be a man."

The voice made an exaggerated buzzer noise. "Incorrect, my friend. The answer is an unlucky giraffe."

"What? How's that supposed to work?"

"This poor giraffe has lost not one but two legs, in separate incidents in a day. You telling me that's not unlucky?"

"But, I ..."

"Don't worry, fella," continued the voice, "all still to play for. Unfortunately, you're back to zero, but I have faith in you."

"Ara, for—"

Before Bunny could get into his stride with losing his temper, a female voice cut across the exchange. "Bloody hell, Jelly, what have I told you about getting stoned on door duty?"

"But I was bored," complained the voice.

"And, as previously discussed, that is not a reason."

"I feel very attacked right now."

"And I hear that you are feeling attacked." The female voice was lacking a great deal of enthusiasm, as if reeling off lines learned by rote. "I respect that feeling and hope we can come to a peaceful resolution built on mutual respect from a place of love."

171

"OK."

"Now, piss off, there's a good lad."

Bunny could make out the shuffling of feet behind the door before the face of a white woman with hair in twists appeared in the slot. "And who might you be?" she said.

"My name is Bunny."

"Course it is. Now, let me guess," she continued, staring at him with piercing brown eyes, "you're here looking for Sean."

"I am."

"Would you be surprised to know you're not the only one who's interested in him?"

"No," he said. "In fact, right now, there's a man watching this place from over the road."

She nodded. "Indeed there is. There's been a couple of them on rotation, and eyes on the back, too. I've been run— co-ordinating this co-operative for eight years, and through four different locations. I can smell the jackboot of the oppressor from a mile off."

"Right," said Bunny, not knowing what else to say but really not wanting to get involved in a discussion about fascists' foot odour.

"Come to that," said the woman. "You're a copper."

Bunny was genuinely taken aback. It wasn't even postulated as a question, rather as a statement of fact.

"I am, in Ireland, but I'm not here as one. I'm here because Sean's mother is really worried about him and I'm helping her."

"Judging by the fascist in the Golf who's been peeing in a jar for the last couple of days, she's right to be. You're not with them."

Again, it wasn't a question.

"No, I amn't," said Bunny anyway, feeling as if he should still be contributing to the conversation.

"I can tell that by looking at your aura."

"Oh," said Bunny. "Right."

"Well, that and the fact you hopped garden walls to get here, crushing my Cornus sanguinea in the process."

"I'm sorry about that."

"Just the latest indignity to be inflicted on Mother Earth by the tyranny of male oppression."

"Is Sean here?" asked Bunny, because this was starting to feel like a Karl Marx meets the Marx Brothers sketch.

"Whoa, whoa, whoa," said the woman. "My enemy's enemy don't make you a friend of the people. Before we can grant anyone access to the co-operative, we'll have to have a meeting where the majority will need to agree. Given your self-confessed status as a tool of the oppressor, we'll have to give this very careful consideration and allow for a harmonious convergence where your presence does not trigger anyone's previous life-experience-based anxieties."

"Right. Will that take long?"

"It's not a matter of time."

"The thing is," began Bunny, "it really is. Sean is in trouble and I'm one of the few people who can help him, but I really need to find him to be able to do that. So, with all due respect to you and your co-operative, I don't have the time for you all to form a drum circle and chant it out, because I think this lad is in serious danger."

"That's just typical of the—"

Before the woman could launch into the full-on tirade that was definitely coming, an urgent whisper from behind interrupted her, and her face disappeared from view. There followed what sounded like a very quiet argument, which seemed to conclude with the woman snapping, "Fine, but don't come running to me when you've been corrupted by the patriarchy," before storming off.

After a couple of seconds, a new face appeared in the slot. This time it belonged to a girl with a mohawk, the tips of which were blue. She also wore a bolt through her nose and had a couple of other piercings. Bunny's pulse quickened. She was the girl Daniel Martin's ex had described as being with Sean the night she met him. Had to be.

The girl spoke in a soft accent that Bunny thought might be from Newcastle or Sunderland – somewhere in the North East. "Who are you?" she asked.

"I'm a friend of Sean's mam," said Bunny, matching the quiet quality of her voice. "Well, a friend of a friend, to be completely honest. She's not well and she's really worried that Sean's in trouble, so I agreed to come over and look for him."

Her eyes, under the piercings and heavy eye shadow, looked scared. "How do I know any of that is true?"

Bunny pulled the bundle of letters and photographs out of his pocket. "Look, she gave me everything he sent home." He picked out the photo of Sean and his mother, and held it up to the door. "And look, here's a picture of the two of them together." He kept it there as he continued to speak. "I understand he's probably scared shitless. He's right to be. I don't know what, but I think he's got himself mixed up in some very dangerous business. Honestly" – Bunny pulled the picture away, so she had a clear view of his face – "I swear I'm here to help him, and I can, but I need to know what's going on. I promise whatever it is, we can sort it out."

"Easier said than done," murmured the girl softly, before chewing on her lip.

"Can I speak to him?"

"He's not here."

"OK, but – I don't have to come in. I could stay out here."

"I said he's not here." Her voice was stronger this time. "We've got the fuzz camped outside. Do you think he's going to sit in here waiting for them to come knocking?"

"OK, where—" They both jumped as Bunny's mobile rang. "Shit, sorry." He checked the screen. Milton Fisk. He rejected the call. "OK, look, I'm willing to do whatever I can to help. You just—"

The phone rang again. "Fucking hell! Sorry," he said, jabbing the button to answer. "Not now, Fisk. Kind of in the middle of something."

"I'm afraid you're about to be in the middle of a whole lot more, *kemosabe*. Two vans full of the boys in blue just pulled up at either end of the street."

"Shite!" said Bunny. "How long have I got?"

"It's happening now."

He hung up without another word. "You're about to get raided by the police," he told the girl.

"Shit," she echoed, her eyes wide with panic.

"I can get you and Sean out."

"He's not here." As she turned away from the door, she began shouting, "Raid, raid, raid!"

"Let me give you my number."

"No time," said the girl. "I can't be here." She pulled the slot closed.

Bunny stared at the sheet of steel, panic gripping him. A thought struck him. "The Duck and Trumpet pub in Shepherd's Bush," he shouted at the closed door. "I'll be there. Come and find me. The Duck and Trumpet—"

He turned as he heard Fisk's shouts on the road. "Thank God you're here, gentlemen – I've been complaining about all the bird shit for months. You seem to have come rather heavy—"

Bunny swore under his breath and ran a few steps down the house's side passage before grabbing the wall, heaving himself over the top and dropping down into the neighbour's garden. He lay there in someone else's flowerbed, inflicting yet more damage on Mother Nature with his oppressive arse. Thirty seconds later he heard a ram battering against the squat's steel door. He gave it a minute before getting to his feet and quietly limping away.

Chapter Twenty-Six

B
unny studied the pint of Guinness in front of him but didn't lift it. It felt like a reward he'd not earned. He'd come so close to finding Sean Malone, only to fail to make any real progress. It was like he was trying to chase a ghost. Outside, it was raining heavily again, the downpour matching his sombre mood.

Once he'd pulled himself out of the flowerbed he'd landed in and made his way around and over a few more garden walls, Bunny had rejoined Fisk up the road from the squat. From behind the cordon they'd watched as, one by one, the police officers in rather over the top riot gear dragged people out of the house. What was of most interest to Bunny was who *wasn't* there. No Sean Malone, and no sign of the girl with the mohawk either. Fisk had wandered within earwigging distance of a couple of police officers and reported back that a couple of the "crusties", as they'd been referred to, had climbed out of an attic window and managed to escape across neighbouring roofs. Bunny also saw Gareth watching and glaring at them from the far side of the police cordon. Fisk being Fisk waved back cheerfully. Gareth wore the expression of a man who'd just realised he'd been messed around and was plotting his revenge.

The only moment of levity came when an individual Bunny strongly suspected was Jelly – the hairy man who'd quizzed him through the squat's front door – was left unattended and managed to climb out of the back of a police van. He casually made his way down the road, hands still handcuffed behind his back, then exhibited a remarkable turn of speed and sprinted around the corner, his captors only belatedly realising what had happened. The gathering crowd of spectators had cheered him on, because everyone loves an underdog, even one in a Ramones T-shirt who looked like their last bath had been before the Berlin Wall came down. Jelly's escape would have been flawless, had he not somehow managed to come running around the same corner five minutes later, straight into the police van from which he'd originally escaped.

Once things had died down, Bunny and Fisk headed back to the Duck and Trumpet. The mood was glum. The reason they were sitting in the corner at the same table they always occupied was because they'd nowhere else to go. No leads to follow. Bunny blamed himself. If only they'd found the squat earlier, maybe he'd be talking to Sean Malone right now.

The two Daves were back at the bar.

"Shouldn't you two be off keeping an eye on the gym?"

"What's the point?" said Flat Cap, nodding at the TV. "They're all at this thing. Well, apart from Theakston's fit sister."

"She's a definite eight," said Woolly Hat. "I would."

"Assuming she has retained her sight, sense of smell and dignity," snapped Babs, "I'd guess whoever this woman is, she wouldn't. And if I ever hear any of that rating-women-out-of-ten crap from either of you two sad sacks again, you'll be drinking in a new pub. Possibly through a straw."

"What's eating you?" asked Woolly Hat, shocked.

Babs gave him a pointed look. "What am I out of ten?"

A wave of tension rippled through the entire pub as every man in the room that wasn't Woolly Hat Dave tried to psychically transmit the message to him that this question had no right answer and his best courses of action were either faking a heart attack or having a real one.

Fisk broke the silence that had fallen. "Wait a second – how do you know Theakston's sister isn't there?"

Grateful for the escape route, Woolly Hat pounced on it. "Because she was in the gym earlier on."

"Yeah," agreed Flat Cap. "Ran in and out."

"And when were you going to mention this?" asked Fisk.

"We're mentioning it now," said Flat Cap defensively.

Fisk shook his head. "Unbelievable."

Seeing a source of revenue that involved doing as close to nothing as possible in serious danger of disappearing, Flat Cap took a belated stab at customer service. "Dave reckons she was doing a runner."

"That's right," agreed Woolly Hat. "She ran in when I'm guessing she knew nobody was in there, and she was out a couple of minutes later, with a carrier bag I'm guessing had the contents of the safe in it."

"You can't know that," protested Bunny.

"I don't know," began Babs, "if anyone knows what a woman making a run for it looks like, it'd be him."

The pub collective winced as the verbal blow to Woolly's proverbial proverbials was delivered with an assassin's precision. Bunny guessed that Babs's tight smile was an indication that all accounts were now square, and Woolly should definitely not try to make any more withdrawals.

"Besides," said Flat Cap, mustard keen to move the conversation on, "she had suitcases in the back of the car."

Bunny turned to Fisk. "What the hell does that mean?"

He shrugged. "I'll be damned if I know, *compadre*. Maybe she's decided that whatever bullshit her brother has got them into is too hot to handle, and she'd rather be elsewhere if and when the shit hits the fan."

Bunny considered this. It was one of those annoying pieces of evidence that looked like a clue at first, but, on closer inspection, revealed itself to be a fact that was of absolutely no use.

Eventually, he turned his attention back to the TV. "Why do heavyweights even have a weigh-in?" he asked. "Like, there's literally no limit to how much they can weigh. There are WeightWatchers' weigh-ins where there's more at stake than there is at this thing."

Fisk shrugged. "It's boxing. Everything they do is part of the circus. Got to have the parade beforehand or else the crowds won't turn up to gawp at the spectacle."

Bunny gave his companion an assessing look. "I'm starting to think you're not much of a boxing fan."

Fisk picked up his whiskey. "I love it. Doesn't mean I have to like it."

On the screen, Ricky Drake was making his way towards the stage through the assembled members of the press. He did so surrounded by his entourage, one of whom was holding up a boom box while Drake danced backwards and forwards to the music, going nowhere very fast. His outfit was an ostentatious gold, complete with an ornate crown that even Liberace might have said was a little much.

"Don't they generally only do the big production on their way into the ring?"

"Yes," said Fisk bitterly. "Mister Drake is trying to break new ground. The guy's ascent to the top of the game has been orchestrated through a series of has-beens and never-weres, and he acts like he's the twenty-first-century Muhammad Ali. I got no problem with showmanship but, even by boxing standards, this guy is all sizzle and no steak. By all rights Stevie Brandon should destroy him."

The camera cut to a shot of Brandon already standing on the stage. "He certainly looks like he wants to," observed Bunny.

The big man was standing motionless, his dark eyes smouldering with a contempt he was making no effort to hide as his opponent danced around a hundred feet away. Bunny was having a hard time remembering that this was the same man he'd spoken to in the hospital room the night before. Behind Brandon, Sparky Theakston wore a glassy grin as he watched matters unfold.

"You notice who isn't there?" asked Fisk. "Gabriel Fuentes. Yesterday, one of the so-called journalists finally asked where he is, then reported the party line that he'd gone home a couple of days early to deal with a family matter." Fisk's contempt was clear for anyone to hear. "Like Gabby Fuentes is leaving a fighter on the eve of a bout. It's all such bullshit, and nobody – not the press, not the police – is questioning it."

"Maybe you should have gone there and tried to?"

Fisk laughed bitterly. "You think there's any chance they'd let me in that building? Even if I got in, there's no chance to ask a real question at these things. They're more stage managed than a Super Bowl half-time show. The assembled press you see are all Pavlov's dogs, unthinkingly answering the bell for dinner."

As they watched the TV footage cutting between the two fighters, Bunny spotted the figure of Lawrence Cooper in the background, behind Theakston and Brandon. The low murmur of the barely audible commentary on the TV was taken up with people in the studio busking to fill time – Drake's little stunt was clearly throwing off the timings for everything. There was plenty of hot air given over to the contrast in the two fighters' styles – the showman and the slugger.

"Hey, Dave," said Bunny.

The two men at the bar looked up from their ever-present copies of the *Racing Post*.

"Which one?" asked the one in the woolly hat.

"Either. Both. I was just wondering, what're the odds on this thing?" He nodded at the TV.

The one in the flat cap answered. "Three to one on the Yank. All the smart money says Brandon might kill him – actually kill him. Vinny at the bookies said a bloke came in last week trying to bet on that exact thing happening."

"Charming," said Bunny.

"Those odds have moved a lot," said Fisk. "It was five to one at the start of the week."

"The dancing fella was on a chat show a couple of nights ago," said the other Dave. "Must have impressed the grannies and they're all putting their pensions on him."

Behind the bar, Babs rolled her eyes. "Oh, here we go – anything that doesn't agree with you experts is because daft old ladies are placing bets. Always the way."

The first Dave looked affronted. "We were merely giving our opinion as professional gamblers."

"Professional gamblers," echoed Babs mockingly. "Not having a job doesn't transform what you spend all day doing into one."

"We have dedicated ourselves to forensic research in the sporting arenas," said the woolly hat.

"Yeah, and speaking as the woman in charge of your ever-growing bar tabs, I'm beginning to think that you two getting a job digging ditches might be a more worthwhile use of your time. How much of the money Fisk paid you have you got left?"

Both Daves fell into sheepish mumbling.

Bunny returned his attention to the TV, where both boxers were finally on the stage together. Drake danced towards Brandon, bobbing and weaving, air-boxing and grinning like a Cheshire cat. Finally, the two men came nose to nose. To be more accurate, it was forehead to chin as Brandon was nearly a full head taller. While his physique was considerably less chiselled, verging on fat, he was also far heavier than Drake and, to Bunny's untrained eye, had an advantage in reach, too. Drake was still smiling and talking, smiling and talking, whereas Brandon's lips remained motionless as he glared down at his opponent with absolute and utter burning hatred. Even on TV, it sent a chill down the spine. At least it did to everyone except the apparently impervious Drake. The smaller man leaned in to Brandon and whispered something. Before anyone could react, Brandon snapped, shoving Drake in the chest and sending the smaller man tumbling backwards off the stage.

"Bloody hell!" exclaimed one of the Daves.

Absolute chaos erupted as Brandon surged forward, right fist cocked back and looking like a man intent on finishing a job, only to be enveloped by a wall of people diving in to restrain him. The camera jerked around to focus on where Drake lay on the floor. As Brandon attempted to shake off those holding him back, Drake shielded his head with his hands in a textbook example of a cower.

"He looks like he's about to shit himself," observed Bunny.

"He does," said Fisk thoughtfully. "I wonder if it's just dawned on him that he's not in a dance contest."

The broadcast returned to the studio coverage as the two fighters were escorted out of different doors and the rest of the people in the room milled around. The talking heads wore sombre faces.

"Here we go," said Fisk. "They'll all give their 'there is no place for such violence in the noble sport of boxing' soundbites, while none of them acknowledge the obvious. That footage will get shown all around the world and shift more tickets and pay-per-views than anything else could manage."

"Do you reckon it was faked?" asked Bunny.

"Nah, I think Stevie Brandon really hates that cocky son of a bitch. He's going to win that fight at a canter."

"No, he isn't."

They both turned towards the voice, to see the girl with the mohawk and the facial jewellery standing in the doorway, soaking wet and panting heavily as if she'd just run there.

"He isn't," she repeated. "That's what Sean found out."

Chapter Twenty-Seven

Bunny and Fisk sat in silence as the girl dried herself off with the towel Babs had given her. They were sitting on the sofa in Babs's lounge, a room Bunny had never been in before. There was a photo on the wall showing what he was ninety percent sure was a much younger version of their landlady throwing a javelin, but now was not the time to ask questions.

The girl with the mohawk looked nervous. She was trying to hide it but as she sat awkwardly on the over-stuffed armchair, there was a shaking in her fingers that was only partly due to getting caught in the torrential downpour. Bunny realised that under the blue hair, the make-up and the piercings, she was probably not much older than Sean. Maybe eighteen, and absolutely terrified. This whole thing would have to be handled carefully.

Babs came in, carrying a tray bearing a cup of tea, a doorstop-sized sandwich and a plate of chocolate biscuits.

"Oh, no, I'm fine, thanks," said the girl.

"I'm sure you are, sweetheart," said Babs kindly, "but if you're under my roof you don't get to look that skinny, so get these down you. I've also got a warm jumper, which you'll absolutely hate, that you're going to be wearing while your denim jacket dries out."

Babs set down the tray then pulled a green jumper from a chest of drawers. "Count yourself lucky. Hideous though this thing is, I've got a pink one with bunny rabbits on it upstairs that my bitch of a sister-in-law knitted for me. Until I saw it, I thought we got on."

Smiling nervously, the girl eased the jumper over her head.

"Excellent," said Babs. "Now, do you want to eat first and then talk, or vice versa? Don't worry," she said with a pointed look in the direction of the sofa, "these two can wait."

"No," said the girl. "I ... there's not much time."

Bunny and Fisk exchanged a look.

"Right enough," said Babs. "Talk first, but before that, you listen to me, my girl. This here is my pub and nobody, and I mean nobody, comes through them doors without my say so. This is my way of saying, you're safe as long as you're here, and you're here as long as you like. Alright?"

The girl nodded and gave an embarrassed but grateful smile.

"Now, I'm Barbara but everyone calls me Babs. What should I be calling you?"

"Tina. And thank you very much."

"Don't mention it, love. For what it's worth, these two might not look like much and I ain't known them that long, but they're decent men and, as far as men go, pretty trustworthy. I mean, don't go lending 'em money, but otherwise, you're alright."

Tina smiled again and Babs gave Bunny a look as she took a seat in the other armchair. She'd done a far better job of relaxing and reassuring their guest than either he or Fisk would've managed.

"OK, Tina," began Bunny. "This fella is Fisk and I'm Bunny. It was you I was chatting to earlier, through the door, wasn't it?"

She nodded. "Aye."

He'd known that, but it was always good practice to kick off interviewing a witness with some simple questions to ease them in. "Did you manage to get out over the roofs?"

184

She nodded again.

"Did Sean?"

"Like I told you," said Tina, "he wasn't there. He's been sleeping rough to keep safe because they've been looking for him."

Bunny nodded. "Who, exactly?"

Her face darkened. "Them lot from the gym. That Cooper fella. Sean says he's got a loada people out searching for him. Says they've offered a reward. Five grand."

Bunny resisted the urge to meet Fisk's eye – that was a serious wad of money to offer to locate someone. They clearly wanted to "talk" to Sean in the worst way.

"Right. I understand you want to protect him and—" He stopped himself. "Before we go any further, how about I finish explaining what I started to earlier on." He took out the letters and photographs, and told Tina everything.

When he'd finished, Tina sat there for a long moment, chewing on her fingernails. "Oh, God, he's going to be so upset. He's mad about her. Always saying how he's going to go home and see her and all that." She blushed. "Saying how he was going to introduce me to her."

Bunny nodded. "Are you and him an item, then?"

"Yeah," she said, looking suddenly bashful. "I s'pose you could say that."

"Fair play, Sean. Done well for himself." Bunny cleared his throat. "So you see, I was only here looking for him to give him the bad news and take him home to see her. I didn't know anything about the trouble he's in, but I can help. If you wouldn't mind, would you tell us what exactly has happened?"

Tina studied the tea tray and kept quiet for long enough that Bunny was about to start backing off, when she cleared her throat. "Sean was working there, at the gym. Y'know, helping out. Stevie Brandon, he got him the job. Sean says he's nice, despite everything everyone says about him. Said he was just sorta shy, really."

"Right," said Bunny.

"His dad – Sean's, I mean..." Tina looked up at him again. "You know Sean came over here looking for him?"

"I do."

"I was with him – first time he finally met him. Got his number from someone in a pub he'd been told he drank in." Her face clouded over again. "I didn't like him – Danny. Soon as I met him. Sean had come all this way to find him and the bloke wasn't keen. You could tell. Least, anyone who wasn't Sean could. I guess he'd built him up in his mind so much that he couldn't see what he really was. Sleazy fucker." Tina's eyes darted across to Babs. "Sorry."

"Nothing to apologise for, sweetheart," Babs replied, flicking the ash off her cigarette into a nearby ashtray. "Sounds a lot like my piece-of-shit ex."

Tina nodded. "Like I said, he wasn't bothered. Sean went to see him again. He even took him to the pub a couple of times. He wanted a lot more from the whole thing than Danny clearly did. Told Sean not to call him dad and all that. I said to Sean, I didn't trust him, and he got mad at me. He kept going to see him, but he didn't take me along after that." She stared down at the carpet. "Like I said, Danny wasn't interested in Sean until suddenly he was. It was about the time he found out Sean was working at the gym."

Bunny nodded. "Right. Yeah. For what it's worth, we met Mr Martin. Didn't strike me as Father of the Year material."

"You can say that again," said Fisk. "He and Bunny didn't exactly hit it off."

"Don't blame you," said Tina. "He told Sean to keep his ears open – that's how he put it. He wanted to know what was going on at the gym. Told him to do a bit of digging."

Bunny could feel Fisk tensing beside him. The American was about to say something, but Bunny shook his head subtly. Better to let her get there in her own time.

"Sean was working there late one night," Tina continued. "Cleaning out the locker-room area. He was in there at all hours. I don't think he was that busy so much as he just loved being there.

Watching the training and all. Anyway, he heard Sparky, Stevie's manager. He was arguing with, ehm ... I don't know the guy's name. Manny?"

"Gabby," said Fisk in a hoarse whisper. "Gabriel Fuentes. Stevie's trainer?"

"Yeah, him," confirmed Tina. "They were shouting at each other. Like, vicious. Sean said the Gabby fella was screaming about how he wanted no part of this, that he wouldn't do it. Sparky was saying how Stevie had to throw the fight. Said there were these Mexican guys – like, some gangsters – Sparky's dad died owing them a load of money and this was the way it had to be. He was banging on about them doing this or they'd all end up dead. Sparky was furious that Stevie had told this Gabby fella about it, said it was none of his business. Gabby explained that it was and that he was going to tell everybody."

Bunny glanced at Fisk again, who was staring at his hands folded in his lap. His face unreadable.

Bunny cleared his throat. "Then what happened?"

"Then," continued Tina, "that Cooper bloke sees Sean listening in, so Sean legs it. He always said Cooper scared the shit out of him. Cooper chased after him and nearly caught him too, but Sean is fast."

"And since then?" prompted Bunny.

"Sean's been hiding out. Cooper and them lot are looking for him, and then there's all that shit today. I mean, police raiding the co-op? Said it was for drugs, but that's rubbish. Mabel doesn't let anyone in if they're using anything serious. Sean was..."

"He was on drugs?"

"Yeah. He used to be, but he got clean. I helped him. I used to be ..." She thought better of finishing the sentence. Instead, she ran her fingers through her mohawk, now floppy from the rain. "Staying clean was part of Sean's deal with Stevie to get the job. He said he wouldn't have Sean using and working there. Sean loved that job." There were tears in her eyes now. "Then, all this happened."

"Thanks for telling us, Tina."

She leaned back into the armchair and hugged herself. "It's all got so fucked up. I mean, the fuzz watching the co-op and then smashing the door down – what's that about?"

"'Tis a good question," said Bunny. "Could I talk to Sean, do you think, Tina? I reckon I can get him home and away from all this. You too, if you'd like to come?"

"That's the thing," said Tina. "After I got out of the co-op, I went and met him. I told him about you. I told him he should talk to you, but he said he'd been in contact with his dad and it was all getting sorted out."

Bunny leaned forward. "What?"

"I know. I said not to trust him, but Sean wouldn't listen. Said his dad had sorted a meeting. All he has to do is tell Cooper that he isn't going to say nothing to nobody and he'll be free and clear."

"Oh, shite," said Bunny. "Did he say when and where this meeting would take place?"

She shook her head.

"Where is he now?"

"Said he was going to see his dad. Said everything was OK and not to worry. And before you ask, I don't know where the dad is. Sean only ever met him in pubs before." Tina put her hands to her face. "This is all so fucked up and I just know Sean shouldn't be trusting that prick. It's so ..."

She broke down in tears. Without saying a word, Babs moved across and sat down beside the young girl, looping an arm around her shoulder.

Bunny turned his attention to Fisk. He was taken aback to see tears in the man's eyes too.

Before Bunny could say anything, Fisk spoke in a hushed whisper that only he could hear. "Gabby is dead."

Bunny leaned towards him. "We don't know that."

"The hell we don't. You've got to understand who you're dealing with. The man would rather die than have anything to do with a crooked fight. He wouldn't just go home or anywhere else. He always said all a man has is his reputation, and he would never put one of his

188

fighters in the ring if they were going to take a dive. Never. Boxing is his life and that, *that* is the unforgivable sin."

Bunny wanted to argue but Fisk spoke with a terrible certainty, and he couldn't think of a counterargument worth the breath it would take to offer.

Gabby was dead, and the chances that Cooper or his boss were going to take Sean's word for it that he'd keep his mouth shut were somewhere between slim and nothing. Especially if he had been the last person to see Gabriel Fuentes alive.

"What are we going to do?" asked Fisk.

"Find Sean."

"How?"

Bunny ran his fingers through his hair and scratched at his scalp.

"Babs?" he said. The landlady looked up at him, Tina's head still buried in her chest as the girl sobbed. "If I was of a mind to borrow money from a Russian called Ivan, where would I go?"

Chapter Twenty-Eight

Bunny and Fisk stood side by side on the pavement in what the taxi driver had assured them was the dodgy end of Peckham. They looked up at the sign above the door.

"This is the place," said Bunny.

"Looks like it," confirmed Fisk.

"Looks like it, alright."

Fisk paused. "You don't have to do this."

"Can you think of a better way to find Sean? Or, indeed, any other way to find Sean?"

Fisk said nothing.

"Then I do."

Babs had taken some convincing, and had repeatedly made the point that this was a terrible idea. Bunny didn't disagree – it was just that it was the only idea he had. In truth, "idea" was giving this far too much credit. It was, at best, a notion. And, quite possibly, a suicidal one at that.

Daniel Martin owed some Russian called Ivan money, which they knew because when they'd chased him down at the dog track, he'd initially thought they were collecting for him. In Bunny's experience, if you wanted to find somebody, the people most likely to know where that person lived were the people they owed money to. That wasn't to say those people would be willing to share that information, but that was another problem.

Sean was with Daniel Martin and, seeing as his father was unlikely to have Sean's best interests at heart, Bunny needed to find them before Sean could be convinced to do something really bloody stupid. The irony was the only way to prevent that from happening was to do something really bloody stupid himself – like walking into a gangster's den with nothing to bargain with.

With great reluctance, Babs had made a few calls, which was how they'd ended up standing in front of a buzzing neon sign as the dull light of a wintry afternoon faded into night.

"You don't have to come in with me," said Bunny.

"How dare you say that to me."

Bunny turned to face Fisk, taken aback by the vehemence in the man's tone. "I was just—"

"You think I'm going to let you walk in there alone? Is that it? And how am I supposed to feel if you don't come back out?" Fisk shook his head. "I've already lost one friend today." He surprised Bunny by blessing himself. "I sure ain't losing another. Also, I'm the only one who can squeeze some justice for Gabby out of that Theakston piece of shit, so don't you dare tell me to step aside."

"Alright. Sorry." Bunny paused. "And for what it's worth, 'tis an honour to be considered your friend."

"Likewise," said Fisk. "But do me a favour and refrain from hugging me, because the two goons on the door have clocked us and I don't think it helps us establish the steely-eyed vibe we're going for."

"Right, so," said Bunny, eyeing the two standard-issue, neckless slabs of muscle staring at them from their positions at the door. "Here we go. What have we got to lose?"

"Our lives, our limbs, our dignity."

"To be honest with ye, Fisky, that was one of them rhetorical questions."

"Sorry. You know me. I'm a talker."

One of the goons had started walking towards them. "Speaking of which, best if you let me do the talking from here on out."

* * *

The air inside Abdul's Shisha Café and Retro Gaming Emporium had a sickly sweet smell to it. Bunny couldn't tell if it was from the funny smoking stuff or a poor choice of disinfectant. Given the state of the stairs he and Fisk were marched up, he was inclined to think it was the former – it'd been a while since this place had seen a deep clean. The stairs led to a surprisingly spacious room that, in other circumstances, might have filled Bunny with a childish delight. Old-school video games lined the walls, beeping and trilling away, enticing the inner child to come and play. Most of the ceiling lights were off, which just added to the allure of the machines.

None of them were in use except one at the far end of the room – a dancing game with pads you had to place your feet on. The last time Bunny had seen one was when he'd taken the St Jude's team bowling. Incongruously, a portly man in a green tracksuit was dancing around on it, panting heavily while trying to mimic the actions of an anime character on the screen in front of him. A half-dozen men in similar but, crucially, not-as-nice tracksuits were splitting their time between watching the dancing and watching the newcomers as they approached across the floor.

Flanked by the two bouncers from outside, Bunny and Fisk came to a halt and watched as the man sweated and swore his way through the game. The animated figure finally made a crying face and said something Bunny didn't understand but which nevertheless made clear that the game was over. One of the other tracksuited men handed the dancer a towel and he passed a few remarks in Russian, at which they nodded and smiled. This guy was clearly the boss.

His black hair formed a widow's peak above his brow, over a five o'clock shadow and sharp eyes that belied his casual smile. One of the other men offered him a tall glass of what looked like lemonade, which he drank a couple of sips from before returning it to the silver tray on which it had been presented. Only then did he turn his attention to his visitors and give them a long look.

Bunny felt much like how a mouse must on its first, and possibly only, time meeting an owl. He cleared his throat. "Lovely place you have here."

"Oh," said the man, "it is not mine. It is Abdul's. Hence the name."

"Right."

"I would pass on your compliments but sadly he disappeared several years ago. However, we" – he turned to a man in a blue tracksuit – "live in hope?"

Blue Tracksuit nodded. His boss turned back to Bunny and Fisk. "We live in hope for his safe return."

A few smirks appeared from his entourage, who were all leaning against machines or sitting in deckchairs, appearing largely disinterested in proceedings. Those in the deckchairs were all seated in the same way, their legs spread as wide as humanly possible. They resembled a display to illustrate the concept of manspreading. Either that, or the waiting room at a specialist STD clinic.

"So you would be Ivan, then?" asked Bunny.

"Most perceptive. This, I think, is not our usual type of visitor, boys. Something smells off. I wonder what that can be? I am sure Lev and Andrei will have patted you down before they let you in here." He threw a glance at the two men standing behind Bunny.

"They did," Bunny confirmed.

"And yet ..." Ivan wafted his hand in front of his nose like a wine connoisseur drinking in a bouquet. "And yet something, I feel, is off."

Bunny cleared his throat. "Well, while the lads searched me – thoroughly – they didn't check my ID."

"I see. And what would they have found if they had?"

Bunny drew a deep breath and tried to run through the phrasing of his next sentence in his mind before he uttered it. The wrong way round and there was a chance he might not reach the end of it. "I am from Ireland and, over there, what I do for a living is, I am a police officer."

"And there it is."

The man's entourage shifted their body positions, now considerably more interested in proceedings. A lot of them appeared to be glaring at the men behind Bunny and Fisk. One of them hissed something in Russian but Ivan held up his hand for silence.

"Thank you for your honesty. What is your name, please?"

"'Tis ... It's Bernard McGarry, but people call me Bunny."

This garnered a raised eyebrow. "Indeed. And please, tell me, what has brought the Irish police to my door?"

"Oh, I'm not here in an official capacity. In London, I'm just another Joe Bloggs."

Ivan pursed his lips, then tasted the words as if they were exotic fruit. "Joe. Bloggs."

"I just meant—"

He held up his hand again for silence then looked at Blue Tracksuit once more. There followed a brief conversation between the pair, which ended with Ivan saying something that resulted in all his men chuckling. After a beat he refocused his attention on Bunny and Fisk. "Joe Bloggs," he repeated. "I like that. So—"

A clock chimed somewhere in the background. This really did attract the attention of the assembled tracksuits, who started talking excitedly among themselves. Ivan barked one word and the chatter ceased.

"Forgive my men their rudeness. You have joined us at an auspicious time."

He looked at the same guy he'd consulted before, who nodded and repeated, "Auspicious."

"Yes," continued Ivan, "an auspicious time. We have a rule in my ... group of friends, that we handle a dispute between friends in a certain way."

As he spoke, two of the men took out a table and chairs and

placed them in the centre of the room. On some silent cue, two further men emerged from the darkness at the back of the arcade. They were both wearing vests that revealed arms so covered in tattoos there was more ink than skin. As they stopped on either side of the table, their eyes locked. The one in a blue vest was gym big, emphasised by the fact he could do the thing where his pecs jiggled up and down. Normally, Bunny would howl with laughter at that, but this wasn't the time. Having said that, his opponent did snort a laugh. This guy was also massive but in a different way, resembling a bear who'd carb-loaded for the winter and been given a light shave. Across the Irish Sea, the Thai lady who worked in Kanin was probably feeling an inexplicable urge to start heating a gigantic tub of wax. The man also sported a full-on handlebar moustache that Bunny found rather impressive.

At the bark of a one-word instruction from Ivan, each man pulled out their respective chair and sat down. Next, they placed their right elbow down on the table and tucked their left hand behind their back. Bunny was pretty sure there was about to be an arm-wrestling contest. Blue Tracksuit approached the table, said something then pulled the two men's hands together, confirming Bunny's suspicions. After a little bit of jockeying around, the two right hands were locked as one. Jiggly boobies guy was smiling across the table, giving his opponent the "full-on psycho" he undoubtedly practised in the mirror on a regular basis. Handlebar responded to this by belching loudly.

Blue Tracksuit nodded at his boss, who barked another word in Russian, and they were off. For about twenty seconds, while the assembled tracksuit mafia cheered them on, the two men were in a stalemate. Then, Jiggles started ranting and raving at his opponent, who remained silent. Jiggles literally got the upper hand and actually whooped in delight, only to see his opponent calmly bring him back to parity before slowly lowering his arm, yawning and then slamming Jiggles's arm into the table so hard that he lost his balance and fell onto the floor. Among the assembled tracksuits, money changed hands, accompanied by grins and grimaces. Clutching his arm and without a jiggle in sight, the loser eased himself off the floor while his vanquisher scratched his nuts, pulled out a bar of Dairy Milk chocolate and started eating it.

"And there we have it," said Ivan. "Another dispute successfully resolved in a non-violent manner."

Bunny glanced at the big fella still rubbing his non-violently resolved arm but said nothing.

"And now," said Ivan, "before we were interrupted, you were about to tell me why an Irish policeman is coming to me looking for money?"

"Actually," said Bunny, "I only said that so your lads would let me come in. I'm alright for money, thanks."

"Good, as I would not have given you any. Whoever told you I do such things was mistaken."

"Right. Apologies for the confusion. I'm looking for an acquaintance of yours."

Ivan glanced at Blue Tracksuit, who quietly uttered one word.

Ivan nodded. "Ah, I see. And you think this is a service I provide?"

"I should explain," said Bunny. "I'm in London looking for a young lad, only seventeen years old, called Sean. His mother asked me to find him. He's fallen out of contact and sadly she is sick, really sick. It's stage four cancer and she desperately wants to see her son again."

"And what has this to do with me?"

"Sean's father is a man called Daniel Martin, who I believe may, after a friendly loan, owe you some money."

Ivan squinted. "I am failing to see your point."

"Sean is with him, and I reckon if anyone would know where Daniel Martin was, it'd be you."

"I see. And let us say I do, what would be the benefit to me of sharing that information? Money?"

Bunny felt Fisk shift slightly beside him, but he answered firmly. "No."

If they made this a negotiation, they'd get bled dry and still not get the information they needed.

"Aha. Have you got information you would like to share with me, perhaps?"

"No," said Bunny again.

Ivan nodded. "So, are you saying that you would" – he looked at Blue Tracksuit again – "owe me a favour?" Blue Tracksuit nodded.

Bunny shook his head. "No. With all due respect, you know who I am and I know who you are, and I'm not going to be in debt in any way to you."

Ivan folded his arms. "Then tell me, why would I help you by giving you this information?"

"Because this woman has stage four cancer and her dying wish is to see her son one last time. We all live in a harsh world, but we all have mothers, and I figured I would appeal to your better angels."

Ivan went to glance at Blue Tracksuit again, but Bunny beat him to it. "Sorry, I mean that I would appeal to your humanity, your compassion. That you would help this poor woman because you can and it does not harm you to do so."

For the first time, Ivan showed some emotion – a flash of annoyance passed across his face. "So, to be clear, this Irish cop comes in here, offers me nothing and demands to know how to find this man. Have I got that right?"

"I wouldn't put it that way, but yes, I'm asking for your help. Man to man."

Ivan turned away, shaking his head, and hissed something in Russian, before picking up his glass of lemonade and taking a sip. "Get the fuck out and do not waste my time."

Fisk went to speak but Bunny put out a hand to stop him.

"Alright," said Bunny. "How's about we resolve this?"

Ivan narrowed his eyes. "Excuse me?"

"I'll arm wrestle for it. I win, and you help me fulfil this dying woman's wish. You win, and I'll do whatever you want."

"I do not arm wrestle."

"One of your men, then." Bunny nodded towards the table. "I'll take on your man over there."

Ivan nodded and looked at Jiggles. "I think he may have a sore arm."

"Oh, not him," said Bunny. "I meant the lad with the moustache. The winner."

A genuine gale of laughter passed through the assembled group. "You want to go against Aleksandr?"

"Sure."

More laughter.

"He has not lost in ten years. You do not want to go against Aleksandr. I think you should leave."

"Fair enough," said Bunny. "If you're too scared."

* * *

Two minutes later, Bunny was sitting opposite Aleksandr. The handlebar moustache looked even more impressive close up. Each man put his left hand behind his back and the pair joined their rights together. Aleksandr's grip felt like it could turn coal into diamonds. As they readied themselves, Aleksandr jerked his hand and smashed Bunny in the face.

"Hey!" shouted Fisk.

"'Tis OK," said Bunny. "Aleksandr here was just saying hello." He spat some blood onto the floor. "Just a bit of banter."

The two men locked eyes and tightened their grips even further. Ivan himself stood over them. "You sure you don't want to run away, Irishman?"

"No. I'm going to attempt to carry out this woman's dying wish if it kills me."

"OK, but it just might. Ready ... steady ... go!"

Chapter Twenty-Nine

Bunny slid into the back of the taxi beside Fisk and told the driver the address he'd just been given.

"That's just around the corner, mate," said the driver, none too happy.

"Don't worry, fella. We're just dropping in there quickly and then we're off somewhere else."

The cab pulled off and Fisk spoke for the first time since they'd exited Abdul's Shisha Café and Retro Gaming Emporium. "Alright, McGarry, how in the hell did you do that?"

"Do what?"

"Do what? You just managed to beat the undefeated Russian bear in an arm-wrestling contest. That was incredible!"

Bunny waved away the compliment. "Ah, rode my luck."

"Rode your luck? Rode your luck? Are you, like, secretly an Olympic arm-wrestling champion or something?"

"Nah. To be honest, I don't think I've even had an arm-wrestling contest since I was a kid. I mean, seriously, who arm wrestles in this day and age?"

Fisk gesticulated with such ferocity that he nearly fell out of his seat as the cab took a corner. "Who arm wrestles? They do. Those Russian gangsters. The ones whose champion of champions you just beat. I have to know – how did you pull that off?"

The taxi came to a sudden halt. "This is it," said the driver.

"Blimey," said Bunny, "it really was around the corner." He looked out the window at the row of terraced houses before them. They were right in front of number 16, the address they'd been reliably informed was Daniel Martin's place of residence. "OK," Bunny continued, opening the cab door. "Just wait here, we're nipping in there for a couple of minutes and then we'll be back."

"I'm keeping the meter running."

"I'd insist on it."

And with that, Fisk and Bunny alighted, Fisk following in Bunny's wake as he strode purposefully across the road towards number 16.

"OK," said Fisk. "Do you want to discuss how we're going to handle this?"

He received his answer when, without breaking stride, Bunny kicked in the front door of number 16.

"Never mind," said Fisk. "I'm up to speed."

* * *

Bunny located Daniel Martin just as he was attempting to exit via a small window in the bathroom. Judging by the fact his trousers were around his ankles, Martin had been interrupted at a particularly inopportune moment.

Bunny dragged him back inside and threw him roughly against the wall. Hard enough that Martin yelped.

"Where's Sean?"

"He's not here!"

"No kidding. Where is he?"

"I don't know."

Bunny spun Daniel Martin around and kicked his knees out from under him, forcing him into a kneeling position. Then he shoved his head into the toilet bowl and flushed.

"Jesus," said Fisk from behind him, but Bunny paid him no heed. He pulled up Martin's now sopping-wet head and held him by a fistful of soaking hair.

"Let me save you some time," said Bunny. "You've sold your son out and sent him to a meeting with people who want to do him harm, because you're a worthless piece of shit. So, before I keep going until I can flush you away, I suggest you start talking."

"It's not what you think," squealed Martin.

Bunny made to push his head back into the bowl again.

"Wait. Wait. It isn't. He's OK. They're watching him."

Bunny glanced at Fisk then dragged Martin back up onto his feet and slammed him into the wall again. "Who?"

"Them," said Martin, his eyes wide like a terrified animal's. "They're the government or police or whatever. They came to me. Asked me to get Sean to help them. Said they needed somebody inside the camp. To help them."

"Smith?" asked Bunny.

"What?"

"Did the guy say his name was Smith?"

"I ... I never asked for a name."

"Bowler hat?"

"Yes," said Martin. "Yes! That's him."

"And what motivated you to do this?"

"They said it was important."

Bunny tightened his grip on Martin's T-shirt. "Not what I asked."

"Alright," said Martin. "I ... I was in a little trouble, and he said he'd make it all go away if Sean helped them."

"And there it is." Bunny moved in until his face was a few inches from Martin's. "Father of the fecking Year. Using the son he was ignoring to get himself out of the shit."

"McGarry," said Fisk quietly behind him, but Bunny ignored him again.

201

"It's not—" started Martin.

"Bollocks it isn't. Where's this meeting Sean's gone to?"

"I ... I don't know."

Bunny pulled Martin towards him then slammed him into the wall once more. "Lie to me again. I dare you."

"I ... I ... They've got him under surveillance. He's perfectly safe."

"See," began Bunny, "that is based on the assumption that Sean's safety is the number-one concern of whoever the fuck those people are. I can guarantee you it isn't. Now, don't make me ask again – where is this meeting?"

"I don't—"

Bunny placed his face even closer to Martin's. "I'll be honest with you here, Danny boy. Normally, in this situation I'd be working hard to pretend. To make you think I was going to do something incredibly fecking violent that I wouldn't actually do. You see, normally, I rely on the threat alone, as I pride myself on not actually being a man of violence." He lowered his voice and moved to the side so he could whisper in Martin's ear.

"Here's the thing, though. With you, I'll be honest, I'm hoping you don't believe me, because this time I'll do it. I swear to God, I will. And I'll enjoy it. Maybe, at some point in the future, I'll lie awake at night and think back on this moment, and it'll turn my stomach, but right now – right now, the chance of kicking the ever-living shite out of the man who put the son he treated like crap into harm's way to save his own skin, that feels like a dream come true. So, I'm asking you – begging you, in fact. Let the next words out of your mouth not be where this meeting is taking place, because that is all the excuse I need."

"Abney Park," said Martin. "They're meeting at the abandoned cemetery at Abney Park. It's over in Stoke Newington."

"Ah, a fecking cemetery," said Bunny. "And who is he meeting?"

Bunny could see Martin internally debating whether to lie and then deciding against it. "That Cooper fella. The big Black guy with the dreads."

"Time?"

"Eight."

Bunny turned his wrist to check his watch. It was already after seven. "If I find out you're lying to me, so help me God."

"I'm not," said Martin with a whimper.

Bunny released his grip and Martin crumpled to the floor. "Let's go," he said as he pushed past Fisk.

"What did I ever do to you?" roared Martin.

Bunny spun around but Fisk put out his hands. "McGarry! Time."

Bunny stopped himself, turned on his heel and stalked out the front door. "Where the fuck has that taxi gone?" he barked.

"I think he hightailed it once you kicked the door in." Fisk pointed the way they'd come. "We should head back to the main road. See if we can get another one."

Bunny started walking in that direction, so quickly that Fisk needed to jog to keep up.

"Do we want to discuss what happened back there?" asked Fisk.

"Not even a little."

"That's what I thought."

Chapter Thirty

Bunny sat in the back seat of the taxi, jiggling his leg anxiously. It had taken too damn long to find another cab. It was now nearly 8pm and they were stuck in traffic. Only London could have a traffic jam at this time of night, and they'd somehow managed to find it. "Is there any way around this?"

"There is," said the taxi driver cheerfully, "but it involves not going to where you're heading." He laughed at his own joke. "Don't worry, always a bit sticky round here but we'll soon be past it."

Beside Bunny, Fisk was unusually quiet.

The taxi driver took the silence as an invitation to keep talking. "I don't know if you know much about Abney Park, but it's a fascinating place. Graveyard for dissenters and non-conformists. Mostly them that didn't toe the party line of the church back in the day. The bloke who founded the Salvation Army is buried there." The cab moved forward about twenty feet and stopped again. "Might not look like the area for it, but it's a spectacular nature reserve. They reckon there's over two and a half thousand varieties of shrubs, and a thousand types of roses. Imagine that."

"You don't say," said Fisk on automatic.

"Oh, I do. I take an interest, you see. It started back when I done the Knowledge, y'know. Us cabbies have to learn London like the back of our hands, and I just sorta kept going. In fact, if you gents happen to be keen taphophiles – as in cemetery enthusiasts – I've started doing walking tours on a Sunday morning—"

The taxi moved forward again and stopped.

"How much further?" interrupted Bunny.

"Well, when we finally get through these lights, it'll be just a left up there. I meant to say, though – you know it won't be open this time of—"

The taxi driver stopped talking as, when the cab came to a halt again, he heard the clonk of the doors' locks disengaging and Bunny was out his side, shouting to his friend who remained inside the car, "Pay the man, Fisk."

* * *

Narrowly avoiding taking out a cyclist, he hopped over a couple of bin bags left out on the kerb and started sprinting down the pavement, weaving his way around pedestrians. As he ran, the steady drizzle increased in intensity until, a few minutes later, by the time he reached what a sign on the railings told him was the edge of Abney Park Cemetery, it had been upgraded to full-on shower. Given its centralish North London location, Bunny had pictured the cemetery as being quite small, but in reality, it stretched out of sight into the distance. Unsurprisingly, there wasn't any lighting inside the grounds, but the lights of the city around it bled in from all sides.

Daniel Martin had mentioned a church. In the distance, on his left, Bunny noticed the outline of a spire. He made his way along the railings until he found the gap he knew would be there. It was an immutable law that wherever there was a set of railings, there would be a gap wide enough for a teenager to fit through, even if they had to make it themselves. This one was a tight squeeze, and his overcoat snagged on the bars as he battled his way through.

Bunny scanned the grounds ahead of him as the rain pelted down on his face. The graves appeared to be mostly overgrown. In fact, the whole place had a returning-to-nature vibe to it. He walked through the wet grass until he found a path, and then, above the treeline, he was able to spot the top of the church spire at the cemetery's centre. He set off at a steady jog, unable to risk anything faster, as the darkness grew thicker around him the further he ventured in. When he stumbled over something, he slowed to a steady walk.

It was eerily quiet. The woods around him cushioned the sounds of the city until it felt like he could be almost anywhere. A plaintive ambulance siren in the distance became the only testament to the existence of modern life.

Bunny jumped as something moved to his right. When the form shifted again, he realised that what he'd thought was a pile of rubbish was in fact a man, buried under a tarpaulin and other unidentifiable layers, bedding down for the night in front of a bench. Bunny watched as the man's shining eyes observed him move past, wary of this intruder onto his patch.

The path turned, the clouds above parted and the moon threw its silver light down on the church. It was an impressive building, and not at all the ramshackle affair Bunny had been expecting. There was no sign of anyone around, but then it was well past eight o'clock now. As he approached the entrance, Bunny thought he caught sight of a lithe figure moving quickly through the trees on the far side.

"Sean?"

No response.

He quickened his pace, the sense of dread that had been sitting in the pit of his stomach growing heavier with each step.

Scanning the treeline, he tried to make out where that person had gone. So it was that when he rounded the corner of the church, he almost tripped over Sean Malone. The boy was half lying on the ground, propped awkwardly against a cold stone wall. His hooded eyes attempted to focus as Bunny fell to his knees beside him.

"Sean, Jesus."

The lad moved his lips, but no noise came out. His left hand was clamped to his stomach. He managed a breathy groan as Bunny shifted it to take a look. His T-shirt was stuck to his skin with blood. So much blood.

"Christ. Hang on, Sean. Hang on."

Bunny pulled his mobile from his pocket and dialled 999. As he listened to the ring tone, Sean tugged at the collar of Bunny's coat.

"Ambulance," Bunny shouted into the phone. "I need an ambulance."

He looked into Sean's face, the boy's eyes pleading as he stared back up at him, appearing even younger than his seventeen years. His lips were moving again.

Bunny leaned in. After a moment he realised the word Sean was trying to say. Mum.

He pushed his right hand towards Bunny. His fist was clasped around a couple of sheets of paper, already covered in blood, and written in the same hand as the ones in Bunny's pocket.

"I'll give it to her, Sean. You'll give it to her yourself. You'll ..."

Bunny saw the moment that the light went out of the boy's eyes and his form slumped back. He felt for a pulse he knew was no longer there.

He knelt there as, somewhere in another world, a voice tried to speak to him from the phone he held in his hands. He looked down and wept for the boy he'd just met. The one he'd been sent to save. The one he'd failed.

He wasn't sure if it was two minutes or two hours later that the torch found him and hands were on him, pulling him away and pinning him to the ground, slapping cuffs around his wrists. All the while, he kept his eyes fixed on the unmoving figure of Sean Malone.

Chapter Thirty-One

Bunny allowed the custody sergeant to plonk him down in the chair. "Thanks very much, waiter. I won't order food yet as I'm expecting company, but a bottle of the house white would be lovely." Without a word, the sergeant set a paper cup in front of him.

"Well, if you recommend it, I'll certainly give it a try."

The sergeant muttered something under his breath. In Bunny's experience, custody sergeants were some of the most miserable people you could meet. He was unsure if the job made them that way, or if something attracted them to it. Probably the latter. It was certainly a job that, if you already weren't a fan of mankind, would confirm all your worst suspicions.

Bunny picked up the paper cup. "Ah, excellent – tepid. Just how I like it." He took a sip and grimaced. "Feck's sake, is this even tea?"

The sergeant shrugged as he left the room. "No one knows."

Bunny sat there for a couple of minutes, alone, supping on the tea as some form of self-harm, and considered the interview room he found himself in. As far as these things went, it was rather spacious. Something about it put Bunny in mind of a hospital. With a shock he realised what that thing was. The place was clean. Unnaturally clean. There were no stains on the walls, and the tabletop hadn't even had something witty and misspelt carved into it yet. He'd a mind to do it himself but sadly they'd not left him with any sharp objects.

In fact, as well as taking away all of his clothing, they'd taken his shoes and given him a pair of these rather snazzy slip-on things. A tracksuit that didn't quite fit him completed the outfit. For reasons modern science could not fully explain, Bunny had never found a tracksuit that fitted him. It was the reason he didn't wear one while training the St Jude's Under-12s.

He stood up and, using the large and in no way suspicious mirror on one of the walls, he adjusted the tracksuit bottoms, inadvertently mooning the definitely-just-a-mirror in the process. After he was done, he sat back down and mimed juggling for a bit. Along with the mirror, there was a camera in the top right-hand corner of the room, and its little red light presumably meant that it was working.

Eventually, Bunny looked up at the ceiling and sighed theatrically. "Jesus, you're not half dragging this out, lads. Can we move things along?" He checked the clock on the wall and started to laugh. "I just realised – I'm on a flight to Mauritius soon."

Something in his own laughter rang a little warning bell in Bunny's mind. He was pissing about because in any situation it paid dividends to confuse your opponent and have them underestimate you, but on this occasion there was more to it. Somewhere inside him, voices were screaming, and he was doing everything he could to block them out. His mind kept flashing back to the image of an innocent lad – not much more than a boy, really – bleeding out in his arms. Bunny had trapped his boiling rage behind a dam, like he'd trained himself to do, but the cracks were already showing. It was a case of when, not if. The flood was coming. What scared him was that when his anger came crashing through, he wasn't sure if he'd be able to restrain himself.

He leaned forward and studied the two empty chairs opposite him.

"I bet they're outside right now, discussing tactics," he said to no one in particular. He then formed his left hand into a sock puppet minus the sock and spoke in a deep, growly voice. "Let's leave the paddy in there for a few more minutes. Make the toilet sweat."

He did the same thing with his right hand, his voice a high-pitched female this time. "Are you sure he'll crack, Inspector? After all, he's a police officer himself."

"Don't you worry, Penelope, it's very different when you find yourself on the other side of the desk. He'll crack. I guarantee it."

"You're so wise, sir."

"You learn a lot in this job, but it costs. Boy, does it cost. I don't know my own kids. The wife has left me. I've developed a drinking problem and a crippling addiction to Cadbury Creme Eggs because I just care too damn much."

"Oh, Tony," said the right hand, "don't be so hard on yourself."

The two hands started moving towards each other.

"I'm your commanding officer, Penelope. We can't do nothing inappropriate."

"I know. You are the haggard but brilliant detective with a drink-and-Creme-Egg problem, and I'm the young, uptight, fresh-out-of-training detective with a stick up her arse. And yet there's such undeniable sexual chemistry between us. Take me now, Tony. Make me feel like a real woman!"

The two hand puppets were mid passionate snog when the door to the interview room opened.

"Fecking hell, you two," said Bunny in his own voice. "Cut it out, we've got company."

A woman in her forties, who looked only marginally happier to be there than the custody sergeant had, was followed into the room by a male detective in his mid-twenties, with a punchable face and a tea stain on his tie.

The two hands broke apart and the left one looked up at Bunny. "Turns out I'm a woman and you're a sexist pig."

"Having fun entertaining yourself, Mr McGarry?" asked the woman as she sat down.

"Well, it was either that or grow old and grey sitting here waiting for you two to show up."

"Apologies," she said, lacking all sincerity. "It's been a busy night."

"Well, if you will go around arresting people for no reason."

"No reason?" echoed the younger man as he also took a seat.

"Oh, Jesus, you let him speak?"

"Occasionally," said his boss, setting down on the table the folder she was carrying. "By the way, I'm DI Chambers and this is Detective Nettleton."

"Charmed, I'm sure," said Bunny. "So, will you be charging me or can I leave?"

Chambers opened the folder and started leafing through the paperwork inside. "Let's have a little chat first, shall we?"

"Sure, why not waste everyone's time?"

"Waste everyone's time?" repeated Nettleton. "You were found holding the victim, covered in his blood."

"Fuck me, Columbo is on the case. The reason your boss knows this is bullshit is poor Sean Malone was stabbed well before I got there, and you can establish that easily because there's a ton of witnesses who'll have seen me running towards the cemetery. Also, if it was me, where's the murder weapon that you haven't found?" Nettleton went to say something, but Bunny spoke over him. "Yeah, you're going to search the area when the sun comes up. Let me save you some time – the killer took it with him, although I'm guessing a certain someone took it off him soon after. And if even all of that wasn't true, which it is, your boss already knows that you will not be charging me with this crime."

Chambers finally looked up from her paperwork. "And why is that?"

"D'ye know what," said Bunny. "Normally, I'd be inclined to play along with this pantomime, out of professional courtesy, but it's been a long night and I happen to think a large part of a copper's job is not allowing themselves to be used as pawns in someone else's little game." Chambers' face showed just how much that one hit home. "So why don't you stop pissing about, get out and send in whoever's standing behind that mirror?"

"Paranoid, much?" said Nettleton. "There's nobody behind there, Mr McGarry."

"That's Detective McGarry to you, sunshine, and pull the other one, it's got my sweaty bollocks attached to it."

"Easy," warned Chambers.

"Or what?" asked Bunny. "You're going to charge me with being aggressively innocent?"

"I'm sure we could find something."

"Well," said Bunny, "wouldn't be the first time your lot has done that, now, would it?"

This particular jibe earned him a long cold stare. "Calm down."

"No, I don't think I will. I've still got the blood of an innocent young man under my fingernails, so why don't you two piss off?" Bunny pointed at the camera in the corner of the room. "Turn off the camera then send them in." He addressed the mirror directly. "And word to the wise, I'd leave the fecking bowler hat outside. I'm really not in the mood."

"You've got—" started Nettleton but was silenced with a look from Chambers.

The DI glanced at the mirror then got to her feet. "If you'll excuse us, Detective McGarry."

She made her way towards the door with the now positively surly Nettleton trailing in her wake. Once the door was closed, Bunny's left hand turned itself into a puppet again. "I thought that went really well."

"Ah,' said Bunny, "we'll see. That was only act one of the panto. Buttons and Cinderella have buggered off but let's see what happens when the wicked witch turns up."

On cue, Bunny noticed the red light beneath the camera go out.

"Oh, quiet down, children, the interval is over."

The door to the interview room opened once more and, as Bunny had fully expected, Gareth and his female colleague trooped in, followed by Smith.

"I stand corrected," said Bunny to his left hand. "It's the three ugly sisters."

Lefty turned in the direction of the trio then back to Bunny. "I can't believe it – the fucknugget is still wearing that fucking bowler hat."

"Jesus, Lefty!" said Bunny in mock outrage. "Mind the language." He looked up at Smith. "I cannot apologise enough. I really think it suits you."

Gareth took up his position behind Bunny while Mr Smith and the woman took their seats in the freshly vacated chairs opposite him.

"I'm beginning to think there is something seriously wrong with you, Mr McGarry," said Smith.

Bunny folded his arms. "That's Detective to you, and blow it out your arse."

"Mind your manners," warned the woman.

"Or what? You'll have me arrested again?"

"We didn't—" started Smith.

"Ara, shut up, would you? I had some of the pieces, but I think I've figured it all out now. Spent my time in your rather lovely holding cell productively."

"Did you?" asked Smith, running a finger along the edge of the table before studying it disapprovingly.

"I did," confirmed Bunny. "Maybe if I'd put it all together faster, poor Sean Malone might not be dead now. I'd blame myself but there are a few more people worthy of that blame sitting not a million miles away. And I'd like to deal with them first."

Smith said nothing, just tilted his head and met Bunny's gaze from across the table.

"Let me know if I've got anything wrong," Bunny continued, "but here's how I see it. Theakston Senior, renowned drug kingpin, made a deal with some dangerous people – drug dealers being the nefarious characters that they are and all. Something went wrong because of – well, don't know, don't care. He's either dead or hiding, but most likely dead, and the naughty people in question have decided that daddy's debt now belongs to his kids. They made a deal. They'll come in and take over the family business and make everything right, but first – as an act of contrition – Stevie Brandon, the jewel in the crown of Junior's boxing empire, must lose a world title fight to their boxer, Ricky whatever the feck his name is. The lad who does all the dancing. I don't know if they're making enormous amounts of cash out of that, but it's a hell of a way to force someone to show their contrition. I've had to hypothesise some parts of it, but I bet I'm pretty close, amn't I?"

Smith's face remained a study in blankness.

"Which brings us to your role in this tawdry affair. I'm guessing you saw an opportunity. You're not trying to nab Theakston, because that'd be police work and you're not police. My guess is you've seen an opportunity to sink your claws into this other organisation – the one Theakston's trying to cosy up to. Maybe your end game is some record bust, or perhaps these naughty people don't just move drugs. There's a lot of other reprehensible activities organisations can get involved in if they know how to get things in and out of countries undetected.

"Those other activities are of a lot more interest to you cloak-and-dagger types. You needed a spy and the best one you could find was a young kid. You weren't sure how to control him, though, so you figured out his dad was the best way in. And he did it, Daniel fecking Martin, piece of shit that he is. He got his son to do your bidding as a way to save his own arse, and the poor lad was so desperate for daddy's approval that he agreed, never realising that, ultimately, it was you he was working for."

The taste in Bunny's mouth was decidedly bitter now and he couldn't even fake the levity any longer. "It all goes tits up, though, when young Sean hears Theakston Junior and Gabriel Fuentes,

Stevie's trainer, having a full-on barney. Gabby is old school, and he doesn't care what Theakston's reasons are, he wants nothing to do with his boxer throwing a fight. Sean runs and Gabby disappears because Theakston – or I'm betting his right-hand man, Lawrence Cooper – knows how to get rid of a body. You'd have your in right there, but I'm guessing you genuinely don't know where Gabriel Fuentes's body is. So you need to get something to hold over Theakston or someone else in his crew."

Bunny leaned forward. "Here's where you had your big idea. Find the kid and use him. Again. They're worried about what he knows – about Fuentes and the fix – and they need to shut him up. You persuade Daddy dearest to get involved again and convince the lad to wear a wire when he goes to meet Cooper: 'You'll be safe, we'll be watching, blah, blah, blah.'" Bunny turned his focus to the woman sitting beside Smith, and who he noticed was avoiding making eye contact. "Perhaps you didn't realise Cooper would just kill him. Should have asked me. I could have told you how fast he goes for his knife. Was it the butterfly knife he used? I'll bet it was."

Bunny broke off for a second and drew a deep breath before sitting back in his chair. "I'll give you the unearned credit of not expecting Cooper to be the full-on psycho he is, but I'll bet you were quick to take advantage of it. It does rather suit you, seeing as I imagine you've now got, oh, I don't know, video footage of him killing Sean Malone? That'd be enough to put him away for life, so you snatched him up either right away or soon after, and had a little chat. He's your man on the inside now, willing to do whatever the hell you want in order to avoid spending the best years of his life as a guest of Her Majesty."

He tapped the table in front of the woman. "Just before I found Sean, I thought I saw a figure running away through the trees. It was bothering me. Cooper's a big man and it wasn't him. I think I just got it. Someone had to go and pull the wire off the dying boy's body, didn't they?"

The woman averted her gaze again.

Bunny nodded. "That's what I thought. Bet they didn't mention you'd be doing fun stuff like that when they convinced you to join the service. Not all exploding pens and underwater cars, is it?"

"Are you done?" asked Smith wearily.

"Oh, I'm just getting started, you pompous arsehole." Bunny's voice was rising now, the vitriol burning in his chest. "This all worked out great for you, didn't it? The risk of anyone finding out about the fix is gone, you've got your all-important mole inside Theakston's organisation, and a better one than you could have hoped for. Everyone's a winner. Well, except Sean Malone, who's never going to see eighteen because you shower of pricks used him like he was nothing."

From behind, Bunny felt Gareth's heavy hands on his shoulders, holding him down.

"Get your fecking hands off me now or I'll rip them off and feed them to you."

"If you're quite finished, Mr McGarry," said Smith.

"Detective!"

"Detective," repeated Smith with a nod, before signalling for Gareth to move away. "While this version of events you've come up with is a fascinating story, that's all it is. You have no proof. Nothing."

"I've got my word and I'm an officer in An Garda Síochána."

Smith actually smiled. "Yes, and if you throw in five pounds that might just get you a pint in one of our less salubrious establishments." He cracked his knuckles. "There are things going on here of which you have no understanding. People such as me, who are charged with keeping our country safe, have to make difficult decisions in order to make that happen. The death of this poor chap—"

"Sean Malone," snarled Bunny. "At least have the decency to use his name."

"Sean Malone," continued Smith, "is of course a tragedy. Sadly, this city, like most other cities on the planet, has a terrible problem with young people becoming addicted to drugs. The crime and violence that go along with that is one of the great scourges of modern life. Poor Sean is just the latest in a long line of victims."

"Yeah," said Bunny, "you're right. That'll be an easy sell, and I'm sure if I kick up a fuss, you can destroy me too. Won't be as easy as destroying Sean, but I've no doubt you'll manage it. Let's be honest, there's nothing I can do here, and we both know it."

Smith nodded.

"Here's the thing, though. People like you, and the people who work for you" – Bunny looked pointedly at the woman – "you justify the Sean Malones of this world to yourselves with phrases like 'collateral damage', don't you? An unfortunate, caught in the crossfire between you, the goodies, and whoever you're using as the baddies right now. I've no idea what the end game here is – maybe it's just one of those photo ops beside a massive pile of drugs where a minister can give a speech and get some votes for being 'tough on crime'. Or maybe, like I said, there's a whole other plan in play.

"I don't care, because you know what? Sean Malone isn't collateral damage. Not to his mother, his poor dying mother, who sent me here to find him because she was so desperate to see him one last time. He loved her so much that with his final breath he was trying to give me, a man he'd never met, the last letter he wrote to her. He might be collateral damage to you, but he was her whole world. You, Theakston, his piece-of-shit father and whoever else is involved in this, you used him because he was convenient and easy, and hey, who's going to miss another junkie runaway? There's a dozen of them getting off the bus every day. Ultimately, I couldn't save him and I couldn't help his mother, and that's going to haunt me until the day I die. Still, as clever as you no doubt are, Mr Smith, there's one vitally important thing I think you've forgotten."

Bunny leaned forward again. Instinctively, Smith did the same, mirroring Bunny's body language. Just enough.

In a flash, Bunny's right hand shot across the table, grabbed Smith's silk tie and heaved it downwards, sending the man's face smashing into the table. The howl of pain, accompanying the crunching of a nose being shattered, was deeply satisfying.

A half-second later, Gareth hauled Bunny to his feet and, with the help of the woman, pinned Bunny up against the wall. Between them, Bunny could see Smith, his hands held up to his broken nose as blood poured down his face.

"Sorry about that," Bunny roared. "Collateral damage."

Gareth threw a heavy body blow into Bunny's ribs, which sent him crumpling to the floor, but as the pain shot through him, he didn't care.

"Get this arsehole on the first plane out of here," screamed Smith, his voice sounding oddly nasal and entirely unhinged.

From his position on the floor as he struggled to draw breath, Bunny saw the interview-room door open then slam closed again. He spotted something on the floor and laughed.

"What the hell?" asked the woman.

Bunny pointed. "He forgot his fecking stupid hat."

Chapter Thirty-Two

DI Fintan O'Rourke pulled onto the large gravel driveway of the well-appointed house in Seaport. The two lads from the Garda protection unit nodded at him from the front seat of the patrol car permanently stationed outside. It was three thirty in the morning but he was expected. His anticipated arrival was further confirmed when he reached the front door, on which he found a pinned note that read simply, 'Fintan. Hot tub.'

O'Rourke had visited Commissioner Ferguson's hot tub on a previous occasion, although not in a social context. Not that this occasion was a social visit either. The last time he'd been here he'd expected to be fired; this time he didn't know what to expect. No, that was only partially true. When he'd received the commissioner's call about forty minutes ago, he'd hung up immediately after being instructed to drop around for a little chat, but O'Rourke knew full well that nobody rang you in the middle of the night with good news.

As he walked around the side of the house and across the lawn, security lights overhead flared into life, making the assemblage of gnomes in numerous locations around the large garden look like contestants in a children's game of statues. The lights were rather bright, which apparently divided opinion.

"For Christ's sake," yelled a voice from over the fence, "turn those bloody lights off."

In response, the very distinctive voice of Commissioner Ferguson boomed from the gazebo O'Rourke was making his way towards. "I'll turn my lights down, Quirke, when your nitwit of a son gets rid of that idiotic exhaust off the back of his car. Waking the whole neighbourhood at all hours."

"It's like Dublin bloody Airport over there. You're visible from space."

"Good. Then right now, astronauts will be able to see the gesture I'm making to show you exactly how much of a shit I give about your opinion."

"I'd phone the guards," shouted back the neighbour, "but we all know they never do anything except sit on their fat arses."

"That's because the council deals with disturbances. The Gardaí deal with things like boy racers who mow down swathes of deaf kids because they couldn't hear the oncoming danger over the sound of the bloody stupid exhaust."

"That doesn't make any sense," responded the neighbour. He had a point, but O'Rourke would not have admitted that under torture.

"It makes perfect sense," countered Ferguson. "You just didn't hear it right because you're half deaf on account of your idiot son's exhaust."

Well recovered.

"I'll tell you what ..."

"No, Quirke, you won't. I'm in a meeting."

"Oh. Right. Sorry."

O'Rourke was rather taken aback by the abrupt change in tone.

"He's actually a decent enough sort," offered Ferguson conversationally as O'Rourke approached. "Wife left him a couple of years ago – ran off with our gardener. I think he resents the fact that we still use him."

O'Rourke was now standing awkwardly beside the hot tub in which Ferguson was seated, a cigar in one hand and a large whiskey in the other.

The commissioner glanced across at his phone, positioned safely out of the way, that was pinging repeatedly as a succession of messages were delivered. "Oh, crap," he muttered. "That dipshit has only gone and woken up the wife. This will end up being my fault somehow, you see if it doesn't." Ferguson threw back the rest of his drink and tossed the glass aside. "I can't figure out why on earth those idiot exhausts are even legal, and you'd think of all people I would know. Good morning, by the way, Fintan."

"Sir."

The commissioner's phone pinged again and he looked at it guiltily. "She's going to be in quite the mood. Out of curiosity, how does your missus take to being woken up in the middle of the night?"

"Funny you should ask, sir. She asked me to pass on her warmest regards."

He was surprised to see Ferguson wince. "Ah, yes. Sorry about that. If it's any consolation, you at least got some sleep. I got a call three hours ago and since then it's been virtually non-stop. My good lady wife sent me down here as the swearing was becoming unbearably tedious, and that's an exact quote."

"I see. Given that you've called me, am I correct in assuming ..."

"Yes, indeed," finished the commissioner. "This involves your friend and mine, one detective Bernard McGarry and his trip to good old London Town."

"I take it there's been a development?"

"You could say that. He's been arrested for murder."

"Fuck!"

"Indeed." Ferguson flicked some ash off his cigar and into the water. "Do you know, Fintan, I think that's the first time I've heard you swear. About time. Don't trust a man who doesn't swear. It makes me worry that he doesn't truly understand what is happening."

"Murder?"

"Yes," confirmed the commissioner. "Murder. One involving stabbing, as it happens."

"Sir, there is no way—"

"I appreciate you and he are friends, Fintan."

"Forget friendship. Ask anyone – Bunny is not going to stab someone to death. Kill them with his bare hands, certainly. Shoot them if the need arises, absolutely. Even hit them with a car, sure. But not stabbing. You'll never make me believe stabbing."

"A point well made," said the commissioner. "Although I'm not sure you're the first person his defence team should call if that's your idea of a character reference."

"Who was the victim?"

The commissioner's face darkened. "Do you know, when I received the laughably titled 'courtesy phone call' to inform me one of my people had been arrested, I asked that question, and that utter flaming slurry pit of an assistant commissioner in the Met couldn't answer. Had to ring me back. Turns out the poor victim is a seventeen-year-old lad from Dublin called Sean Malone."

O'Rourke went to speak but Ferguson raised a hand. "Before you say it, I don't for one second believe McGarry would have done that. Quite the contrary. What's more, as became evident over a series of calls, they don't believe that either."

"But ..."

"But why have they arrested a man for a crime he didn't commit?" said Ferguson. "Yes, I rather forcibly made that point too. It seems McGarry has made himself a great inconvenience to people unspecified. I think we can both agree, in contrast, that certainly *does* sound like McGarry."

O'Rourke didn't say it but he had been thinking the exact same thing.

"Nevertheless," continued the commissioner, "I spent a great deal of time shouting at people who didn't want to listen how generally, as law enforcement officials, we were supposed to detain the guilty while making every effort not to inconvenience the entirely innocent.

They didn't want to take my point and, believe me, I made it with quite some gusto."

"Did they give any details as to what exactly McGarry has done to get in their bad books?"

"No, and I certainly asked. They very much wanted me to tip the cap, apologise for something they wouldn't tell me about, and swear on the Holy Bible that it'll never happen again. Let us say, there was a significant disagreement on this point. They even wanted my assurance that when they stuck McGarry on a flight back home, someone at this end would ensure he did not turn around and head straight back there."

"And?"

"And I told them that I wasn't about to start locking up innocent people just because they seemed so inclined to do so. I also asked under what legal jurisdiction were they forcibly repatriating an innocent man." Ferguson scowled. "It was at that point I was informed I was being 'difficult'."

Ferguson paused and took a contemplative puff on his cigar before rolling it between his thumb and forefinger. "Can you guess what happened next, Fintan?"

From his facial expression, O'Rourke could tell this wasn't one of the commissioner's rhetorical questions. Rather it was one of the little tests he liked to randomly throw in the DI's direction. O'Rourke considered the situation for a few seconds before answering. "The minister?"

"Ding, ding, ding!" chirped the commissioner, bitterness lacing his voice. "They went over my head and I have been informed in no uncertain terms that I am to assign at least one senior officer to meet McGarry's flight and to ensure he does not leave the country for at least forty-eight hours."

"I'm not going to—"

"Yes, you bloody are, Fintan," ordered Ferguson, locking O'Rourke into a stare. As the commissioner leaned forward, his eyes suddenly caught the under-lights of the hot tub and flashed red.

223

"Listen very carefully, Detective Inspector. Very carefully indeed. Detective McGarry is going to be escorted from Stoke Newington Police Station to London City Airport and placed on the eight fifteen flight to Dublin Airport later this morning. When that plane arrives in Dublin, should he be on that flight, you will meet him and do exactly as I have instructed."

In O'Rourke's defence, it was the middle of the night and he'd not slept well, which is why he stood there for a few seconds, his mouth open, before realisation hit. "Ahhhh."

Ferguson nodded and sat back. "I don't know what you're ahhh-hing about, Fintan, but I shall not ask any further questions. I've just given you your orders, as have been relayed to me by our beloved Minister for Justice, and I have total faith in you. If McGarry is on that flight, you know what you must do." The commissioner blew on the embers of his cigar nonchalantly before he repeated, "You know what you must do."

O'Rourke bobbed his head then pulled his phone out of his pocket and started looking for a number.

Ferguson coughed loudly. "Perhaps if you're going to make a call, Fintan, can I suggest you use a phone box?"

"Oh," said O'Rourke, looking embarrassed before shoving his phone back in his pocket. "Yes, sir."

"Good man. Off you pop to do whatever you feel you should be doing at this time on a Saturday morning."

"Yes, sir," he replied, before turning to leave.

"Oh, and if next door's driveway happens to have an Opel Corsa with a ludicrously big exhaust sitting on it, and should you happen to set it alight, well, accidents happen."

Chapter Thirty-Three

Bunny spent a few fitful hours trying and failing to sleep, filling the majority of the time by staring at the ceiling of his holding cell. The adrenalin had worn off and now he just felt exhausted, disgusted and, most of all, defeated. He'd seen death before but each time it hit differently. His mind kept returning to the picture of Sean and his mother, sharing a joke, so full of life. He needed to phone Bernadette. Whatever good it would do, the news would be better coming from her than from the poor guard sent round to do the knock.

He was finally nodding off when the cell opened, and Gareth and his female partner entered.

"Up," ordered Gareth.

"Alright, alright," said Bunny. "The bedside manner needs a little work, if you don't mind me saying."

"Hands out."

Bunny complied and his hands were duly cuffed together. "Y'know," he said, addressing the woman, "I feel very rude not knowing your name."

She said nothing.

"Fine," said Bunny. "Have it your way. Let's keep it on theme. We've got Smith, so you're Jones."

"Shut up," said Gareth.

"Or what?" asked Bunny. "You'll hit me again?" He noticed the custody sergeant standing outside the door and raised his voice. "That's right. In case you were interested, this man, who has no legal jurisdiction in your station, assaulted me earlier on. The 'me' in question being a man nobody is charging with anything, in case you'd not noticed."

The custody sergeant looked down at his feet and shifted awkwardly.

"And now they're taking me out of here, in handcuffs, to move me who knows where."

"Alright. Calm down. We're taking you to the airport," said Jones, who then looked at the sergeant. "Exactly like we said we would. Feel free to ring City Airport and you can verify Mr McGarry getting on the plane, if you like."

"Well," said Bunny, "if you can't trust shadowy members of the government-controlled Secret Service, who can you trust? Who was it said that thing about all evil needs to prosper is for good men to stand by and do nothing?"

"You're really getting on my tits."

"Oh, no," said Bunny, "I'm sorry, please don't hit me again, sir."

"People may have also noticed our boss leaving an interview room after you broke his nose."

"Is that right?" said Bunny. "Reckon I'm in trouble, so. I mean, assuming you have that recorded, and sure, how wouldn't you? There are cameras everywhere."

"I'm going to shove a camera up your arse in a minute," growled Gareth.

Jones gave an exasperated sigh and shook her head. "For fuck's sake. It's like I'm running a nursery. C'mon, let's go."

"To be clear, though," said Bunny, as Gareth grabbed his elbow and started guiding him firmly out of the cell door, "I've not been charged with a crime." He held up his cuffed hands as they marched him down the hall. "An innocent man, being led out in cuffs to be taken God knows where. Great day for policing, this!" Then he turned to Gareth. "By the way, that camera-up-the-arse thing is called a colonoscopy. It's a big word, say it with me – col-on-os-copy. Sound it out if you need to."

* * *

Bunny was escorted out of a fire door and into the car park at the rear of the station. The early morning sunlight was surprisingly bright and it took him a second to adjust.

"Jesus, first bit of decent weather since I've been here."

He was directed into the back seat of a black Mondeo. Jones drove, while Gareth sat in the front passenger seat, keeping a very close eye on their prisoner and one hand on his underarm holster. Around them, police and civilian staff were trickling into the station to start their shifts while others were leaving. As the heavy electronic gates to the car park slowly opened, Bunny looked out the car window at pedestrians power-walking into the weekend, a van making an early delivery, and a motorcyclist attempting to ineffectually repair something on their bike. Bunny raised his eyebrows in surprised recognition then casually checked that nobody in the car had clocked him doing so.

Nothing.

Just your average, run-of-the-mill Saturday morning in London. As the car weaved through the light traffic, Bunny watched the city roll by.

"D'ye know what I've always wondered?" he said suddenly. "If you lot are MI5 or MI6 or whatever, who is MI1?"

"Funny you should ask—" started Jones, before being interrupted by her colleague pointedly clearing his throat. "Oh, give it a rest, Garrett. I got this from an article in the paper. Anyway," she continued, "One was Military Intelligence and cryptography; Two was

Russia and, I think, Scandinavia; Three was Eastern Europe and the Germans; and Four was aerial reconnaissance."

"Really?" said Bunny.

"Yeah. This is back in World War Two. I think they were all rolled into the War Office or something, afterwards. There were others too. Eight was interceptions of communications, I remember that, but there were some more as well. The numbers weren't in sequence either, so people assume that means there were other ones that the public never found out about."

"That is interesting. By the way, I'm very sorry, Garrett, I've been calling you Gareth all this time. No wonder we've not hit it off. Although, to be fair, your boss seems to call you Gareth, too. That must be really annoying for you?"

"Shut. Up."

Bunny couldn't be sure, but something about the way Jones shifted her head made him think she was hiding a smile.

The rest of the drive passed in silence until they pulled into the short stay parking at London City Airport. Even at this time of the morning, the car park was relatively full, and people were circling like sharks, looking for spaces.

"Just whack it into the disabled," said Garrett.

"I'm not doing that," said Jones.

"We're here on business."

"Working is not a disability."

"Amen," said Bunny.

"Shut up."

Jones eventually found a space at the far end of the car park. Once she'd switched off the ignition, she turned around and looked at Bunny. "Right, there are two ways this can go. One, we stick a coat over your cuffs, walk you in there, flash an ID and get you straight through and onto your plane. No fuss. Or two, you decide to make it awkward, I make one call, and Security causes a load of hassle and delays flights so we can drive you out right onto the tarmac and shove you on the aircraft, where the rest of the passengers look at you like you're John Malkovich in *Con Air*. What's it going to be?"

"Let's just get this over with," said Bunny.

"That's what I like to hear."

Once out of the car, Garrett pulled Bunny from the back seat. He threw his coat over Bunny's hands and, with a firm grip on his elbow, started to lead him through the car park, with Jones walking beside them. As they headed towards Departures, two drivers who'd found the same parking space were getting out of their cars, already engaged in a lively discussion about who saw the spot first. Behind them, two other cars and a motorbike waited while they sorted it out.

"Oh, dear," said Bunny. "Looks like people are getting a little tetchy. Very stressful places, airports."

"Shut up," said Garrett.

"Are you trying to work that up into a catchphrase or something? I'll be honest, it needs a little refining."

"Shut—"

"Up. Yeah, you said. Thing is, I'm not under arrest and you're not a policeman, so with the greatest respect, Garrett, blow it out your arse."

Garrett tightened his grip.

"Ouch, Garrett. I don't know if you've realised but you're hurting me."

As they reached the front of the car park, Bunny stopped.

"Now what?" asked Jones.

"I'm not moving another step until this gobshite stops trying to rip my elbow off."

"For Christ's sake, Garrett."

"Oh, shut up, Yvette."

Bunny nodded. "Yvette? I had you down as more of a Christine or a Janice. Interesting."

Garrett shifted his grip.

"Thank you, Garrett, I appreciate your co-operation. Now, would you be a good lad" – Bunny nodded towards his own feet – "my shoelace has come undone. Would you do it up for me?"

"Piss off. Tie it yourself."

Bunny turned to the artist formerly known as Jones. "Jesus, Yvette, is he always this charming? I imagine he sweeps the ladies off their feet."

With an irate hand gesture, the helmeted motorcyclist behind the parking fracas wound their way around the stationary cars, as the one at the back laid on the horn.

"Come on," urged Garrett, but Bunny stood firm.

"I need to do up my shoelace," said Bunny, loudly enough that one of the gesticulating would-be parkers glanced in their direction.

"Just do it," said Yvette. "Don't try anything daft, McGarry."

Garrett released his grip and Bunny bent down.

"Thank you, Yvette," he said, raising his voice even further over the cacophony of car horns that was building as the two men at the centre of the kerfuffle engaged in the kind of body language used by grown men who had never been in a fight but had, mistakenly, always thought they'd be good at it. "And I want you to know," said Bunny from the bottom of his lungs, "that I would never hit a woman."

"What?"

"I have her for that."

At that point, a lot of things happened very quickly. Bunny delivered what was more of a ramming of his head than a headbutt, but it had the desired effect as it made fulsome contact with Garrett's groin, causing him to double over. Meanwhile, Yvette was probably wondering why gravity had buggered off, as she went flying through the air. The motorbike rider, still wearing their helmet, had seemingly come out of nowhere, grabbed her arm and executed a judo throw to a near Olympic standard. Then Bunny's head jerked upwards, making resounding contact with Garrett's chin and sending him tumbling backwards onto a nearby parked car.

The would-be contenders and onlookers in the battle for the parking space had all turned their attention to watch the real violence breaking out. Garrett tried to reach for his holstered firearm, but Bunny delivered a double-handed blow to his jaw that sent him sprawling across the bonnet of the Mercedes he'd been leaning against, a spattering of blood ruining the paintwork's lovely shine. Bunny then slammed into him before awkwardly reaching round and grabbing his gun.

As he stepped back, he almost fell over the prone form of Yvette (second name almost certainly not Jones), who was hand-cuffed where she lay, having been subdued in no doubt textbook fashion.

Garrett tried to turn around but Bunny waggled the gun. "Don't. I won't kill you, but I could happily leave you with one less knee."

At this point, the combatants in the battle of the parking space were both cowering behind one of their vehicles.

Bunny nodded down at Yvette and then at the cuffs that were still around his wrists. "She's got the key."

The biker patted down the agent and, seconds later, Bunny was out of the cuffs. He kept the gun trained on Garrett while the hand-cuffs were transferred to him.

All of this happened in record time, but there was already activity at the doors of the airport. "Let's go," said Bunny as he noticed the gathering security.

The biker ran back to the bike and Bunny hopped on the back, pausing to deposit Garrett's gun in a nearby post box.

Fifteen seconds later, the pair was roaring out of the gates of City Airport.

After a couple of minutes, the bike slowed down to something approaching the speed limit.

After another ten minutes of classic pursuit-evasion driving, including nipping beneath an underpass or two, the bike pulled into the car park of a B&Q that was already busy with weekend warriors keen to wade into the never-ending battle that was DIY.

Bunny let go of his saviour and heaved himself off the bike. Butch pulled off her helmet and grinned at him.

"Jaysus, Butch. Not that I wasn't very happy to see you but, to put it in the words of Shakespeare, how in the great skuttering feck?"

"Would you believe that I was in London, doing some light, bike-based sightseeing, when I saw two unidentified people placing my colleague into the back of a vehicle without his consent?"

"In the car park of a police station?"

"Is that where that was?" asked Butch. "They need a bigger sign. Anyway, I then followed the vehicle whereupon it proceeded to London City Airport and I confirmed my suspicions that my colleague was being held against his will. Lovely tracksuit, by the way."

"Don't," he said. "My arse has been hanging out the back of this thing the whole ride here."

"I know," she said with a grin, stepping off the bike. "I heard the honking and whistling. Anyway, an altercation between my colleague and these two armed, unidentified captors ensued, and I assisted him in his attempt to defend himself. Ideally, I would have made a citizen's arrest, but I'm unaware of the laws in this foreign land, hence I decided that retreat was the yada, yada, yada, and so on."

"One hundred percent believable. But still, how'd you end up here?"

"Officially?"

"I think I just got that version."

"Ah, you mean unofficially?"

"Yeah."

"No comment."

"Ara, for feck's sake."

"Jesus, Bunny – bit of gratitude. I did just save your arse."

"Fair point, Pamela. Although this does rather play into my theory that you're secretly in love with me."

Butch rolled her eyes as she bent down at the back of the bike. "It's been a long drive, please don't make me throw up." She pulled off some tape and shoved it into the pocket of her leather jacket. "Look at that, some scallywag used masking tape to change my licence plate." She tutted as she eased herself back into the saddle. "Right, we should get moving. The Met has more cameras than Hollywood, so we're not free and clear. Where are we heading?"

"Pub," said Bunny.

"Jesus, McGarry. I'm beginning to think you've got a problem."

Bunny made to climb on behind her, but she held out her hand. "Whoa, there, cowboy." She opened the bike's storage compartment and took out her spare helmet. She passed it to Bunny and gave him a wide smile. "Put this on. We'll have no breaking of the law around here, thank you very much."

He took it and puffed out his cheeks. "We'll need to make a stop on the way. I've got a call to make."

Chapter Thirty-Four

This time, the call was answered on the first ring.

He could have rung from the Duck and Trumpet but given that he was technically on the run, it made sense to take precautions. Besides, he didn't want anyone overhearing the call. In truth, he was dreading making it at all, but knew he had to.

"Yes?"

Hearing Bernadette's voice, Bunny found himself struggling to know what to say.

"If this is another of those heavy-breathing phone calls, rest assured I will hunt you down like the mangy mongrel you are—"

"He's dead," said Bunny, seeing as nothing else came to mind.

Another pause before Bernadette spoke again. "How?"

Bunny took her through the events of the last twenty-four hours. At the end of his explanation, another silence fell, which he felt compelled to fill. "I failed him. I'm sorry."

"Bunny, we've known each other for quite a while now, haven't we?"

"I suppose."

"And in all that time, have you ever known me to sugar-coat the pill? Give a little rah-rah speech? Or attempt to gee someone up in any way?"

"No."

"Good, then listen closely and listen well. Pull your head out of your arse. This is not your fault. It is the fault of the unspeakable brute who did it, and the slimy little coward or cowards behind him who told him to do it."

"If I'd have got to him sooner—"

"But you didn't. It doesn't make you the villain, it just means you didn't manage to become the hero." Bernadette's voice softened slightly from its usual strident tone. "You and I do not have many things in common, Bernard, but there is one thing we do. Neither of us is naive about the unfair game that is life, yet we both try to do whatever tiny things we can to try to make it a little bit more fair.

"We may well be trying to hold back the sea, but it is how we are built. We can't help ourselves from trying to assist others, and when we're unable to, it haunts us. It burns in our souls because that is who we are. It is neither fun nor fair. None of that makes this your fault, and I'm aware that nothing I nor anyone else can say is going to make you feel differently about it. That is the burden we bear. Now, since what's done is done, what is there left for you to do?"

Bunny's voice cracked as he spoke. "Make the bastards pay."

"Revenge won't bring Sean back."

"I'm aware."

"Very well, then."

"Are you going to try and talk me out of it?"

Bernadette gave a small, humourless laugh. "Good God, no. I've been where you are – more times than I'd care to count. Do what you feel you must."

Bunny clenched his free fist, the anger now broiling in his stomach. "I'm going to burn the whole thing to the ground."

"So be it," said Bernadette. "Go start a fire."

And with that, the phone went dead.

Chapter Thirty-Five

While hanging onto the back of a motorbike for dear life wasn't Bunny's preferred method of transportation, he'd say this for it – it was fast. The ability to weave in, out of and around Saturday-morning London traffic was not to be sniffed at. In fact, he was rather counting on it. Smith and his cronies were well aware that he was staying at the Duck and Trumpet, so he was banking on being able to get there first. Also, Bunny happened to know that someone's firearm ending up in a post box was an administrative nightmare. It had happened to one particularly unfortunate member of the Garda Síochána, and he'd spent the day waiting for a post-office worker to arrive, followed by a week of filling out reports and a lifetime of living it down. He didn't know if the James Bond crowd were as conscientious with their firearms, but he lived in hope.

As it was, when he and Butch arrived at the Duck and Trumpet, they didn't have to worry about who was there. In fact, there managed to be both far fewer and far more people than he'd been expecting. Babs was not there, nor was there any sign of Fisk, but the place was rammed. Behind the bar, the two Daves were acting as barmen, although their job was made considerably easier by the fact they weren't taking any money.

Bunny grabbed Flat Cap Dave by the arm and dragged him away from his waiting queue of disgruntled punters, who, now that Bunny had taken a closer look, appeared to all be middle-aged men. "What the feck is going on?"

"Babs has headed off for a couple of days and left us in charge."

"She told you that you could give out free booze?"

"Actually, this is happy hour, where she said there were two kegs on the house. We're holding an emergency reunion of our Sea Scout troop." He raised his arm and roared, "The Fifth!"

The rest of the room roared the phrase back in response.

"An emergency reunion?" repeated Bunny. "Is the country in a naval battle I'm unaware of?"

"Don't worry," said Woolly Hat Dave, "Babs knows all about it. This is all her idea." He leaned in. "She said we could do this on the understanding that if anyone came round asking questions ..." He waved a hand around the room. "Well, there's a lot of boys here who are capable of more than just tying knots."

"Right," said Bunny. "So where is Babs?"

"Funny you should ask. The other part of my instructions was to tell you that her, Fisk, and the young lady we don't know about and never saw, went to this address." He took a piece of paper out of his pocket and handed it to Bunny.

"Thanks."

"Don't mention it," said Woolly Hat.

"Yeah," agreed Flat Cap Dave. "We sure as shit won't. You were never here."

When Bunny thought about it, he could see the obvious sense in it. Fisk, who'd been following behind in the taxi towards Sean's fateful meeting, would have found out what had happened. With Sean dead, it was well within the realms of possibility that someone could come to the pub looking for Tina, and she therefore needed protecting. He wondered if they'd told her about Sean yet? He felt immediately guilty for hoping they had, so that he wouldn't have to be the one to break the news.

The address on the piece of paper was in a place called Chiswick. When they reached the area, Bunny was surprised to find that it looked posh, and the High Street was home to various antiques stores and bookshops. He was less surprised that it took them bloody ages to find the place. Sitting on the back of a motorbike while trying to read the A–Z that Butch had bought for herself was not the easiest or most fun way to navigate.

Eventually, they pulled up outside a rather grand-looking semi-detached property, and Babs opened the door. "So they let you out, then?" she said as she flicked her cigarette ash away on the wind.

"In a manner of speaking."

She narrowed her eyes. "Why do I think I don't want to know what you mean by that?"

"You're right – it's best not knowing," admitted Bunny.

"That lady with you?"

"She is."

"Tell her to pull the bike around the side. It'll fit. This place belongs to my old friend Kath. I'm feeding her cat while she's in Thailand. We were in the army together – me and Kath, I mean, not the cat."

"Jesus," said Bunny, "you've got a whole backstory we've not even begun to get stuck into, haven't you?"

"You got no idea, sweetheart," Babs said by way of reply as she turned to walk back down the hall. "Oh, and I brought your clothes, by which I mean the clothes I gave you previously. Not that you don't look delightful in that tracksuit you're very nearly wearing."

Bunny didn't need to be told that Tina knew about Sean. As he made his way into the front room, he found her sitting on a sofa, clutching a cushion to her chest, her legs tucked under her. She was staring blankly at the TV that was showing some quiz show or other. Fisk was seated in an armchair opposite.

"I'm ... I'm sorry." Even as the words left Bunny's mouth, they felt pathetically inadequate.

Tina nodded and angrily slapped away the tears on her cheeks. "Was it ... was it them?"

"Yeah."

"So why'd they arrest you, then?"

"It's complicated."

"Still a rather pertinent question, though," said Fisk. "Glad to see you again, by the way. I take it they let you out?" At this point Butch walked into the room and Fisk gave her a cagey look. "Or is there yet another twist in this tale?"

Bunny introduced Butch to the others then sat down to take them through everything that had happened since they'd seen each other last. Ideally, he'd have preferred not to do it in front of Tina, but she seemed determined to stay and it was her right to do so. Once he'd finished, they all looked at each other.

"Alright," said Fisk, "what's our next move?"

"First things first," said Bunny, "we need to get Tina out of here."

The girl looked outraged, just as he'd expected. "What the fuck are you talking about?" she said.

"He's right, sweetheart," said Babs softly. "It ain't safe for you here."

"And where are you expecting me to go?"

"Is home an option?" asked Bunny.

"Very definitely not."

"Right," said Babs. "How about Manchester?"

"I don't know anybody in Manchester."

"I do. Mate of mine. Miranda. She's got a clothes shop up there – all vintage stuff – and a big old house with plenty of room to boot. You'll have a job and somewhere to stay while you decide what to do next."

"Why would she help me?"

"Because I asked. She's already said yes. She's excited to have the company."

"And," continued Bunny, "in a couple of weeks, I'll give this Miranda lady some money for you. A nest egg. Help you get back on your feet. Maybe do some further education or whatever you want."

"Why would you do that?" Tina asked, eyeing him.

What Bunny said was, "Least I can do," because what he couldn't say was, "Because I wasn't able to help your boyfriend and this goes nowhere towards making that right, but it's a start."

"And what about these people? Theakston's lot? They just get away with killing Sean?"

"No," said Bunny firmly. "I don't know exactly how yet, but I'm going to make them pay. I promise you."

With that, Babs took Tina upstairs, and Fisk and Butch made small talk while Bunny sat in contemplative silence.

After a few minutes, Babs returned. "I'm running her a bath, poor thing. Doesn't know which way is up right now." She lowered her voice. "What I didn't say before is that Miranda's a recovering alcoholic who now works part time as an addiction counsellor. The next while is going to be hell for the kid, but if anyone can help keep her on the straight and narrow, it'll be Miranda."

Bunny nodded. "That's a great idea. Thanks, Babs. For everything."

She waved away his thanks dismissively. "No bother."

"Which brings us to the rather trickier subject," began Fisk, "of how exactly you intend to get justice for poor Sean and Gabby?"

"I never said justice. At this point I think the best we can hope for is vengeance."

"Alright, that then."

"I need to get into the fight tonight. In fact, I need to get into the dressing room."

"No chance, Bunny," said Butch. "Do you not think they'll be on the lookout for you?"

"She has a point," said Fisk. "The security at these things is tight, and I guarantee Theakston and Cooper will have security keeping an eye out for you. Not to mention that Smith guy. I'd imagine after your little rumble at the airport, they'll be super keen to get reacquainted."

"Yes," said Bunny, "all the above. Oh, I left something out – I broke that Smith guy's nose too."

"Right," said Fisk. "You have been busy since we saw you last. While I applaud your gusto, *mi amigo*, I don't think that will have helped with the rather significant problem of how you'll get into Wembley Arena."

Bunny smiled. "Funny you should ask. It's time for you to break open your little black book, Fisk. You're going to need a favour."

"Oh, God," said Babs, "you're not going to get all his ex-wives together and storm the place, are you?"

"Not quite," said Bunny, smiling. "Not quite. But you're reasonably warm."

Chapter Thirty-Six

Truth is an odd thing. In certain circumstances it is everything, and in others, it is entirely irrelevant. In the few days Bunny had known Milton Fisk, he'd enjoyed the man's company and, in particular, the tall tales he shared about his adventures. Bunny hadn't cared whether they were true or not, they were a fun, if brief, respite in a week he'd look back on as one of the worst in his life. Sean Malone and Gabby Fuentes were dead, and nothing was going to change that. All that was left was to make those who were responsible pay in any way they could. For Bunny to do that, the question of whether or not Fisk was full of crap was all of a sudden incredibly important. In fact, his whole plan hinged on it.

After Bunny had told Fisk what he needed, Fisk had gone off and made a few calls. Then he'd made a few more and, eventually, he'd come back to say that while it wasn't a cast-in-stone certainty, he believed he'd got the message through to where it needed to go. In truth, it was one hell of a big ask, but Bunny couldn't think of any other way. He couldn't believe he'd thought of this one.

As he and Fisk stood on a street corner in Cricklewood, close, but not too close, to Wembley, he could feel the older man's tension beside him as Fisk jiggled change in his pocket and bounced up and down on his heels. He was quiet, which was the most un-Fiskian thing possible. Fisk checked his watch. The person they were waiting for was already fifteen minutes late. It was getting awkward now and, along with everything else, Bunny was feeling bad for pushing too hard and really putting him on the spot. He racked his brain, trying to come up with something comforting to say.

Fisk glanced at his watch again. "C'mon."

"It was worth a shot," said Bunny, wincing internally at how the platitude sounded.

"He'll be here."

"Sure," said Bunny. "I just mean, if for any reason he isn't – it was worth a shot."

"He'll be here."

"Course. Just ... it was very short notice."

"He'll be here."

"Absolutely. I'm just saying, it was a bit of a Hail Mary, as you Yanks would say, and ye know it's nobody's fault if it doesn't work."

"He'll be here."

"I know. I'm just saying, it was a mad plan and we don't even know if he's in the country or ..."

The rest of Bunny's train of thought was lost as a large limousine pulled up in front of them.

"He's here," said Fisk.

The nearside rear window descended and a voice from inside called out, "Shit the bed! Milton bloody Fisk, in the flesh. You mad old bastard, I assumed you'd be dead by now. Get in here."

Bunny and Fisk climbed inside and Bunny said nothing while Fisk and his old friend exchanged greetings.

"Phillip," shouted their host. "The Arena, dear boy." He turned his attention back to his guests. "I'd offer you a drink but I'm terribly boring these days. Having said that, I do have an exceptional lemonade you really must try."

"We're good, thanks," said Fisk. "And may I say you're looking fabulous."

"Fisk, you old flirt."

"Apologies," said Fisk, "shouldn't I be calling you Sir now?"

His flattery earned Fisk a wide grin. "To be honest, love, I'd much prefer Dame, but the monarchy have such silly rules. Now shut up and introduce me to your friend."

"Oh me, oh my, where are my manners? This is Bunny, and Bunny, this is—"

"Elton fucking John!" blurted Bunny, finally finding his voice.

Elton looked at Fisk. "Is he—"

"Sorry," said Fisk, "he might be a little starstruck."

"Sorry, sorry, sorry," apologised Bunny. "I just ... You're ..."

"Elton fucking John," said Elton John, with a smile. "Yes, I fucking know. To be honest, I wanted that as my official stage name, but promoters can be so prudish. Lovely to make your acquaintance, Bunny. Love the name, by the way."

"Thanks. People have been taking the piss out of it all week."

"Screw 'em. Don't let the bastards drag you down." He turned back to Fisk. "Now, Milton, how's the wife?"

The rest of the journey was mainly taken up with Fisk running through his collection of ex-wives interspersed with anecdotes, while Elton John howled with laughter. Bunny sat there, trying hard not to say anything stupid by simply not saying anything. Bunny had asked Fisk to pull in the favour he'd said the piano man owed him – for saving his life from a chemically enraged sumo wrestler – but, evidently, some part of him hadn't thought it would actually happen. Either that, or the part of the brain that came up with ideas involving legendary performers and the part of the brain that dealt with the concept of said performer ending up sitting mere feet from you, were two very different bits.

Bunny tried not to stare, and then felt rude for not making eye contact. Suddenly, he didn't know what to do with his hands and, an even more extraordinary occurrence, he found himself wishing he'd gone along with Fisk's suggestion to wear the fancy suit he so hated. Elton himself was wearing a rather understated outfit in blue – at least, understated in the mental image Bunny had of Elton John, which involved costumes so large he occasionally had to be transported around in the back of a truck.

Fisk was in the middle of the story about his ex-wife who was the exotic dancer with the boa constrictor when the limousine's intercom beeped.

"Apologies, sir," came Phillip's voice, "but we're coming up to the Arena. How would you like me to handle this?"

"Don't worry, Phil. Leave it to me." Elton turned back to Fisk and Bunny. "You boys need in and, no questions asked, I'm your man."

"Should we hide?" asked Bunny, which earned him a laugh.

"No offence, Bunny dear, but you're in the back of a limo with Sir Elton fucking John. Nobody is going to be looking at you."

Elton took a few deep breaths then glanced at his guests. "Sorry, I so rarely let the bitch out these days, it'll take a moment to get into character."

The limousine came to a halt and, after a few seconds, the rear window buzzed down. From his vantage point, Bunny couldn't see the face of the large man in a black suit holding a clipboard.

"Can I help you?" asked the security guard.

"Yes," said Elton. "I'm Elton John."

"Right. Ehm, yes. Of course. This is the performers' entrance."

"I know," said Elton with a tight smile. "I'm Elton John."

"Of course, obviously you'd know that. Obviously. But ... you're ... Tonight is ..." The man pawed through the clipboard nervously. "Are you on the list?"

"I'm Elton John, love," Elton replied calmly, studying his fingernails. "I'm on every list."

"Right. Ehm, yes. I ... I don't have you here. Are you definitely on the VIP list?"

"Am I definitely on the VIP list?" echoed Elton, raising his voice. "I'm Elton fucking John. The only time I'm not on the VIP list is when I'm on the VVIP list or the VVVIP list."

"It's just—"

"Have you checked under Sir Elton fucking John, knight of the fucking realm?"

"Yes. I mean, no. I mean … Let me ring in."

"Let me through this instant!"

"But we've got instructions—"

"Instructions?" screeched Elton. "Instructions? Do you have any idea how many times I've played this Arena?"

"Ehm, no," said the security guard.

"Exactly. Nobody does. That's how many times I've played it. There's even a bathroom in there that has only ever been used by me. That's how many times I've played here. I've got my own private shitter, and I'd very much like to use it. Right now. This minute. What's the point of having it if you can't pop in? Let me make this as clear as possible, I'm Sir Elton fucking John and I'd very much like to pop in and take a shit on the Sir Elton fucking John toilet. It's got a golden seat, which is frankly impractical, and pictures of me on all the walls, which is rather offputting, but I'm still going to use it to drop off one of my beknighted logs because I am Elton fucking John and that's my shitter."

"Absolutely, I just …"

"I recorded a live album here before you were born. And do you know how many times I'm going to play here in the future after this humiliation?" By this point he was nearly hanging out the window.

"Open the gate!" shouted the security guard, his will broken. "Sorry, Elton— I mean, sir. I mean, Sir Elton, sir. Your Majesty … Ehm …"

"No problem, darling," said Elton, all sweetness and light again. As the limousine started to move off, he took something out of the inside pocket of his suit and held it out the window. "Here's four tickets to my show over in the stadium. Bring the kiddies. I do love your hair."

As the window closed, Elton smiled over at his guests. "The one thing about having a reputation for being an absolute diva is that people tend to believe it." He patted Bunny on the knee. "I'm a pussy cat when you get to know me. Now, are you boys sure I can't interest you in a lemonade?"

Chapter Thirty-Seven

It was amazing how far you could get into a high-security building when you're a musical icon who'll tell anyone who'll listen that you just popped in for a shit. Some things people just don't question. Bunny and Fisk simply travelled in the man's wake, with nobody paying them a blind bit of attention because Elton John having people with him when he goes to the toilet seems like a perfectly reasonable thing.

"Right," said Elton finally. "The dressing rooms are just down this corridor. Even I might struggle to get in there on fight night." He pointed at an unmarked door. "This is the Sir Elton John toilet."

"Wow!" said Fisk. "That was true?"

"Of course it's true. Who'd make up something like that? I won't play Madison Square Garden again until they give me my own one there. I'm not going to use the same toilet as Metallica. Lovely boys, but still. Now, if you don't mind, I didn't need it but after telling everyone I did, I find I now do."

And with that, Fisk and Elton hugged their goodbyes, Bunny received a handshake, and then Elton was gone.

"That was Elton fucking John," said Bunny.

"Yes," replied Fisk. "I believe you both mentioned that. Now, does your plan involve a way of getting where you need to go?"

"To be honest with you," said Bunny, looking around, "I didn't think we were getting this far."

Fisk nodded. "It's lucky I'm here. I've got just the thing." He withdrew the object in question from his pocket and showed it to Bunny with a flourish.

"Are you taking the piss, Fisky?"

"Actually," he said with a grin, "I am."

* * *

Two minutes later, Bunny and Fisk were standing in a wide corridor in front of a security guard. The roar of the crowd in the arena filtered through the doors behind him as one of the fights on the undercard played out.

Fisk held up the plastic jar.

"Look," he said to the security guard. "It's real simple, buddy. Either Damon Alvarez pees into this or else he's never fighting in the United States of America again."

"But you're not on the list."

"I'm the drug tester from the FCFFCFC!"

"There's another fella—"

Fisk waved away the protest. "He ain't me and I ain't him. It's two entirely different testing regimes. Welcome to the wacky world of international doping control. And God help us if that guy gets all the pee that Mr Alvarez has to pee, because under *our* rules, I've got to attempt to confiscate it, and under *their* rules, he can't give it to anyone else. We don't want a repeat of St Louis, do we? There was goddamn pee everywhere, and nobody comes out of that smelling of roses, let me tell you.

"Look," he tried again, the very definition of reasonable. "I'm really not trying to be a hard-ass here, and I appreciate you've got a job to do, just like we do, so how's about a compromise? My colleague will stay here to make sure Alvarez doesn't leave, and you can take me to see your boss, just so you can confirm this is all on the up and up."

"Yeah, alright," said the guard who'd clearly decided this was a problem well above his pay grade. Afterwards, in the canteen, he'd be disappointed when his story about hassles with international doping control agents was completely overshadowed by Freddie's story about getting bollocked by Elton John.

Fisk turned to Bunny. "Alright, McGonoble." Only Bunny caught Fisk's slight wince after doing a terrible job of making up a name. "You stay here and, no matter what, Alvarez does not leave, you understand me? Not unless I personally show you this jar filled to the brim with testable pee. Is that clear?"

"Yes, sir."

Fisk nodded then turned to the guard. "Then lead on, and let's keep boxing clean!"

Bunny watched as the two men walked down the corridor, Fisk regaling his unenthusiastic guide with an unrequested tale of how he'd had to try to wrestle a vial of Mike Tyson's pee away from an airport security guard in Las Vegas.

And then Bunny found himself alone. From here on in it was all up to him, and he still wasn't sure exactly what he was expecting. Still, sometimes the truth really did matter. Sometimes it was all that mattered, and while it couldn't change what had happened, at least it could shed its light and send the cockroaches scattering for cover.

A loud roar from the arena carried down the corridor. He glanced at his watch – not long until the main event.

Chapter Thirty-Eight

Stevie Brandon sat on the side of the warm-up table while Pete checked and rechecked his gloves. He was going through the same routine as always – the wrapping of his hands, the re-wrapping because he never liked it the first time. Warm-up drills. Shadow boxing. Normally, Gabby did all of this with him, but it wasn't like Pete hadn't seen them do it lots of times. Any change was bad, but then today, tonight, everything would change. Luckily, Stevie was never a talker, so nobody would be surprised that he wasn't saying anything.

He stared at the tiled floor as Pete droned on. How many boxers had sat here before him? How many would be here after him? He didn't make a big deal out of it, but he loved the history of the sport. He read about it, watched old tapes. He and Gabby used to sit down together and watch fights from the seventies, just for fun. Then, he'd made the mistake of thinking he could tell Gabby what Sparky had said he had to do, and Gabby had left him. He'd thought Gabby was his friend, and then he'd turned around and betrayed him. Everyone leaves. Almost everyone.

Normally, by this point, Sparky would have said his bit long ago and moved out of the way to go sit at ringside, but tonight he was still hovering around. It was getting on Stevie's nerves.

Finally, when Pete looked as happy as he ever did, Sparky moved forward and tapped him on the shoulder. "Hey, Pete, give me and my guy a moment here, would you?"

Stevie gave a slight nod and Pete stepped away. He saw Lawrence take him to one side, distracting him so that Sparky could say his bit.

Sparky slapped a hand on Stevie's gloves. "How you feeling, champ?"

"Like I'm not g-gonna be champ much longer."

Sparky, looking worried, leaned in a little further. "Hey, come on, brother. We talked about this. I know this is shitty – believe me, I do. But there's no other way. These people are not to be fucked with. They're dangerous."

"I'm dangerous."

"I know, guy, I know. And I wouldn't ask you to do this if it wasn't life or death. My life or death. We've been through so much together. Remember when I found you? Nobody else believed in you, but I always did. How I made that thing go away? How I've always protected you? This one time, I need you to protect me. We're family, you and me. It's what we do."

This was pretty much the same thing Sparky had been saying to him every couple of days for the last six weeks. Stevie was trying unsuccessfully to block out that voice in the back of his head. The one that was always there. *Family*, it said, mocking him. *You ain't got family, son. Only me.*

Stevie nodded and turned his head.

Sparky bobbed around, dipping to stay in his field of vision. Smiling up at him. "Look, I was saving this to tell you after, but big news – big, big news! We've already agreed in principle on the rematch. It's gonna be Madison Square Garden. You always wanted to fight there, right? Dream come true. Madison Square Garden!"

Stevie nodded again. It had been his dream, but the thought of it now turned his stomach.

Madison Square Garden, echoed the voice. *You ain't worth Madison Square Garden. Not after you do this. Not after the world sees how weak you really are.*

Sparky reached up and placed his hands on Stevie's shoulders. "You know I wouldn't ask you to do this if there was any other way. Just do this one thing and I swear to you, never again. Just picture knocking this prick out while Madison Square Garden roars you on." He looked suddenly worried. "Then, not now. Just, y'know ... do what you have to tonight. Everybody loses. There isn't any shame in it. All the greats had setbacks. It's the comeback that made them great. He gets a lucky shot in. Big deal. Can happen to anybody."

More than anything, Stevie just wanted him to shut up. Shut up. Shut up.

"Just do what you have to do, and you'll be saving my life. Literally. I'll spend every waking moment after tonight proving to the world you're the best that's ever been. The greatest!"

Stevie nodded again.

Sparky patted him on the cheek. "You're a good boy, Stevie. A good boy. Best friend I ever had."

Good boy? Good boy? He talks to you like you're a dog, son. That's all you are. His pathetic little dog.

"Just, y'know" – Sparky spoke in a near whisper – "make it look good."

Make it look good. Make it look good. Make it look good.

Finally, Sparky seemed satisfied, and turned and headed for the door.

Shut up. Shut up. God, Stevie wanted everyone to shut up. And he wanted a drink. It didn't block out the voices but it helped. He looked into the far corner of the cavernous changing room then back down at the floor.

Pete came back over. "OK, champ, let's—"

"Out," said Stevie.

"Sure, champ. Course. I know you do your alone time, but it's a bit too early—"

"Out."

Pete gave him a look. Did he know? Sparky had promised him that only the two of them would know. It'd be their secret. Still, every time anyone looked at Stevie it felt like they knew. He'd told Gabby and Gabby had left. Pete didn't know.

Everyone knows, son. Everyone is gonna know. You're a loser. A pathetic wimp. Sparky's little lap dog.

Stevie glanced at the far corner of the room again. It was where they kept the privacy screens used by doctors to shield people from view.

"OK," said Pete.

"Out!" shouted Stevie, causing Pete to stumble backwards then scurry towards the door. "Right. Sorry. Sorry. Right."

When he'd gone, Stevie kept his eye on the door for a long time then looked back at the screens.

"How the fuck did you get in here?"

Bunny stepped out of the shadows. "You wouldn't believe me if I told you. We need to talk."

Chapter Thirty-Nine

Bunny moved across the dressing room slowly. He'd found a way in through the medical room attached to it and, in his eagerness, had nearly walked in right in front of Theakston and Cooper. As he'd ducked behind the screens, the fire in his belly had broiled. Last night, Lawrence Cooper had killed an innocent kid and now here he was, standing on the far side of the room, chatting to Brandon's trainer like it was nothing.

Finally, Stevie's entourage had left. Bunny didn't know what he was going to say, all he knew was that he needed to say it now.

* * *

Brandon glowered at him as he approached. "I'm about to have the biggest f-fight of my life. Why the fuck are you here?"

"Because I know," said Bunny. "I know that you're about to lose the biggest fight of your life because the fix is in."

As fine a boxer as he was, Stevie Brandon was no poker player. If Bunny had any doubt, the look of unadulterated guilt on his face would have confirmed it.

"That's—"

"Don't bother denying it. To be honest with you, I couldn't give a shit. Win. Lose. Throw it. Who cares? What I care about is when innocent people get hurt. Like your trainer, Gabriel Fuentes."

"I told you – he went home."

"And I now know that's bollocks. Just one of the lies Theakston's been feeding you."

"Bullshit."

"I wish it was. Sean heard Gabby and Theakston arguing because he knew about the fix. Then Gabby disappeared off the face of the earth. You're not naive, Stevie. You might be ignoring it, but you must have some idea of the people you're dealing with."

Brandon didn't – or couldn't – respond to that, he just kept staring at Bunny.

"Just a guess, but when the accident with Marcus happened, when you were sparring, had you just been told that you had to lose the title you've worked your whole life for?"

Brandon's face made Bunny regret the words as soon as they left his mouth. It had been a guess, but a calculated one. The big man went to say something this time, but no words came. Instead, he just looked down at the floor.

Bunny held his tongue. Giving Brandon time to process. After a few seconds, the boxer raised his gaze again, fixing Bunny with hooded eyes. "They use me. Now you want to use me. Everybody uses me."

"You could see it that way," conceded Bunny. "How I see it is I'm telling you the truth, and then it's up to you what you do with it."

"So, G-Gabby?"

"Is dead," said Bunny. "There's a guy here looking for him – Milton Fisk, the writer. He and Gabby were friends their whole life. Gabby hadn't been seen for a couple of weeks, his sister hadn't heard from him and Fisk says Gabby, no matter what, wouldn't have wanted anything to do with a fixed fight. That's why him and Theakston were fighting."

"Sean heard it?" asked Brandon.

Bunny nodded. His mouth was suddenly dry. It wasn't as if he'd been avoiding the next bit consciously, but clearly something in him didn't want to say it out loud. Maybe that made it real again. The image of the young lad's face as he bled out in his arms came back to him, so strongly it brought the taste of bile to the back of his throat.

"He's dead." The words came out so quietly, he couldn't be sure he'd actually said them out loud. "He's dead," he said again, more firmly. "Sean is dead."

Stevie's face crumbled, the rock-hard mask dropped away, and all that remained were the eyes of a scared little boy. "What?"

Bunny nodded. "He'd heard everything, you see. That's why he had to run. Theakston had Cooper, and whoever else, out looking for him. Hunting him down. Eventually, it was his dad – his own fecking father – that set Sean up to meet Cooper last night. Thought he was going to clear the air. Cooper stabbed him."

"That's ... not ..."

"It's true. You know it's true. If it wasn't, then how do I know what I know? Who else knows what Theakston wants you to do?" Bunny felt tears roll down his own cheeks. "Sean died in my arms because I couldn't get there in time. I wasn't able to save him. I couldn't do anything."

"B-but ..." Brandon looked lost. "Why are you telling me this?"

"Because it's all I can do. Cooper is going to get away with it. So is bastard Sparky Theakston. All I can do for Sean and for Gabby, your friends, is tell you the truth. What you do with it is up to you."

There was a knock on the door.

"It's time, champ," shouted a voice from the other side.

Bunny turned around and headed back towards the way he came. "Best of luck, champ."

Chapter Forty

As Bunny exited the medical room, lost in thought, he almost ran into Yvette Probably-not-Jones. The agent's hand flew to her holster but she didn't draw her weapon.

"Can we handle this calmly?" she asked.

Bunny sighed. "Sure. Why not? Are you going to ask me to leave? Arrest me? Can you lot do that?"

"Someone would like a word."

"Yeah, I bet he would."

She scanned the corridor. "Where's your friend?"

"Friend?"

She gave him a look. "The woman who kicked the crap out of me at the airport."

Bunny made a show of looking puzzled. "I think you've got me confused with someone else."

Yvette nodded. "Sure I do. Come on, let's go."

"Alright. Lead the way."

She stepped to the side and waved him forward. "Oh, no, I insist. After you."

"Fair enough."

Bunny started walking.

"And seriously – don't try anything."

"Relax, I would—"

"Never hit a woman," she finished. "Yeah, I remember."

* * *

Bunny was shown into a room where Milton Fisk was sat on a sofa, his fedora down over his eyes, seemingly enjoying a light snooze under armed guard. The guard in question looked perplexed by this show of ease. In the background, the low chatter of a commentary team could be heard coming from a speaker on the wall.

"Ah," said Bunny, sitting down beside Fisk and giving a genial nod to the new guy, "could Garrett not make it?"

Fisk shifted his hat and winked at Bunny.

"The last I heard," said Yvette Probably-not-Jones, "he'd been found on the green in Shepherd's Bush, bollock naked and tied up with some extremely secure knots. Don't suppose you'd know anything about that?"

Fisk and Bunny looked at each other.

"No," said Bunny.

"Probably kids," said Fisk.

"Yeah. I blame the parents."

Fisk lowered his voice. "Did you?"

"I did."

"How did it go?"

"Honestly? No idea."

Fisk nodded. "Well, I guess we'll find out soon enough."

"I guess we will," agreed Bunny.

The door flew open and in stormed Smith. "Unbelievable. You two are unbelievable."

"Thanks," said Bunny. "Milton Fisk, this is Smith. Smith, Milton Fisk. He used to have a hat."

Fisk tipped his own headgear. "Milton Fisk, lowly scribbler,

259

highly regarded, dishonourable discharge national guard, two-time recipient of the LaBroxi award—"

"Shut! Up!" hissed Smith.

Fisk pointed at the extensive bandaging on Smith's nose. "What happened to the old hooter there, chief?"

Smith clenched his fists. "Do you two have any idea how much trouble you are in? How the hell did you even get in here?"

"Sir Elton fucking John," said Fisk cheerfully.

"Oh, piss off," said Smith.

"Jesus, Smith," replied Bunny. "You're swearing now? What happened to the gentleman-spy routine? Rather uncouth behaviour."

"Disappointing," agreed Fisk.

"Laugh it up, you idiots. You're doing your best to mess up a complex operation that was months in the making."

"What?" asked Bunny. "Us? We're just trying to see the fight."

"I'm actually covering it for *Cigar Aficionado Monthly*."

"Is that right?" asked Smith, a rather unhinged smile spreading across his face. "Does that include trying to get a urine sample from a boxer?"

"We pride ourselves on our in-depth coverage."

"Do you two have any idea who you're messing with?"

"Actually, no," said Bunny. "I've no idea who you people are. You've never identified yourselves."

"Now that you mention it," said Fisk, "that gentleman did just point a gun at me and tell me to come with him. I'm starting to worry for my safety."

Smith, almost foaming at the mouth, made a noise that wasn't made up of any recognisable words.

"Sir," said Yvette Probably-not-Jones.

"What?" he snapped.

She pointed to the speaker. "I think it's starting." She reached up to increase the volume just as they heard the bell sounding.

* * *

Thirty-six seconds later, Milton Fisk and Bunny McGarry stood up from the sofa.

"M'lady, gentlemen," said Fisk. "Charmed as always, but I think we'll be going."

Smith pulled his battered face out of his hands. "The hell you are."

"I think it's best they do, sir," said Probably-not-Jones.

"Who asked you? I'm in charge here."

Smith's phone rang.

"I'd answer that, sir," she said. "I suspect that might be about to change."

As they walked down the corridor, Milton Fisk pulled a flask out of the inside pocket of his jacket and offered it to Bunny.

"Drink?"

"Don't mind if I do." Bunny took a swig and handed it back.

"Sorry about your holiday, by the way."

"Ah, to be honest with you, I burn easy and them little umbrellas they put in the drinks always get stuck up my nose."

Chapter Forty-One

The next morning, Bunny sat at the gate, waiting for his flight back home to Dublin. He was trying to ascertain whether or not he was going to throw up. Last night, he and Fisk had returned to the Duck and Trumpet where they were joined by Babs, Butch and some incredibly drunk former Sea Scouts. To the Sea Scouts it was a reunion, but to the four people in the know, it was a send-off for two fallen innocents. Drink and death going hand in hand was possibly the oldest of all Irish traditions, and Sean Malone and Gabby Fuentes were sent off in fine style.

It had been about 3am when things took a turn for the unexpected. Bunny had just waved off Babs and Fisk at the airport, their flight to Las Vegas departing earlier than his. It turned out Fisk, the old dog, may have been getting a bit more with his room than the full English breakfast. He'd popped the question and Babs had said yes. This had led to a lot more drinking as they all toasted the good health of the soon-to-be latest iteration of the ever-evolving entity that was Mr and Mrs Milton Fisk. The couple had invited him to the wedding and, while it had been very tempting, he'd declined. He had a funeral to attend.

Butch was going to Bath of all places, to see a friend for a couple of days, before biking her way back home via the ferry. She'd been "gifted" some extra holidays and fully intended to make use of them.

Bunny took another sip of the bottle of Lucozade he'd got for himself and fantasised about conking out on the flight home. He fully intended to spend most of the week sleeping. He was tired to the very core of his being.

Someone sat down in the seat beside him and Bunny shifted over slightly. Then he looked up and groaned. "Ara, for feck's sake."

"Relax," said Yvette Probably-not-Jones. "I come in peace. In fact, I'm not here officially at all."

"In that case, how'd you get past security?"

She gave him a look. "I said I wasn't here in an official capacity. I still have the identity card."

"And what is actually on that?"

"No comment," she said. "Although I can tell you Mr Smith no longer has one."

"Couldn't happen to a nicer fella. Speaking of which ..." He left the question hanging, guessing she didn't need the rest of it spelled out.

Yvette chose to speak while looking out the departure lounge's floor-to-ceiling windows with the view of the runway. "Following Stevie Brandon's emphatic victory by first-round stoppage, his manager Alex Theakston and head of security Lawrence Cooper have not been seen since, and their location is not known."

"Any guesses?"

"They're either running, which they're going to be doing for a very long time, or ..."

"Or they're not going anywhere, ever again."

She nodded. "Pretty much."

"Still not enough," said Bunny. "Not nearly enough."

"For what it's worth," she said, "I agree. And, not that I'm trying to absolve myself of any blame here, but I pushed hard against putting Sean in that situation. It'll haunt me until the day I die."

"It should," said Bunny. "You failed him. I failed him."

She didn't respond to this and they both sat there in silence for a few seconds. Eventually, she broke it.

"For the record, I think you did all you could."

"It wasn't enough."

"You can't blame yourself for that."

"I do."

"Well, OK, I guess. That's your choice."

"Don't get me wrong, I blame a lot of other people too."

She nodded. "There's plenty of it to go around. Oh, before I forget ..."

She handed him a large carrier bag and Bunny looked inside it.

"Is this ...?"

"Your coat, yes. It's been processed and cleaned. I got them to rush it back to you when you were confirmed as no longer being a suspect. Turns out there's video footage of Lawrence Cooper that means, should he ever be found by someone other than a certain organisation, he'll be going to prison for a very long time."

"Good to know."

"And then there's this ..." She reached into her inside pocket and pulled out a couple of sheets of folded paper.

"Is that ...?"

"Sean's letter," she confirmed. "Yes. Well, not the original, obviously, but we were able to scan it and clean it up, so I thought you might want to ..."

She held it out and he took it, slipping it carefully into his pocket without looking at it. Whatever was in it was between Sean and his mother, and no longer any of his affair.

And with that, Yvette Probably-not-Jones got to her feet. "Well, I should leave you to it. Glad seeing you off this time went a bit smoother. Are you ever going to tell me who your friend yesterday was?"

Bunny remained a blank slate. "I still don't know what you're talking about."

"Have it your way. Actually, before I go, can I ask one last question?"

"Sure."

"This might sound mad, but ..."

Bunny raised both hands. "Let me stop you there. Yes, seriously – Elton fucking John."

"How did—"

"I'm not at liberty to say."

She nodded. "Well, if you ever find yourself over this way again – and I hope for both our sakes you don't – you're owed a favour should you need it."

"I'd say thanks, but I don't have your name or number."

"One of those two things is written on a piece of paper in your coat pocket."

At that moment, Bunny heard someone sit down in the seat behind him and loudly proclaim to the world at large, "Unbelievable. Absolutely unbelievable."

He winced. "Can I cash in that favour right now?"

Yvette shrugged. "Maybe."

Without turning around, he pointed over his shoulder. "We're even if, right now, no questions asked, you shoot that guy."

Free Yummy Easter Egg

Hello there lovely reader,

Caimh here. Ever wondered what's going on in my mind when I write a book? Well, now you can find out. Scan the QR code on the next page or visit my website and come with me on a journey through my warped imagination!

In this exclusive video – which is only available via this link – discuss the process behind the writing of *Fortunate Son,* what inspired me and my thoughts about the characters.

This video contains tonnes of spoilers for Fortunate Son, so if you've skipped ahead and you haven't read the book yet, turn back now, ye weirdo!

You can also view the video at **www.whitehairedirishman. com/knockout**

Drop me line if you have any questions or let me know what you think and if you'd like more behind the scenes content.

Free Stuff

Hello again, lovely reader-person,

So there we go, Bunny's ventured out of Dublin and I've succeeded in stretching the definition of both Dublin and Trilogy. Hope you enjoyed his escapades in that there London. The big fella will be back soon in either America or Dublin so stay tuned!

If you're new to the Bunny experience (get you, you renegade starting on book eight) make sure you've signed up for my monthly newsletter for free short stories, audio stories, and the latest goings on in the Bunnyverse.

You'll also get a copy of my short fiction collection called ***How To Send A Message***, which features several stories featuring characters from my books. To sign up go to my website:

www.WhiteHairedIrishman.com

Oooh, and you can also listen to the Bunnycast and The Stranger

Times podcasts too for more audio exclusives and short stories. They're available from all the usual places or through my website or **thestrangertimes.co.uk.**

Cheers muchly and thanks for reading,

Caimh

Also by Caimh McDonnell

Made in the USA
Columbia, SC
22 November 2024

47317795R00167